Thomas De Quincey, Alexander H. Japp

Memorials

Vol. II

Thomas De Quincey, Alexander H. Japp

Memorials
Vol. II

ISBN/EAN: 9783744688437

Printed in Europe, USA, Canada, Australia, Japan

Cover: Foto ©Raphael Reischuk / pixelio.de

More available books at **www.hansebooks.com**

THE POSTHUMOUS WORKS
OF THOMAS DE QUINCEY.

Volume I.

SUSPIRIA DE PROFUNDIS.

WITH OTHER ESSAYS,
CRITICAL, HISTORICAL, BIOGRAPHICAL, PHILOSOPHICAL,
IMAGINATIVE, AND HUMOROUS.

Volume II.

CONVERSATION AND COLERIDGE.

WITH OTHER ESSAYS.

Edited, with Introduction and Notes, from the Author's Original
MSS., by

ALEXANDER H. JAPP, LL.D., F.R.S.E.

London: Wm. Heinemann, 21 Bedford Street, W.C.

DE QUINCEY MEMORIALS.

Your affectionate father,
Thomas De Quincey.

DE QUINCEY MEMORIALS.

BEING LETTERS AND OTHER RECORDS,
HERE FIRST PUBLISHED.

WITH

COMMUNICATIONS FROM COLERIDGE, THE WORDSWORTHS,
HANNAH MORE, PROFESSOR WILSON, AND OTHERS.

EDITED, WITH INTRODUCTION, NOTES, AND NARRATIVE,

BY

ALEXANDER H. JAPP, LL.D., F.R.S.E.

IN TWO VOLUMES.

VOLUME II.

LONDON:
WILLIAM HEINEMANN.
1891.

Ballantyne Press
BALLANTYNE, HANSON AND CO.
EDINBURGH AND LONDON

CONTENTS OF VOL. II.

CHAPTER XXVII.

CHAPTER XXVIII.

CHAPTER XXIX.

CHAPTER XXX.

¡CHAPTER XXXI.'

APPENDICES.

LIST OF PLATES.

VOL. II.

————◆————

DE QUINCEY MEMORIALS.

CHAPTER XVIII.

"*Wednesday, May* 17, 1809.

"MARY has been reproaching me the whole week for not writing to you, which is a great shame, because your last letter was to her; and, besides, you owe me some three or four already. After all, I don't know what it is she is so desirous I should impart to you, except that there is no reason why you should not come to us in ten days, as you say, or in one day if you please; but I conclude there is no reason for repeating so old a truth, that we are always supremely happy in the honour and pleasure, &c., &c., &c.

" I observe you always say ten days, a distance which as regularly recedes so that it is constantly at the same standing. We have heard of you to-day; that is, from your favoured friend, Miss Wordsworth, through Mrs. Kelsall. When shall we hear anything more of this beautiful cottage? I can't approve of the sitting-room being upstairs. Why did it not open on a sloping lawn, buried in the shade of

 A

venerable beeches, through which one should here and there discover the lake with the western sun sinking into it? Here indeed would be a retreat worthy a philosopher! I should like to know how you will pass your time—whether you mean to bury yourself in total seclusion, or only in an elegant retirement, embellished with every unsophisticated pleasure. I can tell you that you will never endure it alone for two months. I should much like to know Miss Wordsworth, and to see what sort of a woman you admire. —I look with no small pleasure to the seeing all the divine things in Grasmere which you mention. I think that pleasure which I *feel* from beautiful country, or from anything in country not strictly beautiful, which I have associated, however remotely, with my ideas of fine scenery, would have power to rouse and delight me even at moments (if any such there were) when every other thing would be disgusting to me.

"I think you will be pleased with our views from Westhay, though they are certainly of a very mild sort of beauty, and may appear tame after the northern sublimity. If you have any dislike to the worldly bustle of removing, I again conjure you to come immediately, since our time is finally fixed for leaving Clifton entirely at or rather before Midsummer, and cannot now be altered, because this house is *let* from that period, and therefore we must leave whether we are so disposed or not. You can go with us to Westhay if you please, for we shall have rooms enough finished, though the house will be half full of workmen. How often have I told you that 'hope deferred maketh the heart sick'? I am sure no mortal ever had so many prayers, adjurations, and imprecations showered upon them in vain as you have had. Above all things remember the *Bible*, as you value your peace on earth.[1] I hope you will bring some books with you, for we are in a dry and barren soil, where to this hour I believe it is the fashion to talk of nothing but 'Marmion' and 'Cælebs.' I suppose we shall have some more of Walter Scott's stolen goods *soon*. Do you know anything of him? or can he prosecute me for a libellist if I say he borrows his ideas, often his words even sometimes? You have not told us whether you understand Spanish. Mary has got the most stupid master in the world, and so unlike a noble Spaniard, he might rather pass for a low and vulgar Francese. Have you any Italian books with you? I can get none, and I much wish to increase my slight acquaintance with the language. People sometimes argue with me that there is no use in learning Italian and Spanish, because there are so few books worth reading. You have given me a different idea; at all events they are so easy to learn, and I have not the dislike that people in general have to languages.

"Do you remember that you are to teach me German? We hear by letters from India that my Uncle is just made a Major, so we expect he will come home. Richard is still in the Baltic with

---

[1] A Bible in chaste and superb binding for a present to be given by Miss Brotherton (see "Memoir," pp. 105-6).

Admiral Keats. I fear you have never written to Miss Brotherton. Oh, if you break your promises to the fair unknown as you do to us, you will certainly be disgraced. I long to question you on some interesting topics which in a letter you would elude, but the truth cannot escape my penetrating eye. Can you tell me why Foster has never brought out the work which you said was preparing? I suppose it will never come now. I do not think even of inquiring for the 'Friend.' Adieu.—Your ever-affectionate sister,　　　　JANE DE QUINCEY.

"I have heard that Miss Seward has left all her own letters, and all those of her correspondents, for publication—I thank Heaven I was not one of them—to come out 2 vols. a year. If it is true, what must have been the supreme vanity of the creature ! [1]

"I have been reading Miss Lee's 'Recess,' and was foolish enough to be interested at the time, though, on cooler reflection, I find great fault with it for being so full of miseries and written in such a confused style.

"THOS. DE QUINCEY, Esq.,
　　"82 Gt. Tichfield St., London."

---

[1] Anna Seward was a well-known writer of the earlier part of the century. Her works consisted of dramas, poems, biographies : "Louisa, a Poetical Novel," was perhaps the most popular of them. She wrote the Life of Dr. Darwin. She was the daughter of the Rev. Thomas Seward, himself a poet of some repute, and editor of "Beaumont and Fletcher." She was born in 1747, and died in 1809. Sir Walter Scott, of whom she was the friend and correspondent, wrote a Life of

" *Monday,* 23*rd.*

"My dear Brother,—Enclosed I have sent you the ground plan of Westhay, though I own I am a little surprised at such a requisition from you—a Metaphysician and an Architect! A monstrous incongruity! I should almost as soon have thought of sending you the newest and most approved plan for making a Petticoat. If you really understand these things, you will perhaps think many improvements might be made. This is true, but all I have to say is, that though I could fancy many plans which I should like better, yet this is perhaps the best possible arrangement for us, with our numerous requirements and the comparatively small sum which must complete them. Above we have seven rooms, and one in the roof; behind are the coach-house, stable, and offices, intended to be concealed by the infant trees, of which we have planted about fifteen hundred. After all, if you were to come to us immediately from Westmoreland, you would think all our southern views very insipid, though they are beautiful in their style. I am determined, if ever I come into possession of a grand castle, which lives in my imagination only at present, it shall be in Cumberland or Westmoreland; but I shall prefer the former, as being rather more removed from the wicked haunts of men. Whenever I am in possession of the talisman which is to raise it, I shall

her prefixed to her poems, and her letters were collected and published at Edinburgh in 1811, in six volumes, under the editorship of Mr. A. Constable, as arranged by herself. They were very carefully and critically weeded out, however, by herself: report had magnified her pistolary bequest, which still was large enough, in all conscience.

request you to point out to me the most beautiful of the lakes—small, rocky, and wooded to the very edge. The name of Ullswater pleases me, if it answers to my idea of it. You must also tell me the best place on the sea-coast of Wales, that I may fix my marine villa there. I never knew before this winter that a very fine effect may be produced by the snow covering a number of high trees, or a wood still more. I had always execrated snow as the only thing in nature totally foreign to every sort of beauty.

"I have begun to learn Spanish by myself, and though it is indeed so easy that I can almost read it without translating, yet I am under a continual difficulty from the impossibility of teaching myself the pronunciation by any rules that can be given. And there is no master can be got here except one who is in reality a Frenchman. Mary has bought Gonsalvo de Cordoba, a dictionary and grammar. I don't believe I shall ever think, as I have heard some people say, that it is worth learning merely for the sake of 'Don Quixote,' which I have read lately in English, and am never much delighted with this kind of book. But it is an amusement to me to learn, and I suppose there are many books which I should like. I can't meet with any Italian Books but Metastasio. I was in hopes I had sprung a mine of them in opening your box to look for the copying machine, but judge of my horror when I discovered them to be all Greek, Latin, or German. Don't alarm yourself; I replaced them carefully in the tomb, and shall never more trouble their repose. The only exceptions were 'Decameron,' which a Gentleman told Mary was not fit for a young Lady to read, and a French treatise on Logic, which I have opened several times in horror and despair. H. More has just published 'Cælebs in Search of a Wife,' which we have read ;—very good advice to masters and misses, but quite out of your way. I don't know what she would think of me for learning Spanish when I don't half understand Italian, for she hates superficial ladies. This reminds me, though it would be too long a history to explain the connection to you ; but pray explain to me why Milton dares to make Eve inferior to Adam before the fall, when we *know* that they were created equal, and that her punishment was that she should be in 'subjection to her husband.' Allow me to observe that this is a mistake which only a man, proud man, could have made.

"I have been reading all Burns's works. I like his letters extremely ; only I wish he was not quite so wicked. As to his poetry, I meet here and there a few stanzas which please me, but all the Scotch pieces (and these are almost the whole) are perfectly unintelligible to me; and even if I should take the trouble to know the meaning of all the words, still I should have no pleasure, I think, because it would be ages before I could associate agreeable ideas with such uncouth-sounding words. I have been reading all Miss B.'s [1] plays. I could read 'De Montfort' a thousand times, and 'Basil' is a favorite ; none of the others do I ever wish to see again. I believe

---

[1] Joanna Baillie, born 1762, died February 23, 1851.

I have heard you mention some others of her writing besides the series, but I do not know them. I will not say anything about Coleridge's essay, but I am disappointed of a great deal of pleasure by its non-appearance—and everybody is disappointed of something; at least the glories of criticism promised a wide field of pleasure to many.

"This is all very stupid for you, Monsieur le philosophe; but if you will not furnish or inspire me with something to say, why, you must take the consequences. I have not forgotten the long letter, in answer to my dozen and a half, which you promised about two months since, and this, I suppose, is always the case; the few men in the world (and Heaven knows these are few enough!) whom one would desire ever to hear from always make themselves so scarce, that a letter once in a lustrum (isn't this the word I mean?) is all one can reasonably expect.

"I have been building and furnishing the most enchanting cottage for you, in imagination, that you can conceive. Seriously now, what do you mean to do? Only choose your spot and furnish me with a moderate sum, and I am at your service. But then, don't marry—this is the root of all evil, I assure you. Don't you know that you would be deceived? Are you not aware that it would be the easiest thing in the world for any one who had a mind to make you believe her an angel for a few short months, when you would find out the melancholy contrary? And then my cottage is not large enough to accommodate a wife and a dozen *small* children, who, poor things! must all learn to live upon air and philosophise themselves into feeling none of the vulgar necessities of mortals. But, alas! I fear I am preaching to the deaf adder which refuseth to hear the voice of the charmer, charm he never so wisely ! ! !

"I do but counsel thee to the wise resolution which at present I have taken myself. I mean to live and die in the woods which mine own hand hath planted, and to please myself with mine own solitary grandeur. I am delighted to hear you say that Wordsworth understands gardening, and am impatient to know what sort of a thing is a philosophy of gardening. I hope, as he is so well versed in the theory, he does not despise the practice. Mary desires me to say that she is in utter dismay about the prospectuses, and that till they come you well know we can get no subscriptions, for nobody will even offer to subscribe on the mere strength of our recommendations to a thing of which they know not even the nature. Two or three promises only we have had, and many people have been impatiently awaiting the prospectuses, but you are too much of philosophers, all of you too ethereal, not to ruin your own interests. You will let everybody cool, and they will not be easily roused again. Adieu.—Believe me ever your most affectionate Sister,

"JEANETTE DE QUINCEY.

"THOS. DE QUINCEY, Esq.,
      "William Wordsworth's, Esq.,
            "Grasmere, near Kendal, Westmoreland."

"WESTHAY, *Thursday Night, December* 14, 1809.

"MY DEAR BROTHER,—I have been deliberating for some weeks whether I should write to you or leave you to your fate as a punishment for your silence, but my extreme clemency has at length prevailed. I wish very much to hear whether you will have your box sent now. I suppose in that case we may inclose the money for Coleridge. We do not happen at present to have any friend in London who might pay it—is it not a shilling a number? To be sure I should never have guessed that Coleridge would have had patience to carry it on so far, and to talk with confidence of the twentieth number. I know one of his dilatory friends who would not, though a most interesting young man in other respects. I have not been in the way of hearing many opinions about it lately, but I believe all wise and sober-minded people disliked the tale in the thirteenth number, which they say is so unnatural.[1] One Lady I have heard of is going to give it up, after having with difficulty held out till now. For my part, I can't think what the good people expected; but I am tired of hearing their foolish criticisms. 'Coleridge deals so much in paradox; he is so extravagant, so incomprehensible,' is the ceaseless cry of those who have brains enough to make a remark at all. Those who think they have not content themselves with not reading him; they own he is too deep for their humble capacities. I conclude C. gives these latter entertaining numbers

---

[1] The tale in the thirteenth number of *The Friend* was "Maria Eleanora Schoning," and was by Coleridge himself.

to please the Ladies, poor things! He talks, you know, of a female correspondent who complains of the dulness of some of the numbers. I dare say she was compelled to write this by some stupid husband or brother who was ashamed to confess so much on his own account. My mother likes his Taxation number, and wishes he would write politics chiefly.[1] Then, and not till then, shall I call him uninteresting. I like his political papers when they come, but certainly not to the exclusion of a thousand other things.

" When are we to have the long-promised papers upon English literature ? Do you know who Satyrane was ?[2] I like his letters exceedingly. We should be seriously obliged to you to send or order to be sent the two copies of each of the two first numbers.

---

[1] The Taxation number was the twelfth, and is well worthy of the praise given to it ; but it is surprising that we do not find in these letters any queries about or reference to the series of sonnets—now so well known—on the Tyrolean patriots, &c., by Wordsworth, or the " Hymn before Sunrise in the Vale of Chamounia," by Coleridge, which appeared in the eleventh and twelfth numbers, as well as some specimens of Rabbinical wisdom from the Mishna.

[2] Satyrane was Coleridge himself. He wrote under that *nom de plume* a series of letters to a lady, describing his life and experiences in Germany. The letters are reprinted in the *Biographia Literaria* (vol. ii. pp. 182-254) ; and in the same work (vol. i. pp. 211-12) we find him writing : " By a gracious providence, for which I can never be sufficiently grateful, the generous and munificent patronage of Mr. Josiah and Mr. Thomas Wedgwood enabled me to finish my education in Germany. After acquiring in tolerable sufficiency the German language at Ratzeburg, which, with my voyage and the journey thither, I have described in *The Friend*, I proceeded through Hanover to Göttingen, where I regularly attended lectures on Physiology in the morning, and on Natural History in the evening under Blumenbach, a name dear to every Englishman who has studied at that University." Coleridge was born 21st October 1772, and died July 25, 1834.

Now, do for once in your life be a good boy, and defer not till to-morrow that which may be done to-day. Send these numbers, and with them a long letter telling us all about the northern poets and their children, and your own self and cottage. I want a sketch of the latter. Don't you find it very solitary sometimes, or is your friend Johnny sufficient company? With such a dilatory being as you, can I ever hope to see Westmoreland? Not, at least, till grey hairs are nigh and the years come in which I shall say I have no pleasure in them.

"I have been in Bath to visit Mrs. Kelsall, who, after spending a few days at Westhay, is returned to Manchester. We are of opinion that she is half mad. Westhay is very much improved since you were here, but has turned out much more expensive than was intended or feared. It is still in an unfurnished state, but will be a most beautiful place in time. Since you went we have walked so little on the down that we had nearly forgotten your old way to Brockley, and the other day I discovered with mortification that some malicious and evil-intentioned person has removed the old shoe placed by you as a landmark.

"How beautiful your birch woods must look now! We are planting weeping birches to produce the same effect in miniature. Have you any rose indicas? I shall have great pleasure in ornamenting your little garden when I come. I should think Autumn must be a most beautiful season to see it in—to me at least, who am an *Anti-spring-ist*.

"Have you any new communications to make

respecting books? The other day we were at Lansdown's, and with a true scholar-like contempt of dust, turned over all his old worm-eaten books, but we found nothing to please us. An old Tasso, which, being an Elzevir edition, I thought must be correct, I found had lost a volume, and Lansdown himself, civil and obliging as he is, has scarcely a pretension to know one book from another. Ours are all arranged in the book-cases, and look very well, though, to be sure, they are a pitiful collection. When I am rich I shall try to make it more respectable. I have not been tempted to open Hutton yet, except a little in Geometry. Is this the most interesting of the branches of Mathematics which he treats of? If it is, I am afraid my head is as unmathematical as it is unmetaphysical and unmetapolitical, to use C.'s learned and, I suppose, original term. A strange infatuation to have no exclusive taste for these sublime subjects! One would have expected better things from the sister of a Philosopher. Nevertheless I read C.'s papers with more attention and interest than, I dare say, half his friends; and I do mean to try what I can do with Hutton.

"Mary sends her love. She is going to put into the Lottery, and intends to have the twenty thousand; in that case you will hear more of us. Is your avaricious design of growing rich by the same means gone off? I have made particular enquiries on the subject, but the general opinion seems to be that there is not any of the foul play which we suspected. I am still rather incredulous.

"I conclude you have heard by this time from Richard that he is at Plymouth, expected to sail soon, and made master's mate, which is a higher sort of midshipman. Henry is going to spend three weeks with us. He is much improved lately, and reads Homer. Henry Leeves is just arrived from Oxford, and Mr. Elsdale is expected for the holidays. We have very little intercourse with this accomplished family. The Bridgers have been staying with us, and we are going to them for a week. The Mores never fail to enquire '*de vos nouvelles*,' particularly Sally, who calls you 'the sweet young man, Dr. Kantian.' With the Boaks too you are a great favorite; but don't be vain of these perishable honours; if you don't return soon your dearest *freundins* may perhaps forget you. Do you remember Sally More's prophecy that you would be a bishop, if you pleased? I wish you would please to be something which would raise you above the vulgar wants of this wicked world—a counsellor, for instance. You will come to this at last; at least so prophesies your ever-affectionate Sister,

"JANE DE QUINCEY.

"THOS. DE QUINCEY, Esq.,
    "Grasmere, near Kendal, Westmoreland."

"WESTHAY, *Friday, May* 3, 1811.

"MY DEAR BROTHER,—I suppose you are quite amazed that you hear nothing of us and our intended proceedings, and perhaps conclude that we have forgotten Grasmere and its attractions—and its inhabitants, I was going to add, but I recollect I ought to comprehend these under the second head; but you are mistaken, for Mary says we think of them all day and dream of them all night. Change all into every and I will swear to the assertion. Yet, alas! this letter is not to fix the day for our departure, as it ought to do, but simply to regret that this is impossible, for our evil genius, in the form of Mr. Scarth (Lord Darlington's agent), has arisen to torment us. This man is to settle a dispute which you may remember concerning Lord D.'s claim to a part of our land, but, instead of coming in May, as he promised, he has announced the beginning of June for his appearance; and my mother thinks she cannot stir till she has seen him. I will not attempt to describe to you what consternation; yea, what indignation; yea, finally, what calm despair was produced by these arrangements. You will perceive that by them not only is our patience tried most cruelly, and 'hope deferred,' we are told, 'maketh the heart sick,' but also we are thrown upon the hottest or the most rainy, and therefore, at any rate, the most disagreeable season of the year. At the same time neither Mary nor myself could patronise any plan for deferring our journey later than necessity requires, as a fine autumn, though the loveliest of all lovely things, is very uncertain.

"So much for our grievances. Do write and console us—say whether you are prepared to receive us when we do come, and whether you think we can scale your mountains in a July morning. We did talk of staying in Manchester first, but now this must be left till we return,—a delightful contrast to Grasmere and its environs.

"Pray, what do you sanguine politicians say to the evacuation of Portugal? I know you have laid aside your philosophic indifference on this subject, and therefore I may venture to ask the question; and do not you think Lord Wellington a great soldier? I never used to like him, but if his friends in the House of Commons do not exaggerate his merits, I cannot but think there is something very heroic in his disdaining to clear himself from the many aspersions and insinuations thrown out against him at home, and in the unwearied perseverance with which he follows up his own plans, which appear equally well conceived and well executed. Happily, however, he needs not my tribute of approbation, for most people seem to concur in acknowledging his merit now that he is fortunate, and perhaps is sufficiently rewarded in contemplating the effect of his exertions.[1]

"I expect to become a very able politician under

---

[1] And so, for a long period after Wellington's achievements were considerable, discussions arose about his powers and merits. It would seem that, though an aristocrat, he had to fight his way step by step, and in one of his own private papers declares that he was not favoured for a very long period either by the War Office or the Horse Guards; and that, even after he was distinguished, was cumbered by what they pleased to call a second-in-command, which he declares that he could not understand. It is characteristic of him that he declined or even disdained to clear himself from many aspersions and insinuations thrown out against him.

your tuition this summer, especially as I conclude
you and your friends are generally agreed on important points; otherwise, according to an expression
of an acquaintance of yours in this part of the world,
I may chance to be thrown *all abroad.*

" Letters from Richard lately announce that he
has sailed in the *Princess Caroline* in the expedition
for the Baltic. I cannot conceive what employment
they can find for so large a fleet in that quarter.
We have had very dismal weather here for the last
week, which is unlucky; for Mrs. Church and her two
children are staying with us, and town people have
scarcely an idea of the country being good for anything except in a sunshiny day.

" Mary and I returned lately from Clifton, where
we have been staying at different houses nearly two
months, and this period, with that which has elapsed,
makes it three months since we have been alone for
one day; otherwise I should have written sooner.
And now I take to myself some shame for sending an
epistle three hundred miles which has so little in it;
but I beg you to remember that it is written·in a
moment of all others the least calculated for sharpen-
ing the wits; namely, between the utter extinction
and the faint revival of hope.

" My Mother desires her love, and bids me say we
will come as soon as we can. Mary exists in the
same hope. I told them just now, with a sigh, that
it was this very day (4th May) on which in your last
letter you hoped to see us drinking tea in your
cottage. Alack! that ever it should be otherwise.

I must say, however, that *we* are beginning to look very beautiful in our spring dress; the Elms and most of the trees, except Oaks, are quite in leaf, and everything is rejoicing in the rain we have had. Westhay is improving every day, and our friends here say that it is most unsentimental to leave it just the first summer it is finished, but we are deaf to their kind admonitions.

"I mean while I am with you to read *all* the books in your library during the intervals of my climbing *all* the mountains; but my mother still talks of a month, and I fear we cannot do half what we wish in that time. I have no news to send you from our part, except that Mr. Cotterell and J. Pratt have both got livings; that Mr. C. has married Miss Boak, and J. P. is to lead off the other sister in a few months; so that we are likely to have a clear field. Your worthy friend Mr. Leeves is well, and is our great friend also. His brother, I believe, is gone to be a private tutor in some family. We are to have a neighbour shortly in that beautiful field just above us—an East India Colonel (Mackenzie).

"Adieu! I trust the next thing you hear of me will be how I am charmed with the ride from Winandermere to Grasmere. Pray write to my Mother, and believe me yours very affectionately,   JANE DE QUINCEY.

"THOS. DE QUINCEY, Esq.,
    "Grasmere, near Ambleside, Westmoreland."

"ARDWICK, 26*th July* 1811.

"MY DEAR BROTHER,—Any man but yourself would have a right to wonder at our dilatory proceedings, but *you* must consider us only as returning one of the many practical lessons which you in former times have bestowed upon us. I assure you, however, that we are all longing to be at Grasmere ;—to explain why we are not there I must travel back to Westhay. Two days before the one fixed for our departure Mary had been with Mrs. Hannah More to Brockley, and in alighting from the Barouche box of the carriage she fell and cut her face. This delayed us a week. However, it was healed and recovered its looks, and Mary grew impatient to set out, although she had by no means recovered her strength or the complete shock which she had received. My mother acceded, but unhappily the consequences of three days' jolting in hack chaises to an already exhausted frame has been a violent bilious attack, which has confined her to the house almost since we came here, which was last Wednesday week.

" Our intention was to have set off next Wednesday for Grasmere, but you will see the impossibility of this, or indeed of speaking with any certainty on the subject. We have Dr. Jarrold attending, and he gives us hope of a speedy recovery, but we do not know the exact degree of reliance to be placed on his promises. At present she is too weak to bear the slightest exertion. My mother says we will not fail to write again and give you the notice you desire; as soon as she sees any probability of our coming, she means to dispatch a box containing some books of yours, and tracts, &c., for your curate.

"I am very assiduously renewing my acquaintance with the town of Manchester. I think it possible I may never see it again, and I am determined not to be guilty of forgetting the land of my nativity any more. We think it very much improved, and really, on the whole, it is not so vile a place as I imagined. Mr. Kelsall's house at least is airily situated, and one may discover from it something in the similitude of green trees and grass. A slight quarrel I have with the inhabitants for all looking alike; one meets five hundred men in the course of a walk with scarcely, it seems to me, a shade of variety in the expression of their faces, but each appears .to be struck off in the same mould with his neighbour. Lavater would find very little subject of speculation here. We have been finding out all our old friends. Mr. Hall, surprising to say, gave us a most cordial reception, and appears entirely to have forgotten that we have been any other than the best friends in the world. The young men are grown out of all recollection; Rupel especially is a most singular-looking creature; he is going to be tutor to two of the Duke of Beaufort's grandsons. We have been to see also the Belchers, Mrs. Wilkinson, formerly Miss Eason, and several more whom you don't care about.

"We expect Mr. and Mrs. Elsdale from Wrington

to-morrow to enjoy the remainder of the summer in Long Milgate. I know not why I should write any more, seeing that I hope so soon to be with you. I have been solacing my impatience with a view which I have found of Grasmere Church; another comfort is that we have certainly avoided the least agreeable part of the summer and missed no very delightful weather. Mary and all the party send their love.—Believe me ever your affectionate

"JANE DE QUINCEY.

"THOS. DE QUINCEY, Esq.,
"Grasmere, near Ambleside, Westmoreland."

"28 RICHMOND TERRACE, CLIFTON,
"*March* 26, 1812.

"MY DEAR BROTHER,—It may be as well to tell you before I begin to write that my sole intention in doing so at this moment is to ascertain a matter of fact, and therefore you will do well not to expect to be greatly amused. Indeed, however much I might be disposed to exert my wonderful powers, it would at present be a vain attempt, as I am placed in the midst of a confusion of voices compared to which Babel would be a calm retreat.

"To proceed to business. My mother having heard through Richard that you are really agitating a remove to town, a sudden thought has started into her mind: 'What does he mean to do with Mary Dawson?' Perhaps you think of taking her with you, or you may mean to keep her still at Grasmere; or, alas! still more probably, this agitated remove may never take place; but the most distant hope of importing southwards a genius so rare in these parts is not to be despised by us. She promised, if ever she left you, to come to us, but, in such a case, might expect the first advances to be on our part.

"We are now at Clifton visiting the Kempes: we shall stay about a week, and if it is not too much to ask from mortal man, we should be very glad to know how the matter stands on the aforesaid subjects, as we are going to hire servants. This request will appear more modest if you count up the number of months which have elapsed since we heard of you, except indirectly. Your case affords a melancholy example of the degree of moral turpitude which, by continued habit, a man may learn to contemplate with composure. I can't help laughing in my heart to think of the believing sailor who has absolutely resolved to stay in London in the *Ignis Fatuus* hope of seeing you. He may wait long enough, I suspect.

"We have been reading Pasley, and are much delighted. He seems to have a surprisingly clear and comprehensive view of his subject, which, were it a less general concern than it is, must be made interesting by so much talent; nevertheless, though *on the whole* we agreed with him, several things struck us both as contradictory. At first he is in the depth of despair, seems to think nothing can save us but measures which we certainly shall be far from pursuing, and even these would be very risky. In the latter part his spirits seem to rise with the consideration of his subject, and all things, even the conquest of the world, seem to be nothing more than putting one's gloves on. Perhaps a second reading might have reconciled these seeming contrarieties. I should have supposed that you would not approve the high opinions he seems to entertain of Buonaparte's abilities.[1]

"It just occurs to me to remind you of a piece of advice which you have often given me with respect to books—Why, say you, don't you buy books instead of hiring them? Now, I paid fifteen shillings to a Bristol library for six months—three are elapsed, and I find I have read twenty-one vols. How many books, my good friend, could I have bought for 7s. 6d.? and in the meantime I must have vegetated without any. Adieu. My mother will fill this paper. My love to all my friends.—Ever your very affectionate JANE DE QUINCEY.

"We talk much of our enchanting walks in Westmoreland. I have always a strange feeling come across me when I think of Ullswater and twenty other places which take turns in my affections. My mother and I have rung every possible change upon the possible alterations which can have occurred in Grasmere; pray explain. I believe I have written exquisite nonsense, but I am indeed

---

[1] See footnote *in re* Pasley's book.

quite bewildered with noise. Henry Leeves is here,
just been to Oxford to take his Master's degree, and
now very ill of a fever. He desires to be remembered
to you. Mr. Elsdale has lost his election to the
school here by a very small majority, and with great
credit to himself—it is a great disappointment to
the Leeves.

"My dear Thomas, I have managed my acc^ts of
your Uncle's money so badly that I am obliged to
go to everybody for help, and to you to tell me, if
you can, what money you have ever had from your
Uncle as a present through me or Mr. Kelsall. I do
not expect to find any effectual clue in my application to you towards the clearing my acc^ts, but I shall
be obliged to you for a direct reply,—Yrs affect^ly,

"E. Q.

"Thos. de Quincey, Esq.,
    "Grasmere, near Ambleside, Westmoreland."

"Westhay, *Thursday, Dec.* 17, 1812.

"My dear Brother,—By this day's post Mary
has dispatched a letter to you at Grasmere, the
strain of which is to this effect; namely, to beg
that you will exert your influence wherever it may
lie for Henry Leeves, in a way which I will tell you.
You remember he had a cough when you were at
home, which has hung upon him for some months,

but was treated with little attention as a thing which his family ignorantly supposed of small consequence. Some unfavourable symptoms which appeared latterly, however, induced them to go with him to Clifton to consult Dr. Craufurd, who thinks everything depends upon his going abroad immediately, to escape wintering at home. Fortunately he has met with a friend who is Captain of a Sloop, and has offered to take him out with him directly to the Bermudas. He has got an introduction to the secretary of the governor of this island, but is ordered not to remain long on shore, but to proceed from one place to another in a more southernly direction. The result then is, that if you can procure from any of your friends letters to Portugal, Spain, Malta, Sicily, or, in short, any place in that direction, his course being quite uncertain, you will excite much gratitude in the family, who are in the utmost affliction at the possibility of losing this favourite, to which possibility they have only now opened their eyes. We thought that Southey would oblige you in this way, and perhaps Coleridge to Malta. If you are in London you may know others who have connections in some of these places. Need I add that whatever you do must be speedy, as Captain Kennedy is quite uncertain how soon his ship may receive sailing orders, but expects it very soon. To interest yourself you would only need to witness the distress of the family at this unlooked-for destruction of their prospects. Any letter must be sent under cover to us, as Henry Leeves is at Clifton. I shall be dis-

mayed if you do not receive this.   We have just had
a disquisition on the great want of principle evinced
in a man leaving home without the shadow of a
direction where one may find him.   Unless you are
altered in this respect, we think you would hardly
find in your heart to leave London while every day
brings such interesting news from Russia; you will
surely wait the illuminations for the capture of that
varlet, as our paper designates him, though I begin
to fear, alas! that he will take care of his individual
person whatever becomes of his army, which, I think,
can hardly escape.   Surely such a brilliant campaign
in so short a space of time is scarcely recorded in
history.

"I expect to be in London about the latter end of
January.   I want to know whether I am likely to
find you—where and how? and if I should have
occasion to remain a day or two in London, can I be
taken in at your lodgings?   The plan of my journey
is not yet adjusted, for Henry, on whom I depended
as an escort to town, writes word that an unforeseen
circumstance (which is couched in mystery and dark-
ness) detains him in Oxford this whole vacation.
He has sent down a magnificent engraving of the
High St., Oxford, with its college, handsomely
framed ! ! !

"If you pass through Liverpool you will find
Richard at No. 1 Leece St., Renshaw St.   I fancy he
means to take up his abode there, to the astonishment
of his country neighbours.

"Colonel Mackenzie has lost one of his children

since you left us, with water in the head; he is in too much sorrow now to be reproached for his prosing politics about the Russians, but Mr. Boak we do not spare. Really one can't help feeling sorry for the French soldiers, who are guiltless of either pleasure or profit in this expedition. If we can hardly bear the intense cold here, what must it be in those frozen regions almost without clothes!

"We are very busy in the prosecution of Dr. Bell's plan in our school, which improves as fast as we can expect, though we find great difficulty in its organisation from the beginning, simple as it appears to be, but we have all of us everything to learn and a great deal to unlearn. My mother received Southey's book. We lent it immediately to H. Leeves, so have not read it. We dined last week at the Addingtons', who are, on the whole, pleasanter people than the generality of this neighbourhood. I hope the young heir will exert himself for Henry Leeves, who is his particular friend. We are trying in other quarters, but our principal dependence is on you; so, pray, do not fail us. Let us know the particulars of your health. I hope these hard frosts have prevented a recurrence of your indisposition, as I hear that effect ascribed to them in maladies of various descriptions. No news of the Fortescues since you left us. They all hate writing, or I should suppose them ill. I hope the agonies of uncertainty in which the direction of this letter is conceived will be an instructive lesson to your feelings not again to leave us in such perplexing ignorance. If this fail to affect you, add the consideration of my benumbed fingers in a cold room turning over the letters of the last five years to find where Great Tichfield Street resides, or even if there be any Great Tichfield St. All send kind love.　Pray write immediately, I conjure you by whatever consideration is most likely to affect a heart so often flinty in this respect.— Yours very affectionately,

"Jane Quincey."

CHAPTER XIX.

PROFESSOR WILSON.

THE friendship of De Quincey and Professor Wilson was of such a remarkably close and constant character—bore, we may almost say, such a Damon-and-Pythias-like aspect—that, though much has been written of their connection, the utter beauty of it has not probably been even yet fully realised. They were of very different types, but each could make allowances for and sympathise with and appreciate the other. Wilson, with his buoyant vivacity, found much to love in his friend, perhaps on the law of contrast rather than affinity, and never changed though he had certainly much to put up with in the erratic and unpractical character of the Opium-Eater; but De Quincey, in an intellectual sense, had so much to confer; his conversations and letters were so stimulating and suggestive to Wilson, that Wilson on many knotty points to the end found him the one man to whom he could make appeal for advice, suggestion, and aid. And even in their money-matters and "accommodations," which, as was only to be expected, went *ajee*, and through De Quincey's unbusiness-like ways, Wilson, when this was the

case, shows the utmost consideration, and is ready
to make the most affectionate brotherly excuses for
his friend. We ourselves had no idea how much
Wilson had to bear in this way till we read the
letters that are to follow; but we have never pre-
tended that De Quincey in his earlier life, and
whilst prostrated under opium, was anything but a
perilous person to have much to do with in lending
to or in accommodating; and this, as we have said,
from mere helplessness in practical matters. But,
as will be seen from these letters, it was De Quincey
who was first the lender;—another proof that, so long
as he had it, his friends were welcome to his purse.
And this generosity and timely assistance Wilson
never forgot, but stood by his friend in all weathers,
even when the horizon was most cloudy. It will
perhaps be remembered that Wilson, through the
fault of others, was suddenly deprived of his fortune,
and plunged into difficulties, and, instead of peace
and study at Elleray, had to think of making his
way in the world; and by-and-by proceeded to
study for the Bar at Edinburgh. Hence the tone
of the first letter :—

I.

" Tuesday [*May* 1813].

" My dear Sir,—I was prevented from going with
you to Borrowdale by very urgent business in Kendal,
but had not time to tell you so in my note sent per
coach yesterday.—I am at present in greater diffi-

culties about the business I spoke of than I at that
time imagined. I heard on Sunday of several very
considerable bills of which I had no remembrance ;
others are far greater than I thought of; and, to
complete my bad fortune, some money now due to
me cannot be paid for some months. I therefore
cannot conceive any way of settling my bills here
and elsewhere without getting temporary assistance
from a friend. By not settling them, I fear that
very unpleasant effects would follow.

" When you so kindly offered your assistance on
our walk t'other day, my acceptance of it to my mind
seemed impossible. The shortness of our acquaintance renders it difficult for me to think that I can
have any right to request or accept such a mark
of kindness and regard, and, further, I have some
doubt of the *justice* of availing myself of your bene-
volent disposition, or of that friendly feeling you may
entertain towards me.—I hope, however, that on no
occasion of my life have I preferred my own interests
to those of a friend, and I w^d face any difficulty,
rather than be the cause of bringing a similar one
on any Man.—But your kindness suggested the relief,
and when I contemplate the idea I have of your
character, I venture to speak thus to you ; it being
the first time that I have ever spoken it to any
friend.

" £200 would, I believe, with what I shall be able
to raise elsewhere, keep me afloat for the Summer.
At Christmas, I shall be able to repay that sum,
together with the interest. On this plan alone could

my conscience allow me to accept of this sum from you. If you can advance that sum to me immediately, it w^d be a kind of *blessing;* for there are many feelings both of my own, and of one most dear to me, which it would save. I might say much to you on this request, but I cannot.

" If I live till Christmas, you will sustain no loss whatever. If I do not, your debt will be among my sacred ones, and will be paid. Otherwise, I could not have written this letter to you. Let me have a few words from you. I shall be at home on Wednesday afternoon, and also all Thursday. If you cannot come here a day before you go, I will come over if you remain at Grasmere.—Your affectionate Friend,   J. WILSON."

II.

"GRASMERE, *Tuesday afternoon, May* 11, 1813.

" MY DEAR SIR,—Having made my offer to you the other day in perfect sincerity, I am truly happy to learn that you have determined to accept it.

" I have detained your servant for the purpose of sending off by him a letter in time for to-morrow morning's post. Will £200 be enough ? If you are in very *immediate* want of the money, could you not draw upon me at a short date ? The money will most probably reach Ambleside on Monday night next.

" I am proud that you allow me so confidential a

place in your friendship; and, in the midst of my sympathy with you under your misfortunes, am glad that they have furnished me with an occasion for testifying (though by so trifling a service) that I am not unworthy of it.—Believe me, my dear Sir, very faithfully your affectionate Friend,

"THOMAS DE QUINCEY.

"JOHN WILSON, Esq.,
   "Elleray.

"*P.S.*—Excuse me for not writing more at length. I was asleep when your servant arrived,—not having got home yesterday from Borrowdale until midnight, and having had little sleep in the night from toothache. I shall be at home, I believe, all this week, but shall be most fully disengaged from business on Sunday, Monday, or Tuesday next."

III.

And this was the letter that went by Wilson's servant to the post :—

"GRASMERE, *Tuesday, May* 11, 1813.

"DEAR SIR,—I have an opportunity of rendering an important service to a friend by lending him immediately the sum of £200. Can you conveniently furnish me with that sum or with a considerable part of it by next Monday? I leave this place for London next Wednesday, and on Tuesday there is no post from Kendal; so that if your answer does not leave Manchester by Sunday night, it cannot be here before I go away.—I am, dear Sir, faithfully yours,   THOS. DE QUINCEY.

"Mr. JOHN KELSALL,
   "Merchant, Manchester."

IV.

"EDINBURGH, 53 QUEEN STREET,
   "*Friday, December* 17 [1813].

"MY DEAR FRIEND,—When I last saw you I thought it probable that I might pay a visit to Elleray at Christmas, but I find that I cannot do so. The Law Class continues during the Christmas week, and regular attendance on it, tho' of little utility, is necessary to admission to the Faculty of Advocates. I cannot therefore hope to revisit Westmoreland before the middle of April.

"On my arrival here I found that in a few weeks a number of new regulations were to be adopted by the gentlemen of the Law regarding the examination of candidates. It became necessary, to avoid their operation, to pass my Civil Law trials immediately. As I boldly petitioned to be examined on the Corpus Juris, and last week was examined by nine wigs, who were pleased to express themselves satisfied with my knowledge of the Laws of Rome, which are the foundation of much of our Scottish Law. In a twelvemonth from that time I shall be at the Bar, though I have still an examination in Scottish Law to pass thro'—to qualify myself even decently for which will require several hours' daily study. This I am told on high authority, tho' it seems not very consistent with reason.

"I begin to feel myself quite a barrister, and attend Court regularly, where I improve myself in the principles of oratory by listening to the numerous old men eloquent with which the Court abounds.

"In about a fortnight it falls upon me to open a debate in the Speculative Society (composed chiefly of Lawyers) on the question : ' Has the Peninsular War been glorious to the Spanish nation ? ' Now, I am sorry to say that I do not feel myself so well able to discuss this question as I ought to be, and if you have leisure to send me a few hints they will be most acceptable. I wish to be instructed by you in the following points :—First, in what essential respects the Spanish people have shown themselves superior to, or equal to, the Americans, the Hollanders, &c. &c., in this struggle. Secondly, some general reasons to account for their supineness and want of exertion at particular periods of this war. Thirdly, an answer to that objection to the Spanish character drawn from the non-appearance of first-rate men among them. Fourthly, an explanation of the causes w^h have prevented them from ever possessing one great and effective army. Fifthly, some good remarks on their behaviour during the year 1812, and at present. Sixthly, your opinion on what they w^d have done without Lord Wellington at all, and of the value of his achievements. In short, you will oblige me by giving me weapons of any kind to wield against the raw-boned regiment who will attempt to deprive me of ratiocination in this enquiry.

"The whole principle of such a debating Society as this is very absurd, but as all my friends and acquaintances will be present on this occasion, and as a little quackery is useful in the world, I w^d prefer making a good speech to a bad one, and really without your assistance and advice I fear that this will not be in my power.

"On the same night I must also read an essay on some political or philosophical subject. I find that I have not time, inclination, nor ability to write one. If therefore you have any essay by you that you think w^d surprise a Scottish intellect, or if you c^d direct me to one not likely to be known here, I can inform you of the effect which y^r reasoning produces in the Metropolis of Scotland. Something on literature, as Mr. Skeffington says, would be desirable; but if you can accommodate me with a paper of half-an-hour's length, the subject matters not, provided I can read the language in which it is composed.

"I suppose you will receive this on Sunday. I go to Glasgow on Friday (this day week), so I should wish to hear from you about this essay before I go. If you have one, you can send it per mail directed to me at 53 Queen Street. Your lucubrations on the Spanish War will be most acceptable as soon as convenient to you. Perhaps Wordsworth w^d write me a letter on the subject were you to inform him of the public appearance I am forced to make of myself.

"I remain in Glasgow only two or three days. I hope that your domestic concerns at the Town-end go on pleasantly, and that your new handmaid gives satisfaction. In your letter to me, and I take it for granted that you will let me hear from you, be so good as let me know what y^r intentions are about the Spring months. I c^d meet you at Grasmere about the middle of April, or indeed at any other part of the world, for six weeks. If you have any idea of a Highland walk, you can command me later on in the season. But, till I hear from you, no more. Mrs. Wilson, and indeed all the family, remember you with all possible kindness, and believe me, my dear Friend, yours most affectionately,

" JOHN WILSON."

Wilson, however, made up for his enforced absence from Elleray during the Christmas of 1813 by a longer stay in the autumn and winter of the following year, being there from the middle of September till after Christmas. We have one or two records of this stay : and our next letter may be regarded of interest by many as signifying to us that James Hogg, the Ettrick Shepherd, had either accompanied him to Elleray or paid him a visit, for we find De Quincey thus writing, inviting the pair to dinner :—

V.

"GRASMERE, *Friday, September 22nd,* 1814.

"MY DEAR WILSON,—I am expecting Mr. and Mrs. Merritt this evening on their return from Keswick—where I left them on Tuesday last:—so that to-night I cannot possibly come over. Moreover, it appears to me that Elleray is not in the way from this place to Wastwater; but rather *vice versâ.* However, if you and Mr Hogg will come to Grasmere to-morrow and dine with us at $\frac{1}{2}$ past 2 o'clock [I hope that hour will not be too early], we can arrange a plan for going thither in which possibly Merritt might be included; and that would delight him. He can't walk ['damn his body!' as he says]; but I think I can get a horse for him from Allan Bank.

"Mrs. S——r [damn her body!] has it in contemplation to run away from old S——r [damn his body!]. She told this in confidence to Mrs. Merritt —who told it in confidence to me—who hereby, my friend, tell it in confidence to you. Mind that you keep the secret as well as I have done; and then it will stand a chance of coming round to old S——r to-morrow morning, by the Whitehaven coach.—Faithfully yours, THOS. DE QUINCEY.

"JOHN WILSON, Esq.,
  "Elleray."

VI.

And, of course, the festive season of Christmas comes in for due celebration. We find De Quincey thus writing to Wilson on Friday, December 23, 1814:—

"My dear Friend,—I have promised for you that you will meet a party, viz.: young Mr. Jackson, Miss Huddleston, the family from the Nab, and others on Christmas-eve, Saturday, Dec. 24. Now, therefore, I conjure you do not bring me, your sponsor, into discredit, nor disappoint the company [who are all anxious to see you], by not appearing. So may a just God prosper your Law Schemes as you attend to this request. This note will be delivered to you by young J. Simpson, who is kind enough to ride over on purpose.—Most affectionately yours,

"Thos. de Quincey.

"*P.S.*—Come to dinner if you can, but at any rate, *Come.*

"John Wilson, Esq.,
  "Elleray."

VII.

" 53 Queen St. [postmark, *Mar.* 22, 1820].

"My dear Friend,—I begin to fear, indeed have feared for some time past, that you have not been well since we parted. If so, I shall be most sincerely sorry for it, and hope that with the approaching Spring weather you will pick up health and spirits. If not, I shall be extremely glad, and hope that you will let me hear from you at y^r leisure.

"When I last saw you at Bowness I wished to enjoy your society without alloy; and therefore touched as lightly as possible on any topic that might have been uncomfortable—as, for example, pecuniary affairs. The necessities of the situation in which I *now* stand drives me to write of these, and nothing but necessity w^d drive me to do so.

"A good many months ago I borrowed forty pounds from the only quarter which was within my power, to take up a bill or bills of yours, I forget which, to that amount.—I knew that it w^d be necessary for me to repay it at the precise time fixed by me, which time elapsed a few weeks before my last visit to Westmoreland. I did accordingly pay it with a difficulty and a misery of which I do not wish to recall the image to my remembrance. It was the utterly impotent situation in which I was left by that unavoidable payment which obliged me to write to you on the appearance of the two twenty pound drafts presented to me about a month before I visited Westmoreland, stating my inability to take them up. Mr. Cookson's twenty pounds I received only, but I mentioned to you that the twenty-five pound bill was not accepted by the person by whom it was drawn, and that I should have in all probability to refund the £25 which I received for it from the Bank here. This has accordingly happened. The Bill was brought to me a few days ago, and I returned the £25. This I did by borrowing the money from my brother's clerk for a couple of days, and next morning selling as many books as I could muster to an auctioneer for ready-money, by which I repaid the clerk at the time specified. The books did not bring one-third of their value. Soon after my return from Westmoreland the £25 draft of which you spoke to me in the Bowness Bowling Green was presented and paid. The letter from your Mother with money to that amount never has arrived, and a few days after I paid that Draft, a tax-gatherer came to me for £14, which I had not, and he threatened me with an execution in my house. I got the money from Blackwood, and so avoided that evil which would have been ruinous to me all my lifetime. The case therefore stands thus : that, being in debt to the very lips, these last two 25 pounds, £50 and the previous £40 = £90, have done me up : and I scarcely see how I can avoid bankruptcy.

" If I know anything of my own heart at all, I know my affection and my gratitude to you, and believe myself incapable of a mean action. ·Perhaps I ought not to have stated these things to you at all, for I know that it is not in your power to repay that money. I have, however, brought myself, most unwillingly, to tell you precisely how I am placed, and if I accept any more bills of yours, and am left to pay them, the necessary consequence is loss of credit, and an arrest. I declare to you, my dear

Friend, that life is scarcely endurable to me under the ignominious shifts and subterfuges that I have been driven to in order to take up these two last bills. Pardon me, if I have said anything to hurt you—for God knows that I love you, and w^d assist you to the last farthing of what I have. My affairs are at a crisis—not a hopeless one, but one that will be fatal to my whole future life if I should be forced to accept any more bills! As it is, I do not know how to extricate myself from present embarrassments. Yet I do not fear in a year or two to make things square again.

"I had wished to write about the Magazine, but know not now what to say. Unless something has occurred to make it impossible for you to send y^r contribution as you so solemnly promised when we parted, no doubt you w^d have done so. But I can never again mention the subject to Mr. Blackwood, who delayed the printing of the work several days on my assurance of a packet coming from you. It becomes daily a more difficult task for Mr. Lockhart and I to write almost the whole of the work, and when he is married it is not possible that for some months afterwards he can be in Edinburgh or at leisure to write. Your assistance is becoming, therefore, every day more desirable, and I have only to add that payment at the rate of £10, 10s. a sheet shall be monthly transmitted for your communications along with y^r Nos. of the Magazine. This I again pledge myself to do, and for the last time; for were I again to reiterate, I feel that I should be forcing the task upon you. Whatever and whenever you send, it shall be inserted, and nothing can ever come wrong.—With kind regards to all y[r] household, I am, my dear De Quincey, your most affectionate Friend, JOHN WILSON.

"Send y[r] articles addressed to the Editor, No. 17 Princes St., either in letters per post or in parcels per coach."

VIII.

In 1820 Wilson, on the death of Dr. Thomas Brown, was appointed Professor of Moral Philosophy in the University of Edinburgh.

"53 QUEEN STREET, *August 5th* [1820].

"MY DEAR FRIEND,—In your letter of the 26th you proposed to send in a day or two your review of Malthus. It is now the 5th of August, and I am beginning to fear that something may have occurred to stop your composition. *Ebony*, who is the child of Hope and Fear, and who has shown a face of smiles for some days, begins to droop excessively; and if the article does not come soon, no doubt he will commit suicide, which will be some considerable relief to me and many others of his well-wishers. Two sheets of the magazine was a promise that raised the mortal to the skies; so do not draw the devil down!

"I am quite at a stand respecting my lectures, but have been reading some books, some of which even I understand. What is good in Clark's 'Light of Nature'? He is an insufferable *beast* as to style, and seems to me to have no drift but to leewards. If you think otherwise, give me notice of those parts of his book that you think worth reading. As I have to lecture on Moral Philosophy, I should merely give such general views of the intellectual part of our nature as are essential to the understanding of Man as a Moral Being :—and first of the physical nature of Man. What should I treat of in the Senses—appetites and bodily powers ?—It seems to me —perhaps I said it before—that I sh^d have a lecture on 'The Origin of Knowledge' when treating of the Senses.—What are the books? and what theory is the true one? And your objections to Locke.

"Of the Intellectual Powers, I send you to-day a sketch by the late Professor Brown—my predecessor.—He had a great character here, and the book seems exceedingly ingenious. I wish during the winter—probably about the 1st of December, to explain his Theory to my students; and hope that you will read it, at your leisure, and discuss its merits and demerits fully and freely exactly as you opine them to be,—in letters addressed to me. I forget if I mentioned to you that I intend giving half-a-dozen lectures on the Greek Philosophy— Socrates, Plato, Aristotle, &c. Have you any books about them and their systems; or can you write me some long letters about either, or their philosophy ?

"What does, in your belief, constitute moral obligation ?—and what ought to be my own doctrine on that subject ?

" Are there good essays on the Stoic and Epicurean Philosophy, and where? What books ought I to read for disquisitions and views respecting the duties created by society. This branch, if I treat it at all this winter, and I think I must, is most exigeant.

" I sincerely hope that you will not delay, should you not have written to me already, to send me such information as I now seek, for time is flying rapidly, and I have few books.

" I write this letter, which probably contains repetitions, to remind you of the necessities of my present situation; and that nothing in the world w^d benefit me so much as your advice and assistance at the present juncture.

" In what I have said about your articles for the Magazine, do not imagine that I have any intention —however remote—of doubting that you will send them *if you can.*   That, however, I know, does, with all men, depend on a thousand circumstances.   I tried to convince Blackwood that you never *had engaged to* write for the Magazine, and his face was worth ten pounds—for it was as pale as a sheet.—I told him, however, that now you *were* engaged, so that if the articles don't come now, he will become a sceptic even in religion, and end in total disbelief of Earth, Heaven and Hell.—Believe me to be, my dear Friend, ever yours most truly,   John Wilson.

" *P.S.*—Stewart's ' Elements of the Philosophy of the Mind ' consists of 2 vols.—the latter of which contains ' Reason,' &c., and the former ' Imagination,' &c. Whatever of these you have not, I will send to you. There is a third volume of separate Essays, which I will send too immediately if you have it not; do let me know how the matter stands.

"I have received your long and entertaining letter of the 5th, so delayed sending this letter. Not hearing from you to-day (7th), I send it off. I see the necessity of secrecy. But I am working away. Can you give y^r letters a less mysterious outward form; and, pray, do not write anything on the backs. Time flies. I will not write again till I hear from you again. Adopt in your letters some ingenious disguise as to your object in writing.

"J. W."

IX.

"EDINBURGH, *Sunday* [postmark *Feb.* 17, 1821].

"MY DEAR DE QUINCEY,—I feel some difficulty in knowing how to write to you, as I fear you may be, or may have been ill: and it is my wish at all times to write nothing that may be otherwise than agreeable.

"I. I hope that hitherto I have behaved according to the best laws of friendship regarding the bills you have lately been forced to draw upon me. I have subjected myself by paying them to the greatest indignities and degradations. I say no more. Should I, some day or other, refuse to accept a bill of yours, I trust that you will do justice to my motives. I have considered the subject in every possible view, and see no possibility of accepting another bill. I have suffered for your sake that which I w^d not have voluntarily suffered for any other man alive.

" II. With respect to *Blackwood's Magazine*, I do not think that I can press that subject upon you any more, for, if you c^d write for it, surely you would; and therefore I am bound to believe that some cause exists to prevent you. This I most deeply lament, for, as money is necessary, and as £120, £130, or even £150 per annum could be made by you in this way—the fact of your not writing to that amount, obliges me to believe that some distressing cause prevents you from writing. God knows that y^r good is my object in having so often urged this request. Necessity makes me write, and nothing else almost.

" III. I am anxious to know from you, if you have done or still intend to do the 8 —— for me before the 1st of Novem^r. I trust that you will. I wish you w^d write one or two on Cause and Effect, but not unless you choose. I do not wish to say that by not fulfilling y^r promise of these 8 —— you will distress me much, for perhaps it may distress you more to write them, but to trust to them and eventually be disappointed w^d be a most serious calamity to me.

" I wish, therefore, much to hear from you; and speak of them as chapters in a work of your own, if you please, when you write to me. Could you contrive to give your letters a less mysterious outward appearance?

"I am greatly behind in my labours, having been ill of late with headaches and palpitation of my heart. It is in your power to confer a great benefit on me; but, if you do not, I shall attribute it to any other cause than want of inclination. You promised me a scheme and a list of books, but do not trouble yourself about them if it will hinder you from writing. An early letter will be most acceptable.—Your affectionate Friend,

"J. WILSON."

X.

"GLOUCESTER PLACE, EDINBURGH,
" *Thursday* [postmark 1825].

"MY DEAR DE QUINCEY,—We are all well and comfortable in our new house. Thank God, it is so; for between Moss Paul and Hawick my dear wife was taken suddenly ill—a fit of a hideous and appalling kind. I dare not think of the miseries of that hour—night and solitude—nor shall I distress you by any details. You who know her and me will know what must have been my agonies with her lying insensible and convulsed for half-an-hour in my arms in the mire of the road, with none to assist us, and Johnny and Bean weeping and wailing beside us. She is now perfectly recovered. Instead of reaching Edinburgh on Saturday night, we reached it on Tuesday. This fit was a repetition of that Mrs. W. had last summer, but its effects have not been nearly so severe, and the medical men say that nothing can be so cheering as to know that the second attack has been less violent than the first. I am grateful to God for her restoration, and live in hope that His mercy will be shown toward us. Do not speak of this; but indeed you feel on all occasions in such a way that any caution is unnecessary.

"I shall be looking out every day for your communications, which are much needed, I assure you. I almost hope that some beautiful things are winging their way hither at this time from Rydal Cottage. As soon as you have any one thing complete, send it off by *letter*, for the publisher is in a fever, and the volume must be shipped off to London in time to be published there, *some weeks before the New Year*. This, he says, is the meaning of the appellation JANUS. Remember that everything you think good, on whatever subject, and however short, original or translated, will answer our purpose. Without your timely assistance the double-faced old gentleman will assuredly be damped, for Lockhart left Edinburgh this morning, and is all in a bustle about his change of life, and I have been palsied by that late terror.

" Fifty guineas a year will add to your Incomings or Comings-in (which is the most abominable word it is hard to decide), and, if *Janus* prospers, *that* you will receive for 100 pages easily written, being but two sheets of a maga, every 1st of December till Doomsday. Do not disappoint me then, my dear Friend, and believe me to be, now and always, yours affectionately,

" JOHN WILSON.

" *P.S.*—I trust that everything you send will leave Ambleside by post in letters on or before Thursday the 10th, for Saturday the 12th is positively the last day that can be allowed—say then Saturday the 12th the last day on which your pen works. But unless I get copy (accursed word !) the press will be stopped before that."

The following letter is of a date somewhat later, after Mrs. de Quincey had been some time in Edinburgh, and had fallen ill :—

"MY DEAR DE QUINCEY,—I am truly happy to hear that Mrs. de Quincey is much better ; and I hope ere long will be restored to her usual state. Dr. Abercrombie has the first character in Edinburgh for skill.

"I am absolutely enslaved at present by my Political Economy Lectures, but you cannot come amiss any night—*except to-morrow*—this week.—Yours affectionately,   JOHN WILSON."

It may be here necessary to add that, whilst the Editor's aim has been, as far as possible, to let the letters speak for themselves, it must be borne in mind that in hardly any case do we have the letters continuous and complete; and that, if we had, further light might be thrown on some points and first impressions modified. In the case of Professor Wilson's letters, it hardly needs to be pointed out that they belong mainly to a period which De Quincey himself has characterised, in very explicit terms, as one in which other economies besides political economy tended to go to wreck; and that later letters, had they been preserved, would have done much to modify the impression that might be drawn from some of them, as though De Quincey, having once done Wilson a friendly favour, was ever after drawing bills upon him with the most awkward consequences for Wilson. For many years after the date of the last letters here given De Quincey wrote much in *Blackwood's Magazine*, of which Wilson was, in effect, editor; and in this case, as in others, the lapses in business matters in a period of deep prostration were to a great extent atoned for. The handing of their purses to one another, with full faith, as it would seem, that the future would somehow, as if by a kind of magic, work out order for them, is not to be commended, as likely to lead to a deepening of respect and friendship; but it is pretty clear that, at a certain time, it was practised by this circle pretty well all round : it is something to know that accounts were satisfactorily "squared" up, in so far, at all events, that Wilson and De Quincey to the end remained the most attached friends.

XX.

THE letters from Sir William and Captain Hamilton
are very few and short, a circumstance due to the
fact that, after De Quincey became intimate with
them, he was always in close neighbourhood, with
many opportunities for personal intercourse, but the
letters will suffice to show that neither he nor his
biographers have exaggerated the intimacy. The
letters from Captain Hamilton ("Cyril Thornton")
regarding Mrs. de Quincey's illness are those, surely,
of a very attached and warm friend. It may be
mentioned that "Cyril Thornton" was published in
1827, and that Captain Hamilton also wrote a
"History of the Campaigns of the British Armies in
Spain, Portugal, and the South of France from 1808
to 1814," which was published in 1828. Captain
Thomas Hamilton died at Pisa on the 7th December
1842 ; and there appears in *Blackwood's Magazine*
for February 1843 an affectionate obituary notice of
him. His last work was "Men and Manners in
America," of which two German and one French
translation had already appeared at the date of

the *Blackwood* notice; and of the work *Blackwood* then said that it was "eminently characterised by a tone of gentle, manly feeling, sagacious observation, just views of national character and institutions, and their reciprocal influence, and by tolerant criticism."

The letters of Captain and Sir William Hamilton are uniformly without dates, but must belong to the years 1831–7 :—

I.

"5 DARNAWAY STREET, *Saturday.*

" MY DEAR SIR,—I find my brother is engaged on Tuesday, and I think it would be more pleasant for you to come on *Monday,* should you happen to be disengaged on that day.—Believe me ever, my dear Sir, very truly yours,

" T. HAMILTON.

" THOS. DE QUINCEY, Esq."

II.

" MY DEAR DE QUINCEY,—Will you not break thro' your rules and dine with us to-day at 6 o'clock ? *No party.* .Only my brother and perhaps one other gentleman.—Ever very truly yours,

" T. HAMILTON."

[Note by De Quincey :—" *Monday, March 3rd.* Dined there on this day."]

III.

"MY DEAR DE QUINCEY.—Will you allow Maggy [1] to come to us on Monday next, as you were good enough to promise Mrs. Hamilton? I have been often threatening to call on you, but the days are so short, and I do not get out till so late, that I have never yet effected my purpose. I hope, however, your daughter's being here will be an inducement to you to offer us a dinner visit whenever you are so inclined. We are, I may say, always at home, and *always* shall be glad to see you.—Believe me ever, my dear De Quincey, very truly yours,

" T. HAMILTON.

"DARNAWAY STREET, *Friday.*"

IV.

"MY DEAR DE QUINCEY,—Mrs. Hamilton is in bed to-day with a headache, and therefore I fear your little girl would find it stupid work being with us to-day. To-morrow, however, we shall be delighted to receive her, tho' I fear, poor thing, she will find our house dull enough at best. Being absolutely alone, it would be an act of charity if you would come and dine *tête-à-tête*, but this I have not the conscience to press, tho' your doing so would give me

---

[1] Maggy—Margaret, De Quincey's eldest daughter, later Mrs. Robert Craig, then a mere girl.

the greatest pleasure. I hope Mrs. de Quincey is well, and with best wishes and regards, believe me ever, my dear De Quincey, very truly yours,

"T. HAMILTON.

"5 DARNAWAY STREET, *Monday.*"

V.

" MY DEAR DE QUINCEY,—I am very sorry indeed to hear of Mrs. de Quincey's illness. Mrs. Hamilton begs me to say that if there be anything this house can afford either esculent or potable, which would be either useful or agreeable, she begs you will let her know. In short, if she can be of use in any way it will give her and both of us the greatest pleasure. I hope, however, Mrs. de Quincey is already in a fair way of amendment, and I now write to beg that if you can bear the society of a *bookseller* and a *printer* you will dine here in such vulgar company on Wednesday next. I sincerely hope Mrs. de Quincey's health will then be no obstacle. In the meantime I have only to say we shall be most happy to see little Maggy on Thursday. But never mind her dress. Annette will supply her with anything she wants.— Ever, my dear De Quincey, yours,

"T. HAMILTON."

VI.

"My dear De Quincey,—Our Cook calls to know whether she can dress anything for Mrs. de Quincey, who, I trust, is better. I have desired her to see you, and you will of course not scruple to order anything that may be either useful or agreeable to the invalid. If you can get away either to-day, to-morrow, or any other day, I trust you would come to dine with us, for you must be very solitary. We are quite ready for your little girl whenever she can be spared, Mrs. H. and I being quite re-established.— Believe me ever, my dear De Quincey, very truly yours,   T. Hamilton.

"*Saturday Morning,*
        "Thos. de Quincey, Esq.,
        "18 Duncan St."

VII.

"My dear De Quincey,—I write to express my hope that Mrs. de Quincey is again recovered, and that Maggy is to come to us to-day according to promise. Mrs. Hamilton bids me expressly prohibit you from taking any trouble about her dress; it really is entirely unnecessary, as we see no company. Mrs. Hamilton likewise bids me say that she would have called on Mrs. de Quincey, but she is at present not equal to the exertion of paying visits. We both hope Mrs. de Quincey will be good enough to accept this apology, and that we shall have the pleasure of seeing both her and you at dinner as soon as she feels equal to such an exertion. Tell Willy to come at all hours to see his sister.—Believe me ever, my dear De Quincey, very truly yours,   T. HAMILTON."

.

VIII.

"MY DEAR SIR,—I shall send you the book from Colquhoun to-night. He is coming to drink some negus with me to-night. Would you join him— about ten—with the children?—Yours ever truly,

"W. HAMILTON.

"*Sunday Night, Dec. 23.*"

IX.

"MY DEAR SIR,—If you are not better engaged this evening would you come over to Coffee—with the Children?—Yours ever truly,

"W. HAMILTON.

"*Sunday.*

"Give bearer only a verbal answer."

CHAPTER XXI.

LATER LETTERS OF JANE DE QUINCEY.

I.

"WRINGTON, *Saturday, July 3rd,* 1813.

"MY DEAR BROTHER,—An important communication which I ought to have made sooner, I am now afraid may come too late—a certain parcel I left at Miss Hewson's directed to Miss Hazelfoot, Devonshire Place; it was on the chimney-piece of my bed-room. If it was never sent for, can you contrive to convey it as directed? I shall be glad to pay porterage for the same. My mother is much better; she is at Clifton for a fortnight in Dr. Bridge's house, where she can give you a bed if you please any time before next Tuesday week. I can't send you any news, as I am writing from the Rectory, where Henry and I are dining. The latter is still house-hunting. At present the Banks of the Wye preponderate in his esteem, but it is not impossible that the visit of this day may transfer his affections to the *Yeo.* You are much remembered here, and much expected to dance at the Club on Tuesday with Mrs. Elsdale.—Ever your affectionate JANE QUINCEY.

"Miss Leeves says: 'Tell him I *must* doubt his gallantry if he does not come.'"

II.

"WRINGTON, *Saturday, Sept. 9th,* 1815.

"MY DEAR BROTHER,—It is singular to see how long a man retains the power of surprising people, and, contrary to the maxim long established, how prone the wisest are to wonder, since even we cannot take in the circumstance of your three weeks of business being lengthened to three months. Let us hope that it is by this time satisfactorily settled, and that you will not delay your visit till the whole of this fine autumn is fled. Many people have inquired after you, some to promote colloquy, and some from kinder or less idle motives, among whom always reckon the Mackenzies, who are very desirous to see you. Another person interested in your movements is Mr. Haviland Addington, who has thoughts of making a walking tour to the Lakes, and hopes to find you there. I have not seen him for a week, and when I did he was looking out for a companion, which is an article, when it must be found in the shape of a young man, so uncommon that I think he will probably be obliged to give it up till next year—but I told him I should mention it to you. The Addingtons are the pleasantest people, on the whole, in this county, when you get well acquainted with them. I met at dinner there last week a Gentleman who had travelled in a coach with a certain man who told him that Coleridge was separated entirely from his wife and had taken a house at Calne. Did he lie? I hope for the sake of all concerned that this is only the exaggeration of malicious gossip.

"I have bought Southey's 'Roderick,' which I prefer to anything *I* have seen of his poetry. How was it you did not join my mother and Mary in London? They had a pleasant set of rooms in Berkeley Square, with a carriage, &c., which Mary did not enjoy much, for she was very ill during half the time. They were out only ten days.

"I talked over the Lakes with young Addington the other day, till I fanned into a fever the constant desire I have to see them once more in my life, and I regret exceedingly that the state of society will not permit a lady to travel with any companion that may offer. If *brass* had been abundant we should certainly have looked in upon you. I can't imagine what you are doing or why we have never had those C—— we were to expect before Easter. Ah, my friend, how many fair years are passing away! It appears to me that the world is at present in a very decayed state. I don't mean the shell itself, for that seems to me more beautiful than ever, but, in the first place, there is a sort of stagnation in public affairs, neither a war nor a tax to furnish a little excitement to the famishing politicians; nay, to descend to minuter occurrences, there is not an earthquake nor a murder of any note to rouse one. A still more alarming fact, which seems to portend the approaching dissolution of the world, is the very rapid decline of all sorts of sense; the increase of folly in my short experience being so great that I am fully persuaded the next generations will not, except in a few favoured instances, be able to keep

themselves out of fire and water. As a temporary
amendment of this evil, Mary and I propose to
burn all our acquaintances whose mental or moral
maladies place them in the list of incurables, and
it is astonishing how few common honesty would
permit us to save from the grand conflagration.

" We have lived this summer in a state of pleasant
vegetation, solacing ourselves with the charming sun
and the beautiful country, and with visions of delightful people and delightful books, and regions of un-
tried knowledge and travels beyond the seas! Do
send a letter like an angel visit and tell us some
good thing.

" Henry is still at Dulverton, where he has got
acquainted with his neighbours. I wish you could
give me any news of Richard. We don't know
where to write. We are expecting General and
Mr. ——, Indian friends of my Uncle and the Kel-
salls, for a short time on their way to or from Bath.
The Kempes are all at Ilfracombe.

" What more can I say unless you will write? It
is like writing to a man in distant spheres to whom
you are ashamed of communicating the everyday occurrences of poor humble earth, or to a friend of former
years so long unseen that he may be grown over with
hairs and eat grass like Nebuchadnezzar, and of course
any allusion to his former state would be painful.

" Mary sends love. This is the last frank we
shall get this year; remember Mr. A. is not restricted
to any weight, a fact which some of the post-offices
do not know, and one which we sent was charged

7s. 4d. from this mistake. Again I entreat you to send us some good news.—With remembrances to our friends in your parts, ever yours,

"JANE QUINCEY.

"Miss B. bids me say your rug is finished and will be sent in due time."

"THOS. DE QUINCEY, Esq.,
    "Grasmere, Ambleside, Westmoreland."

III.

"WRINGTON, *Monday, May* 31st, 1819.

"MY DEAR BROTHER,—I am sorry I could not at once reply to your letter, which I should have done had there been any money in the house which could render it serviceable. My Mother, intending to go to Bristol to-morrow, waited till that visit should enable her to get a proper bill drawn by her banker there.

"The sum you mention sent last summer as an annual remittance from my uncle is intended to be so, and would have been forwarded to you naturally at the time answering to the date in my mother's note-book—I think the 15th of July, and with it half a year's warehouse rent not yet paid, though due last Ladyday, and which Mr. Kelsall proposed to remit to my mother with her Midsummer quarter. I am surprised you should not have heard of his failure, which happened four or five months since, in consequence of extensive speculations in which you would have fancied plodding John was the last person to have thought of engaging. Of course we are in a degree sufferers by his losses. Most happily in the course of the last 2 years my mother has gradually removed about seven thousand pounds from his hands,—to her no small matter. *Now* he has not above £1000 among us all unsecured. He has compounded with his creditors for 15s. in the pound, to be paid by instalments in 18 months. After this he fancies he shall still have something left to recommence business in a small way, and promises to pay off the remaining fourth part of our debt, but we think it safe not to expect it.

"Mary and Mr. Serle are settled at Brislington, in rather a pretty, well-wooded neighbourhood, 2½ miles from Bristol on the Bath road, and 14 from us. Mr. S. has the curacy and lectureship in the room of Mr. Simpson, who died lately; the last is a perpetuity, and has the advantage of exempting him from residing on his living of Oddington, near Oxford, where there is a mere farm-house in, as you know, a direful country. They have been so fortunate as to get an excellent house, a little out of the village, with a beautiful garden, &c. I have not yet seen them since they went to reside there at Ladyday, but shall soon follow my mother, who is on her way to-morrow to stay there during Mary's confinement, which is to take place in a few weeks. You will probably hear of this event, if not before, when the Manchester money is sent to you.

We leave Westhay, which is now in high beauty, quite empty; Mrs. Brotherton being on a visit to Boston, where it is thought Fitzwilliam cannot last long.

"Henry's address at present is 5 Nelson Place, Clifton, but as he often changes, any letter had better be sent here. His wife, who is a *lovely* creature, has wretched health, and he nurses her with a devotion *rare* in any one, and almost amusing from him, who has not had much credit given him for constancy. He actually *fainted* dead away lately, when Mr. Burrough told him, with as much preparation as possible, that, tho' his wife was better for the present, he was not without fears that her complaints might sooner or later terminate in consumption. I should be deeply grieved if he were to lose this only thing which seems to steady him, and if he were to marry again he would hardly find a person so amiable, circumstanced as he is, to take him, to say nothing of the alarming prospect of children, which she is happily free from. Of course they often get into scrapes about money, but *on the whole* get on better than could be expected.

"Of Richard we have heard nothing since he acknowledged the receipt of the money my mother sent. I suspect he is trying his fortune somewhere in the land of adventure, as he calls America. My Uncle continues at the Cape for his health, which improves. My Mother pretty well.

"I have spent so much time in giving you this short account of our domestic affairs as to have left myself no room to speak of my Swiss tour and the extreme delight it gave me. I never feel *perfectly* satisfied as to scenery except in a mountainous country. I remember I felt the same vivid pleasure when I first opened my eyes on a mountain in Westmoreland, which had also the advantage of being the first that had enchanted me. It is odd that I felt comparatively very little of the same enthusiasm the year before last when we travelled thro' a great part of Wales. Many very fine, very lovely spots we certainly visited, but, in a general way, the objects seemed to me to want that *keeping* and proportion among themselves which holds, according to their respective magnitudes, in each of my other mountain impressions. The vallies are as large as those of Switzerland, without the corresponding majesty of their surrounding mountains. On the whole, I travelled thro' Switzerland with a pleasure almost amounting to pain, when I considered how soon I must leave it; and I live in the hope of some time returning to explore the wild country of the Grisons and other lands of romance which we had not time to visit.

" My mother desires me to leave her a little room, so I must conclude with the fervent hope that you may find another fine summer, such as I hope we are going to have, effectual to the relief of your health and spirits.—I am sure we have had days already which might, as you used to exclaim, ' cure all sadness but despair.' I am a surprising *doctress* in the village, and think I could cure you if you were here.

Everybody, you know, in this generation has stomach complaints, which, tho' they do not kill, are most wearing to the mind and spirits ; and you philosophers go the wrong way to work—when you should take a few simple *pillules* and bitters, drink milk and keep early hours ; you sleep when you should wake, write when you should sleep, in a fit of absence eat the most unwholesome things, and then swallow opium for the whimsical cure of these heterogeneous ills. Lest you should distrust my medical skill, I give you an example quite out of the common way in a cure I have just made of a Cow of ours, who, given over by the *professional* men, was dying in the slow consuming agonies of a stomach complaint. I administered a powerful medicine first, which I do not discover to the uninitiated, and then dosed her with Quercus cortex till, in spite of the physicians, she began to hold up her head, and now eats and thrives like her neighbours.

"I hope you will, however, be able to write—I think 10 guineas a sheet would make me do wonders. And, after all, the performances which you might execute with the least satisfaction to yourself would often be read with very different feelings by those whose spirits and interest in the subjects were more alive. Moreover, if you only got fairly into the midst of *something,* I should think exertion would more and more quicken your powers and make you forget your maladies.

"I hope your family (what an odd word to write to you !) continues healthy and blooming, and that your wife has quite recovered her indisposition. Pray make my kind regards to them all, and believe me your very affectionate   JANE QUINCEY.

"The *Spectator* somewhere says : ' I never *do* pardon mistakes by haste.' I hope you do, as I am in the midst of packing for Brislington, and cannot read over this morsel of eloquence."

"MY DEAR THOMAS,—I enclose a Bill on London value £100, which is your Uncle's £84 and your half-year's Warehouse rent which I am to receive from Mr. Kelsall. The rest I have made up, and it is all I can do. I will pay the interest to your Uncle of the £160 till you have recovered from the pillage of your dishonest serv^t.—With love to your wife and children, I am, your affectionate Mother, E. Q.

" Pray acknowledge receipt to me at Revd Philip Serle's, Brislington, near Bristol.

" THOS. DE QUINCEY, Esq.,
  " Grasmere, Ambleside, Westmoreland."

Jane de Quincey lived to a long age, and was never married. In her later years she, like her mother, adopted evangelical views ; and it was the business of more than one of Mr. de Quincey's daughters to cheer her lonely hours, after she was aged and feeble, by reading to her favourite books, of which she never tired, though not seldom the patience of the reader was so; for they were mostly of the old-fashioned style of trivial dull story or treatise, with but little to meet the tastes or satisfy the cravings of the younger generation. She had a great love of gardening, and soon transferred the homely gardens at the various places where she lived into tasteful and beautifully laid out parterres; and her careful economy and admirable management of her investments were equally remarkable—her solicitor declaring that in these matters she scarcely ever made a mistake. She died on the 10th of February 1873.

CHAPTER XXII.

LATER LETTERS OF MARY DE QUINCEY, AND LETTERS
FROM MRS. HANNAH MORE.

I.

" WESTHAY, *July* 24, 1809.

" MY DEAR BROTHER,—If this letter should meet you, it will inform you that the Queen's Head, Redcliffe St., is the place of rendezvous for the Wrington Carriers.

" What could be in Mrs. Kelsall's head, when she told you we were not on good terms with the Leeves family, I cannot imagine. Be assured, however, it is all a mistake. I conclude from your enquiries about Silver Leg you have not received a letter I wrote to you in the North. He *is* yet alive, the young man of whom ye spake; and talking of *Legs, his* have to-day been splendidly arrayed in white silk hose in honour of his Sister's wedding.

" We shall walk towards Brockley on Thursday evening; to-morrow I think there is no chance of you. You have surely not forgotten the tall Thistle and the old shoe. Pursue that road and we shall meet. Till then farewell, my charming Brother.

" But first I must tell you that Hannah More

69

sends you word she is keeping some of her best Artichokes for you, and desires you will come and eat them without any delay. I met two of the ladies to-night, and told them we expected you on Thursday. Polly immediately exclaimed, 'There shall not be another artichoke ate till he comes!'—Ever your affectionate   M. DE QUINCEY.

"THOS. DE QUINCEY, Esq.

"Miss de Quincey requests Miss Dyer will have the goodness to deliver this letter to her Brother if he should call in Broad St."

II.

"WESTHAY, *April* 26, 1810.

"MY DEAR BROTHER,—I have lately been in Bristol, and have made many enquiries concerning water carriage for your books. I find that there are Vessels frequently sailing from thence to Liverpool and sometimes to Lancaster, but even if they were sent to Liverpool I suppose they would be forwarded northward. I now wish to know where you would have them directed. You mention Kendal in your last, but I have not been able to ascertain whether there be any water conveyance between that place and Lancaster. You, who are so much nearer to the source of information, might easily enlighten yourself on that head. I wish, however, you would let me know soon, as it is really high time poor Mrs. Hall should be disburdened of three ponderous boxes which have remained in her house in Dowry Parade since we left it. I suppose it is in vain to ask you if you remember how many you ought to have. I concluded these three to contain books because of their weight. I hope when they arrive in Westmoreland they will not prove to contain any of our household goods.

" My Mother has been expecting to hear from you ever since you left us. Have you forgotten that you were to write on the subject of your finances ? Are you not horribly poor ? and don't you find house-keeping a ruinous concern ? If you have discovered a mine of gold in your mountains, let me know, and I will come and see you immediately ; otherwise I shall not have the conscience to add to your poverty by increasing your expenses. If this difficulty were surmounted, pray tell me how I am to journey to you. These, alas ! are not the days when one can mount a white palfrey and ride unmolested through woods and vales, over hills and downs. From all this, I think it pretty evident that you ought to come to visit us, and then we might go back in company ; or what do you think of making a walking tour through Wales, by the way ? We have a very backward Spring in this part of the World. The woods are only now beginning to come out. Westhay improves but slowly, though I suppose you would find it much altered since you saw it. We have green grass plots, and budding trees, and a promise of a wilderness of sweet flowers, but unsightly heaps of brick and mortar still meet the eye. The Ladies of Barley Wood often enquire after you. They say you invited them to come and pay you a visit in your Cottage. Sally More says, 'Oh, 'tis a sweet young man!' Henry has just been to enter himself at Brazenose College. He does not reside till next spring. Jane is not at home, so I am not able to refer to your letter, in which I remember you mention several remedies for the toothache, upon which subject I have to observe that I believe all *hot* things apply'd to the teeth, though they will sometimes give a temporary relief, are highly injurious in the end, and as you cannot put anything on one tooth without touching all the rest, you endanger your whole stock. Therefore I strongly recommend you to abstain from using them. Any outward application to the face, I should suppose, must be harmless. A Lady told me the other day that a Laurel leaf made warm at the fire and then bound on the cheek would often produce a very good effect. What is become of 'The Friend'? — Believe me your affectionate Sister,   M. DE QUINCEY.

"THOS. DE QUINCEY, Esq.,
     "Grasmere, Kendal, Westmoreland."

III.

"WESTHAY, *June* 30, 1810.

"MY DEAR BROTHER,—Far be it from me to insinuate that you are a man to be suspected of a deficiency in punctuality. Yet you know, to any

person it might happen that, though they fix to leave
a place the next week, they might defer it to the
next, or the one after that, or even to a more distant
period. These and some other considerations deter-
mine me to hazard a letter to Grasmere; if you
should have left it, I suppose it will sleep quietly till
you return. Before I proceed I must thank you for
your plan and enchanting description of your Cottage.
To give you an idea how ardently I desire to see it,
to range those mountains and to hang in ecstasy over
those clear waters which have been the subject of so
many of my sleeping and waking dreams, is quite
impossible. I do not, however, know whether we
shall be able to persuade my Mother to fall into the
plan which your journal proposes. I trust more to
your eloquence than to my own, and therefore shall
not urge her much till you arrive here. What will
be the *damage* of the journey, think you? I fear
not less than thirty pounds there, and as much back.
I do not quite understand from your letter whether
you intend to visit Westhay before or after you go to
London. I imagine the latter. If you should see any
book bargains in Town, I leave it to your discretion to
make a small purchase for me; any tolerable Spanish
or French work would be useful, as we have so few.
If Mrs. Radcliffe's ' Romance of the Forest ' and
' Italian ' are to be had for little, it would be pleasant
to add them to our Mysteries. I don't mean by any
means to confine your choice to these books.

"I hope you are going to take a degree at Oxford.
Does not your heart dance at the idea of adding B.A.

or M.A. to your name? We had a letter from Richard about a fortnight since, dated from the mouth of the Loire. If you do not already know it, it may be well to inform you that no letter directed to him out at sea will reach him unless *post* and *packet* paid. If you direct to the Crown Hotel, Plymouth, it is still right to pay the postage.

"You may expect to see our garden much improved, though still far from the excellence to which we hope it will attain. The season has been very unfavourable to the growth of our young shrubs. We have had as little rain as you, and of course suffer from a want of grass and hay. The two fields have, however, yielded about as much as will serve the pony and two cows during the winter. One luxury our southern situation procures for us that cannot be had in your beautiful country—I mean the musical notes of the nightingale. Our woods abound with them—they have now, indeed, almost concluded their singing for the season. Can you tell me whether they ever sing again in the autumn, as the Encyclopædia informs me? for I don't think myself bound to believe them, as they also observe that their usual time of beginning to sing is often six o'clock, whereas they are to be heard at almost any hour in the day. Did not I tell you when I last wrote that my Mother had sent two pounds by post to the printer of 'The Friend' at Penrith?—yet you say you have just paid for the whole quantity we have had. By the way, I must here mention that we have never had *any* 1st or 2nd Nos., and but *one* 24. If you do not bring them with you I am persuaded we shall never get them.

"This day (July 1) we have witnessed what is become almost a phenomenon—two showers of rain ; distant thunder is rolling all round us, and the air feels as hot as if we were near the crater of Mount Vesuvius. The news in this part of the world is that Miss Leeves is to be married to Mr. Elsdale in a week or two. Miss Boak also, it is said, is going to lead Mr. Cotterel to the altar, or he is to lead her, if you will. Silver Leg is become much more sociable than he used to be, and occasionally calls in at tea-time. He shall sing a glee for you when you come. My Mother sends her love, and will be very glad if you come as soon as you tell us. Give my love to little Dorothy Wordsworth, and tell her we must be sworn friends. It will be as well if you can write as soon as you arrive in London, for it is very possible we may trouble you with a few commissions if you send your direction. Jane and Henry desire their love.—Ever your affectionate M. DE QUINCEY.

"My parting injunction is, come quickly. Is it not singular that the very day after I received your letter Jane went to Brockley and saw lying on the table the very book you mentioned—the account of Tongataboo ?

"Thos. DE QUINCEY, Esq.,
   "Grasmere, nr. Kendal, Westmoreland."

IV.

"*Monday, August* 12,
"MANCHESTER, 1811.

"MY DEAR BROTHER,—My hand is still weak and trembling, as you will see, but I wish to inform you myself that I am getting well very fast, and am now quite able to travel; only, unfortunately, we are detained by my Mother, who has fallen sick as soon as I have begun to get well, so that when we shall be able to move I am at a loss to guess. Dr. Jarrold urges her to travel, but she says she has not strength. I hope she will feel herself much better in a day or two, but I fear we shall not leave this odious place this week. Mrs. Kelsall says we ought not to run away from her the moment we are beginning to be in a state to enjoy the company of our friends, and a great deal more to the same effect, which your knowledge of her will enable you to supply. She has been so kind during my sickness, and means to be so kind, even when she torments one by her importunities, that we do not know how to act. I am in despair at the thought of remaining here another week, and I know very well I shall neither recover my strength nor lose my pale, sickly appearance, until I breathe your pure air and have the energies of my mind called forth by the glories of that delightful country. We have just heard of the King's death.[1] This is a doleful

---

[1] George III., born 1738 and died 1820, in the end of October 1810 showed signs of derangement of mind; and now and then, whilst he was in the worst crises of this disorder, reports were spread of his death.

letter, but I cannot write otherwise than as I feel. I need not add with what joy I shall announce the day of our departure.—Believe me your affectionate Sister, M. DE QUINCEY.

"THOS. DE QUINCEY, Esq.,
"Grasmere, Ambleside, Westmoreland."

V.

"WESTHAY, *Dec.* 7, 1811.

"My DEAR BROTHER,—I have been talking of writing to you ever since I returned home. Last Monday fortnight I even made a kind of vow that I would not delay beyond the next day, but lo! that very night I was seized with a sore throat, and the next morning was pronounced to have got the scarlet fever, which has been very prevalent in this country for some weeks. As soon as the report got abroad, our house was avoided as though we had the plague. Our neighbour, Mrs. Mackenzie, did not venture to pass the gate, and was afraid to send for vegetables from our garden. The Mores were more courageous; they came twice to make enquiries, and brought me grapes from their vinery. I don't know whether I am not indebted to you for a little of this attention. They were much gratified by your present of Char, though they were not so fortunate as to taste a morsel of it; the reason whereof you shall hear. The two pots, you mayremember, were tied up together and wrapped in paper. When we arrived in Manchester, it was thought advisable to open them, and give them the advantage of fresh air in a cool place, which was no sooner done than they fell to pieces, having, I suppose, been cracked in the course of our journey. Not being able to procure other pots, the luckless Char could not be conveyed any further. You may conceal or impart this intelligence to Mary Dawson as you judge best, and may at any rate tell her it was thought excellent by all who ate of it. The old ladies, however, justly considered that the gallantry of the intention was the same, and they constantly aver that you are a sweet young man. Your picture is hung over the drawing-room chimney-piece, and is universally considered an excellent likeness. I hear from Miss Austin that she has *seen* a gentleman who has *seen* your Cottage at Grasmere. He was told it belonged to Mr. de Quincey, a poet. She entreats me to send her some of your compositions. I beg you will immediately pour forth an ode in her praise, or address a sonnet to her. You may begin to this effect :—

> ‘O thou ! who erst in shining steel array’d,
> My heart in famèd Jericho betray’d,’ &c., &c.

‘ You cannot imagine how dreary I felt for the first fortnight after I returned home. The weather was miserable, and the whole country so saturated with wet that it was impossible to stir out. The hills, which in other times had appeared so respectable in my eyes, being compared with those I had left, seemed unworthy of the name. All this time I maintained a melancholy silence. Everything I saw displeased me, and my soul blessed nothing on this side Orrest-head. These glooms have been greatly dispelled by my late fever, and I can now admire the rich tints which still linger on our Ash woods, and look with pleasure at our grassy nooks and sloping fields. I am visited at times with the most lively visions of particular scenes in your sweet country ; nay, I am even inclined to think that I have more than once been transported by some kind Fairy to several places which I could name. Once during my illness I was at Watenlath with you and Jane. We sat down by the warm stream, and ate the same mutton-bone which erst we gnawed on the descent into Borrowdale. And I have walked with Miss Wordsworth through Tilberthwaite on the beautiful winding road which charmed us so much. By the assistance of my aerial friend it is highly probable I may frequently visit Grasmere, but as I observe I cannot always go exactly where I choose, I beg you will send me all manner of information concerning everything belonging to the valley. Pray remember us all most affectionately at the Vicarage, and enquire after the welfare of my two birch-trees. The roots of the *Osmunda regalis* which we received from Mr. Wordsworth on the morning of our departure are planted, and I hope will appear in the spring. We have been making improvements in our garden, and are building a little rural hut of roots and moss and pieces of knotted trees, in a warm ever-green corner. We have, as far as the nature of the ground would permit, adopted Mr. Wordsworth's hint concerning fruit-trees planted on the lawn, and where these would not grow have planted ornamental forest trees. In a few years we shall have a very woody appearance. There is a great deal of planting going on upon the hill behind our house. I am sorry to say that Larches abound, mixed indeed with Birch and Ash.

"After all that was said on the subject, 'The Friend' was not remembered. We regret this very much, both on our own account and because we have so often promised Burroughs to bring his numbers. Pray send them by any opportunity that offers. If Mr. Johnson should take either of the canaries which my Mother has mentioned to him, he might bring them as far as Bristol. I think he is much better off at Grasmere. I was very much vexed about Mrs. Wordsworth's print and cotton commission. Some friends of ours, for whom we had made purchases when we were in Manchester before, had given Mr. Kelsall a deal of trouble by asking him to change certain articles which did not please them, and he told us, in consequence of this, that he had rather not be employed in this way for anybody but ourselves. After this I could not mention the Grasmere commissions without asking it as a particular favour for them, which, for many reasons you know of, I did not choose to do, especially as I found it would only save a penny a yard. I often wish I had any means of sending poor P. Ashburner a bottle of the Asthmatic medicine. If it is to be had at Kendal, do buy a bottle for me, that she may give it a trial.

"Tell Mary Dawson [1] we continually long for her brown bread and nice mashed potatoes, and that we talk and think and dream of Grasmere without ceasing. How are 'my Parker' and the *young man?* I hope the latter will not give in to the expensive habit of furred and lined greatcoats this winter. I should strongly recommend him to court this acquaintance of our friend Miss Wilson; she is the woman who will teach him to rein in his extravagant habits. We expect Henry in a few days; he has had one of his old inflammatory attacks since he went to Oxford, but is partly well again. The accounts from Richard are bad; his cough increases, and the ship surgeon fears an affection of the lungs. He is endeavouring to get home that he may be able to attend to his health. He is now at anchor in Hosley Bay. When you go to Brathay carry our best remembrances to the Lloyds. When shall you be in London? I shall go through about the middle of June. Pray contrive to go before that time.— Your affectionate   M. DE QUINCEY.

"THOS. DE QUINCEY, Esq.,
     "Grasmere, nr. Ambleside, Westmoreland."

---

[1] Mary Dawson was De Quincey's servant in Grasmere.

VI.

"My dear Brother,—The same ship which brought this letter carried one also for my Mother. Hers contained Bills; and yours being directed in the same hand, we immediately concluded it was of the same kind, and therefore, thinking to save the expense of another letter, I have opened it, for the purpose of using the cover. I delayed acknowledging your last and its valuable contents till I heard whether Henry Leeves had received that and another packet of letters which came soon after the first had been received. They were enclosed in a frank with Mr. Southey's compliments, who sent at the same time several from Miss Kempe. This day a note of thanks came for H. Leeves, who is at P———. He desires his best remembrances to you, and many thanks for your kind exertions. He has given up his intention of going to the West Indies, having had the offer of a passage in the *Aboukir* 74, which is going to the Mediterranean, to touch first at Gibraltar. He has every reason to expect a perfect restoration from a warm climate, since he has already received great benefit by confining himself to a room kept at a certain temperature. Pray make our acknowledgments to Mr. Southey. We were all very much grieved to hear of the affliction which the Wordsworths have sustained in the loss of that sweet little boy. It is not surprising that they should sink under the pressure of such an unforeseen calamity, but it is distressing to hear that they are actually suffering in health. Mrs. Mackenzie has lately lost a little girl in that terrible complaint, water on the brain. The child from the commencement of the attack, which at first was not considered dangerous, refused to take any medicine; and the horror which she felt to it, however concealed or disguised, was so great, that often she would abstain even from tasting water, though parched with the thirst of fever, from suspicion that something was mixed with it, and the strength of two men could seldom force a drop of medicine down her throat. She was rubbed with mercurial ointment to procure a salivation, and her head covered with blisters, which were very sore. The cruel treatment, being the only chance of removing the disease, was rigidly enforced by the mother, though the child was continually calling out to her to let her lie quietly. Poor little Tom Wordsworth was a favourite with my Mother, and she was much affected at the account of his death. I am sorry you think so ill of Richard's appearance. He says his cough never troubles him in frosty weather, but hangs upon him at other times, particularly in damp and foggy weather. This sounds more like asthma than consumption.

"Jane left us last week. She went to London with Mrs. Millard, and from thence to Boston with Fitzwilliam Hodgson. Henry has not left Oxford this vacation. He still thinks himself in love with Bessie Leeves, and he occasionally favours me with a closely written letter descriptive of the 'desolation of his heart, the 'torments under which he suffers,' the 'sleepless nights and the anxious days he passes,' &c. &c. My Mother desires me to say we are anxious to hear that you have brought your affairs into such a state as to be able to make your demand upon us. With best remembrances to the family at the Vicarage, in which my Mother joins, believe me your affectionate   M. DE QUINCEY.

"My Mother says you had better endorse this Bill to Mr. Kelsall, or any other person, because it cannot then be used without a forgery. The Bill has been sent to Mrs. F., but pray write to her—she will be much gratified. Please to acknowledge the receipt of this.

"THOS. DE QUINCEY, Esq.,
    "Grasmere, near Ambleside, Westmoreland."

Mary de Quincey, as has been said, married in 1819 the Rev. Philip Serle, and settled at Brislington, near Bristol. She died in 1820 in childbed; and the two letters from Mrs. Hannah More which follow show something of the impresssion she had made on those with whom she had come into contact :—

I.

"MY DEAR MADAM,—I know not how to write to you, and still less do I know how to forbear. We have indeed been deeply interested in your sufferings, and I have lamented on this, as on some former similar occasions, the impotence of human friendship, which can do so little, can do nothing for us, which can only feel, and whose feelings do not mitigate what they share.

"Just as I had written so far, Mr. Serle's letter was put into my hands. I think I never shed so many tears over any letter, and I doubt whether there were not more joy than sorrow in those tears. There is indeed something so elevating in the tone and spirit of it as makes me consider the subject of it almost as much a matter of congratulation as of condolence. It presents a very striking and encouraging instance of the power of divine grace to raise the devout heart above its sorrows, above its mortality, above itself. Much as I lament the loss of the dear departed (and she has been the frequent subject of our discourse with Mr. Inglis and the Thorntons, who are staying with us), I cannot but feel gratitude, joy, and encouragement in the consideration of such a dying bed. This sublime resignation of the dying Christian strengthens the faith of the survivors; it is an animating evidence that Religion is a *reality*, and the only support, when flesh and heart fail; the only relief and strength in that last great exigence of sinking nature. I feel deeply what the afflicted husband must have endured on witnessing sufferings so exquisite in one so dear to him. I hope her bitter but brief sufferings are over, and she is now, I trust, with those who came out of great tribulation, and who were brought out of it by the same blessed means, the blood of the Lamb.

Such scenes as these, and even the representation of them in this letter, reduce all things relating to this world to their real littleness, reduce everything not connected with eternity to nothing ! Oh that such impressions were commonly more lasting ! I feel much for the widowed desolation of poor Mr. Serle, so soon bereaved ! And this leads me back to the holy resignation expressed by her he has lost. Hers was a real evidence of religion. She was not one who was under trials and difficulties, and those disappointing and vexatious circumstances which help to wean from life. Submission in such cases often passes for more than it is worth ; death may be rather an escape than a trial, and to quit a world so little inviting costs but little. But *she* we lament was young, happy in her circumstances, happy in her husband ; all about her was prosperous, peaceful, and promising ! What a lesson to us all !

" If I had not begun this scrawl to you, I would have written to Mr. Serle, but in writing to one, I write to both. Pray thank him cordially for his letter, which in his situation must have been no inconsiderable effort. I hope I shall be as much *edified* by this letter as I have been *affected*. My sister has been deeply interested for you all, and joins in most affectionate sympathy to all three with, my dear Madam, the same from your very faithful

" H. MORE.

" *Tuesday.*

" Mrs. QUINCEY,
 " Rev. Philip Serle's,
  " Brislington, Bristol."

II.

"My dear Madam,—I have not lately been able to get any information relating to you. And it would be a gratification to us to hear that you and Mr. Serle are as well as can be expected. Alas! how well is that? The health of your sad trio, however, I hope, has borne up under this severe shock.—And so the poor little babe is escaped from all the perils and sorrows of a sinful and suffering world, and is gone to join its dear Mother.

"We shall miss you very much at the Bible meeting on Thursday next. It is on a small concern connected with that meeting that I trouble you with this hasty line. How does Westhay stand at this time with regard to fruit? If it abounds, you will perhaps have the goodness to bestow upon our Thursday dinner a portion of *anything* that can be spared without robbing your garden too much. Will you excuse this liberty?—We shall be deplorably off in the way of speechifying—Bishop of Gloucester at the Isle of Wight, Dr. Randolph in Germany, poor Simpson dead, Biddulph and Boak absent, &c. &c.

"We are under great concern for some other dear friends; our favorite, Dr. Perceval, dying; by this time probably dead! His sweet Wife expecting every day to be confined; several little ones already! Oh! it is a dying world, and that to which we are hastening is the land of the living.

"With our most affectionate regards to Mr. Serle

and Miss Quincey, I am ever, my dear Madam, your faithful and affectionate and sympathising

" H. More.

" Barley Wood, *Saturday.*

"Mrs. Quincey,
      " Rev. Philip Serle's,
          " Brislington, Bristol."

It has to be remembered that Mrs. Hannah More was not alone distinguished for the educational and more strictly moral and religious works with which her name has come in more recent days to be popularly associated.   Mr. Austin Dobson implicitly gives his countenance to this idea in the clever poem, "Lines on a Stupid Picture" :—

> " Maybe this homely face may hide
>   A Staël before whose mannish pride
>   Our frailer sex may tremble.
>
>   .   .   .   .   .
>
>   Or say the gingham shadows o'er
>   An undeveloped Hannah More !—
>   Or latent Mrs. Trimmer ! ! "

In her earlier days she was an intimate of the circle that gathered round Dr. Johnson, Burke, and Garrick, and wrote several plays that were fairly successful ; among them, "The Inflexible Captive," "Percy," and "The Fatal Captive."   She also wrote several novels and stories.   About the year 1799 she came under strong religious impressions, and allied herself with the evangelical revival, in the minds of

modern readers associated with the rise and work of
the "Clapham Sect;" thenceforth she devoted herself
entirely to work of a moral and religious tendency,
or on education with reference to these. She is said
to have realised more than £30,000 by these works.
She was born at Clifton about 1745, and died there
in 1833.

CHAPTER XXIII.

I.

"WRINGTON, *May* 31*st*, 1811.

"MY DEAR THOMAS,—I am much obliged to you
for your long Letter, which ought to have had an
earlier answer. If you are extreme to mark offences
of this sort, I am afraid my excuses will do me no
good, if I fill a sheet with petty interruptions and
sorrowful headaches, from day to day obliging me
to neglect your interesting commission. I have
succeeded to admiration in obtaining the required
information, and that altogether by my evil deeds,
and therefore do not see why I should not follow
great examples, and claim the praise of virtue! I
did not get to Barley Wood till last night, where
company and other objects so engaged the party
that I trembled for my business, and said to myself,
'This is for not coming before,' but at length I had my
turn, and Mrs. H. More (previously ill and languid)
roused up her attention and entered with her usual
benevolence into the Christian politicks of Grasmere.
She could only say that a Sunday School Society
did somewhere exist in London, and that it afforded

"

before marriage.

after marriage.
Mrs De Quincey.

assistance to poor Parishes (as it could, not being itself affluent) in money and Books. Jane and I were coming away disconcerted at our failure on this point, though not without a promise from Mrs. Hannah and her sister Patty of a contribution in Tracts to the School when we come to you. At the very moment of our departure Mr. Venn from Clapham was announced, and Mrs. H. More with great readiness welcomed her guest and asked our questions in the same breath. I hope the answer will be to the purpose as far as it goes. The Grasmere Clergyman must write to the Society's Secretary, Mr. Smith, No. 19 Little Moorfields, and will entitle himself to favor by simply stating the inadequacy of his means, and the great objects depending on support, at least till experience recommends the Institution to more effectual patronage at home, where at present it is an experiment, and viewed with indifference, if not with suspicion, by people who must very feebly comprehend the value of religious instruction. We shall bring our little aid along with us, and I hope the encouragement and strength of Hannah More's name will cheer your good Pastor under his difficult labour.—When we shall begin our journey I cannot yet ascertain."

II.

"June 8.

" Your letter to Jane is just received, and has spurred on my lazy pace to make a very great attempt at a conclusion this night, which I should certainly effect but that a curious little Boy is just arrived with a Note in his hand from Hannah More, begging us to receive him for a couple of days (Barley Wood overflowing with company). This Boy is the Son of Mr. Macaulay, Editor of the *Christian Observer;* he is now sufficiently pleased by himself among the Books, and if he can be quiet without drawing upon me for attention, I shall deliver my conscience and relieve you from your various apprehensions.

"First, I assure you the Letter upon which Mary Dawson has exercised her inquisitional talents to the death of your miserable Cobler, and the implication, I suppose, of many beside, came safely and without any delay, as well as the one to me which I now answer. Your Boxes likewise are resting in peace where you left them, but Jane, under the quickening impulse of your complaints, is resolved to cord them forthwith.

"We stay to see Mr. Scarth (my Lord Darlington's Steward), and to know assuredly whether he persists in his claim upon your Uncle's Land or gives it up. If he claim, I shall receive an ejectment and must take advice, and put the defence of our right into proper hands. How long this will take I cannot guess. Mr. Scarth is expected in a few days. I think I may safely say we shall not quit Wrington till the very last of this month. We have many things to arrange if this most important affair wind up ever so smoothly, and then we shall come *immediately to*

Grasmere.—Ask Mary Dawson if other Articles, such as Table Cloths, Sheets, Knives, Forks, Spoons, not to mention Kettles and Pans, which we cannot accommodate, must come.

"We enter sufficiently into the general joy at Lord Wellington's victorious career; the dullest clod in Wrington understands it is better to win a battle in Portugal with great loss than try our strength here with the horrors of war at our doors, whatever might be the result; but our honest neighbour, Colonel Mackenzie, could never be tutored to your view of things, tho' he is very candid, and of course if we press him he will own his mistake. The question which Captain Pasley's Book[1] will stir, I think, will be hard to settle between the Politicians and Moralists; I have thought about it, but am as much 'abroad' as Madam Leeves. I recollect a paper in the *Friend,* upon the affair at Copenhagen, which perhaps, if I had a better memory, I could bring to bear upon the present point, but you can better tell where the *Friend* is than anybody else. After all, Captain Pasley's arguments may probably stand too much on the support of expediency to satisfy my

---

[1] Captain Pasley [afterwards Major-General Sir Charles William Pasley, K.C.B.] wrote extensively on military matters and mathematics. He saw a geat deal of service—was at the siege of Copenhagen and distinguished himself at Corunna. The essay on the "Military Policy and Institutions of the British Empire" (referred to above) was only the first part of the work as originally planned, and the continuation never appeared. It gave rise to much discussion—Wordsworth discussing it in a letter to the author of it which will be found in " Prose Works," vol. i. pp. 197–208. Pasley was born in 1781, and died April 19, 1861.

feelings, yet I should read the Book if it came in my way.

"This little Macaulay is a clever Boy, and puts me in mind of the elder Coleridge, but he says such extraordinary things that he will be ruined by praise.

"We hear his Majesty the King of Rome (little beast), as Mr. Hughes says in a Parenthesis, has the Crown of England suspended below his royal canopy to accustom his eyes and fingers betimes to their proper object !

"Wrington weather has maintained a good correspondence with Grasmere ; however, I think it has been the sweetest spring I ever remember, pleasanter for the hundred changes in a week. The verdure is quite perfect, the nightingales all in song ; very melancholy.   I understand Jane shall give Mary Dawson satisfactory notice of our approach.—Poor Lansdown is dead after three days' illness.

"Mary is gone with the Bridges, who have been here all the Week.   Miss Brotherton and Jane unite in kind regards with, dear Thomas, your very affectionate Mother,   E. Quincey.

"Mrs. H. More tells me, with great indignation, that Southey's Uncle has left his fortune to a stranger.

"This Macaulay has half read over the 'Mysteries of Udulpho' this evening ; he travels post, and amuses me inexpressibly with his motions and emotions.

"I have scratched out much of our Baby genius [1] to tell you that a Baronet's Son has written what he calls the 'Necessity of Atheism.' He has sent it with a Letter to Hannah More, requesting, 'if she find the proof satisfactory, that she will not hinder the circulation of the Book by her intolerant Religion !'

"THOS. QUINCEY, Esq.,
"Grasmere, near Ambleside, Westmoreland."

In a conversation with Mr. Ernest Hartley Coleridge, which we were recently privileged to have in London, he described to us a visit which he had paid, with his father (Derwent Coleridge), to Lord Macaulay at Holly Lodge, and he remarked that he was then struck with the likeness in form of face and head to the portraits of his grandfather. It would thus appear that the general resemblance maintained itself to the end. Mrs. de Quincey was the first we are aware of to note the likeness, or, at all events, to make record of the impression.

This Pasley book referred to in the above letter indeed caused a great stir. The minds of the

Macaulay was born 25th October 1800, and was therefore in his eleventh year; but what a pity De Quincey's mother should have scratched out anything about him, even to make room at the end of a letter to tell, what, of course, we now know so well, that Shelley was a most irrepressible propagandist of his then atheistical opinions ! But fancy the idea of Mrs. Hannah More propagating them ! Yet, it seems, she could not help talking of them and of him.

Doubtless it was of this passage De Quincey was thinking when he wrote as follows in the essay on Shelley : "My own attention was first drawn to Shelley by the report of his Oxford labours as a missionary in the service of Atheism " (" Works," vol. v. p. 18).

people were possessed as with a sense of some demoniac visitation in the person of Napoleon ; and every word spoken by a practical man was listened to and discussed in all quarters with an eagerness and keenness hardly credible to us now. No other topic rose into any competition with it. That Wordsworth was led to discuss the book at length is a proof of the interest it excited. His letter to Captain Pasley published in vol. i. of the " Prose Works " as a kind of supplement to the " Convention of Cintra " pamphlet is a good illustration of his power as a publicist : had he chosen to devote himself to work of this kind, he would have left a precious legacy of clear and yet impassioned writing, of which doubtless political writers and historians would have had to take note. And his speciality is, that, like all the true philosophers of the past, he desired to raise the level of the discussion to a higher platform than that of politics or military policy only. We are glad that the above reference has given us the opportunity to signalise, so far as we may, the remarkable qualities of Wordsworth's earlier prose, and his keen interest in national development, true liberty, and social progress.

Wordsworth, in his letter, acknowledges the interest he felt in Captain Pasley's book, but deals rather with the points on which he disagrees with him than on those in which he is agreed ; and the burden of all is, that our policy is war with France so long as she maintains the spirit of domination and military pretension ; that war is likely even to be cheaper and better for us than peace; and that our efficiency for this purpose depends more on elements—moral and social elements—that did not properly come within Captain Pasley's purview as a military critic, than he is likely to believe. Wordsworth in the outset says:—

"You seem to wish to frighten the people into exertion; and in your ardour to attain your object, that of rousing our countrymen by any means, I think you have caught far too eagerly at every circumstance with respect to revenue, navy, &c., that appears to make for the French. This, I think, was unnecessary. The people are convinced that the power of France is dangerous, and that it is our duty to resist it to the utmost. I think you might have commenced from this acknowledged fact; and, at all events, I cannot help saying that the first 100 pages or so of your book, contrasted with the brilliant prospects toward the conclusion have impressed me with a notion that you have written too much under the influence of feelings similar to those of a poet or novelist, who deepens the distress in the earlier part of his work, in order that the happy catastrophe which he has prepared for his hero and heroine may be more keenly relished. Your object is to conduct us to Elysium, and, lest we should not be able to enjoy that pure air and purpureal sunshine, you have taken a peep at Tartarus on the road. Now, I am of your mind, that we ought not to make peace with France, on any account, till she is humiliated and her power brought within reasonable bounds. It is our duty and our interest to be at war with her; but I do not think with you that a state of peace would give to France that superiority which you seem so clearly to foresee. In estimating the resources of the two Governments, as to revenue, you appear to make no allowance for what I deem of prime and paramount importance, the character of the two nations and of the two Governments. Was there ever an instance, since the world began, of the peaceful arts thriving under a despotism so oppressive as that of France is, and must continue to be, and among a people so unsettled, so depraved, and so undisciplined in civil arts and habits as the French nation must now be? . . .

"The spirit of Buonaparte's government is, and must continue to be, like that of the first conquerors of the New World who went raving about for gold— gold! and for whose rapacious appetites the slow but mighty and sure returns of any other produce could have no charms. I cannot but think that generations must pass away before France, or any of the countries under its thraldom, can attain those habits, and that character, and those establishments which must be attained before it can wield its population in a manner that will ensure our overthrow. This (if we conduct the war upon principles of common-sense) seems to me impossible while we continue at war; and should a peace take place (which, however, I passionately deprecate), France will long be compelled to pay tribute to us, on account of our being so far before her in the race of genuine practical philosophy and true liberty. I mean that the *mind* of this country is so far before that of France, and that *that* mind has empowered the *hands* of the country to raise so much national wealth, that France must condescend to accept from us what she will be unable herself to produce. . . .

" We must go deeper than the nature of your labour requires you to penetrate. Military policy merely will not perform all that is needful, nor mere military virtues. If the Roman State was saved from over-throw, by the attacks of the slaves and the gladiators, through the excellence of its armies, yet this was not without great difficulty;[1] and Rome would have been destroyed by Carthage, had she not been preserved by a civic fortitude in which she surpassed all the nations of the earth. The reception which the Senate gave to Terentius Varro, after the battle of Cannæ, is the sublimest event in human history. What a contrast to the wretched conduct of the Austrian Government after the battle of Wagram ! England requires, as you have shown so ably and eloquently, a new system of martial policy ; but England, as well as the rest of Europe, requires what is more difficult to give it,—a new course of education, a higher tone of moral feeling, more of the grandeur of the imaginative faculties, and less of the petty processes of the unfeeling and purblind

---

[1] " *Totis imperii viribus consurgitur,*" says the historian, speaking of the war of the gladiators.

understanding, that would manage the concerns of nations in the same calculating spirit with which it would set about building a house."

III.

"WESTHAY, *Monday, March 1st, 1813.*

"MY DEAR THOMAS,—I am going to write to you about business, and as I am not likely to be very luminous, nor you very attentive, I can assure you my credit in my neighbourhood is suspended upon the execution of a certain Bond, which is coming to you from Mr. Kelsall without a moment's delay. This is to make you lay down your Book and take up your Pen ; and I will explain to you on what acc^t you are called upon to sign such a Paper. I have bought the Land on both sides of this place, or rather I have bought other Land for which my Lord Darlington gives me Land on each side this House, so that, as our old Clerk said to Mary, " I do zweere, Miss, that your ground do go to thick little orchert of Mister Leeves's to thick here gate," which is true ; and as soon as your Uncle sends me Money to make up the whole purchase, I shall transfer it to him. In the meantime I am obliged to borrow of the Quincey estate, but so fearful is Mr. Hall of being hurt, and I suppose he requires no more than is strictly in order, that on Saturday Night the Bond of Indemnity arrived, and was signed by us and sent on to Jane. I had so little notion of this Bond being to prove anything more than a simple requisition that all my Children should engage not to trouble the Guardians if any loss should eventually be incurred to the Estate, which I knew was impossible, unless I should turn a robber of my Children, that I did not think it needful to ask any of them whether they would consent to sign; but now I see that the Paper is for the whole sum borrowed, namely, £2000, and doubled according to the usual tenor of Bonds, and you have never heard for what you were to become responsible. I think it is but decent to let you know that I expect to receive the whole money from India probably in two or three Months, but certainly as soon as your Uncle can remit in answer to my Letter by the Fleet just gone out, and the Land is safely mine till he can pay for it; and I have also an India Bill of seven hundred pounds due in June to cover any loss if your Uncle should die in the interval. Therefore I conclude you will not see *any* hazard. Mr. Gee requires no such security, but Mr. Hall has put him into the Bond, and from Mr. Kelsall's Letter, I am almost afraid he (Mr. Hall) will not let the money be advanced till he sees every name to 'his bond;' and you may judge how I feel when you are told that the Lawyers on both sides are appointed (according to the terms of the purchase and the exchange) to meet on the 25th of this month, for the conveyance to be made, the papers being now ready and the money paid. I therefore beseech you to sign the Bond and send it off as directed instantly, and if you get this Letter first, enquire every day for it.—If I am forced to appear without money, I shall be utterly dishonoured.. I have written very strongly to Mr. Kelsall to remonstrate with Mr. Hall against suffering me to be exposed to such a calamity, for it would be no less to have the story fly all over the county, and that merely because Mr. Hall is a trifler. Mary and Jane having signed certainly secures him from the very worst which my utmost knavery could bring upon him. Your Uncle, too, would be much injured, and most likely lose the land which he has constantly been desiring me to buy, and would have long ago sent the money for but that I assured him there was no prospect of ever having it. It is by a strange chance now that I have got it, and every Gentleman who has seen it says your Uncle's estate is increased in value £500 beyond the cost of the Land, which, as land, is quite dear enough.

" Mary sent you a Bill of £105 from India long since, and hopes you got it.—We are both sincerely sorry for the Wordsworths. ' For young Children whom I never knew, I am more apt to feel how happily they are laid up in Heaven than to grieve that they have tasted little of life ; but for little Tom, whose image is very vivid to my recollection, especially that day when he drank tea with his Father and Mother at your Cottage with me, when you and your sisters were out, and upon Mr. W. giving him some slight reproof he was covered with blushes, and laid his face down in his poor little hands upon the Table, shedding many tears before he could be joyous again. I could have been glad and thankful for his recovery, though, of all Children, one of such sensibility was least fitted by Nature for living an easy life.—We are much obliged to Mr. Southey for his exertions in favor of Henry Leeves. He is really almost well, except his tossing and sickness in the Bay of Biscay, where he has been heard of.—We remember, and hope you do not forget, you are under some sort of promise to come here this spring or summer. We shall be very glad to see you. I have been expecting to hear from you any time since Christmas, and am in all ways wishing and ready for your communication.

"I congratulate you on Bonaparte's disgrace; I examine every paper and sift every sentence to find out something worse than is shown upon the surface.—Mary sends her love to you.—I am, my dear Thomas, your affectionate Mother,   E. QUINCEY.

"There is no sort of news here; only a few old, very old people dead ; and the chief object of interest in Wrington is the school upon Mr. Poole's system, which is Dr. Bell's with some alterations. I expect a large party of Children to-night, who are so athirst for learning as to come out here twice a week.

" Mr. Belcher is dead. I am afraid his family are quite thrown upon the kindness of their friends, all able indeed, and I hope willing, to help them.

" THOS. QUINCEY, Esq.,
    " Grasmere, near Ambleside, Westmoreland."

IV.

"WRINGTON, *Feb.* 9, 1814.

"MY DEAR THOMAS,—The Post arrives so late since it has arrived at all, that Letters cannot well be answered by its return ; at least not by me, for I cannot see to write by candle-light.

"I will give you Henry's direction at the foot, but as to Richard's wishes about his Trunk I can say nothing ; he is lodging at No. 2 Lower Church Street, Bath, and I suppose there may be time before he leaves it for Henry to receive his orders. Richard has bathed and drunk the waters so successfully that after spending one fortnight here he means to take another dose. What then I have not heard. Jane is with Richard.—If we had not interpreted your silence by the old comfortable rule of 'no news being good news,' we should have added this to our dreary winter's musings to fear some evil had befallen you, and after the best use of our rule we were not a little glad to hear by the Elsdales that you had appeared in Manchester.

"The chief event, which at the time enlivened the monotonous sadness of being shut up in the snow, was that on Thursday the 2nd January, after midnight, we had the happiness to be instrumental in saving a family from the danger of perishing. A Father, Mother, and their two Daughters were on the way to Congresbury in a Chaise, when the party were quite buried. Their cries at length roused all the Sleepers, for all were fast asleep, and Moses by great efforts of strength dragged out the Women, who were in fits.

The Men were sadly exhausted by their endeavour to reach the House from the back of our garden Wall, where the Chaise was wedged in. At last all were got in, and after due cherishing put to bed; the Postillion, who was almost a dead man, was the longest before he recovered. Moses finished his patient labours at last by bringing the Horses out of their snow tomb into the Stable. We had the party till the next evening, when the road was cleared for their departure with four Horses; and we were almost as glad to part as to meet with the Drawing-Room Guests; the Postillion and his Horses were the best of the Company.

"I am terribly out of love with our flocks; they are much like the Ladies and Gentlemen of the rational creation, so restless that they require a Man's time to be spent in bringing them home from broken bounds. They have torn and eaten all our shrubs, and the beautiful Ivy, which had reached the top of the hothouse, they have eaten down to the ground. Three lambs are dead, and considering the still likely accidents and consumption of Hay, the profit will be little and the mischief lasting.—Your Grasmere news is all doleful. Poor Mary Dawson! I fear she was never the same internal woman at least from the time she looked with favor on such a Man, and probably continues unchanged and unrepentant, as it does not appear, from what you say, that either she or her Visitors made much account of the sin. The shame of her disappointed vanity and all her bitter anger against the Man may leave her where she is, and without other proof of repentance, I think Mr.

Lloyd was quite right not to visit her.—I cannot but be sorry for your loss of this poor Creature, for besides her housewifery, her age and homeliness rendered her a more proper person for the situation than a very young one.—We shall be very glad to see you, come when you will. It is in vain to ask you who are the base or the foolish Men of whom you prophesy that they will waste our golden opportunities.

"I was casting about how to send the enclosed Letter to Mr. Salmond without giving him postage to pay. Read it, as you will see by it what your Uncle ought to reap for his services. He has already sent a Copy to Salmond, but fearing it might be lost, sends another to be sure that his Masters may hear of his Merits enough. He does not expect much, as he has no great friends or powerful interest to help his suit.—I suppose the twopenny post will be safe enough. You will put a Wafer in the Letter of course.

"Mr. Kempe being just arrived, I must not say several things I had in store. I am half afraid that I may forget something relating to the document which you may perceive is of importance to your Uncle. Henry's direction is 35 Whitehall.

"Mary desires her love. She says she has written by this post to Richard telling him about his Trunk, and both she and I think it had best be sent to Henry's Lodgings if he will receive it.

"Besides Salmond's Letter, I send also a Note to a Man in the Haymarket which encloses a £1 Note for

a parcel of Pills, with which I doctor my good neighbours so successfully that I am thought the most
skilful Physician in these parts. I am, my dear Son,
longing to see you.—Your very affectionate Mother,

"E. QUINCEY."

V.

"WRINGTON, *Sept. 9th*, 1816.

"MY DEAR THOMAS,—So many times when I
reckoned upon seeing you have passed in disappointment that I seem to have no chance of exchanging a
kind greeting; therefore I catch the present opportunity to tell you how much the hope of seeing you
in London spurred me to the undertaking! It was
right for me to go, as your Uncle's affairs required it,
but I assure you neither I nor my companion (your
sister Mary) counted upon any pleasure unless we
could find you there; and indeed we had no pleasure,
but great discomfort, for she was alarmingly ill, so
that I thought for a short season she would surely
die. I should except the satisfaction of having
effected what I went about, and the positive refresh-
ment and delight of hearing a Preacher after my
own longing mind, whose Sermon seemed, at least to
me, to contain deeper matter and sublimer views
than one often meets with. As Ann Kempe said on
hearing Robert Hall, who has lately been in Bristol,
'It is at such times we are made to feel what our
nature is capable of, and to blush at the low and

little objects which so generally absorb without satisfying us.'

"We saw my Friend Nancy's Brother in Town, whom we thought less amiable than ever, inasmuch as by making himself coaxed and courted among his fashionable Parishioners, his pride is desperately fed and his principles starved. It happened on the day that this piece of divinity dined with us, and by appointment escorted us to the British Gallery of Paintings, young Thatcher from Madeira was of the Party, and perhaps you can hardly believe me, but indeed it is true, so gross was M.'s insolence that I was obliged to let the poor Madeira Lad go away from our Hotel in Berkeley Square into the City, and dine with us the next day.

"The frank in which this goes was begged for the sake of your India Letter, and is a parting one, as Mr. Addington is summoned to Town on Monday. I have not a word from your Uncle, and as it appears by the Paper that the Gov. Gen. has his head-quarters at Futtyghar, where he is stationed, I am spinning hopes that his Excellency may be scattering favors. I therefore beg you will write to tell us if my Brother tells you that he gets aught. I do not expect it on any other ground but as a bribe to get his place for another who would make better use of it. So little does my Lord Moira like Reformers, that when my Brother went up 800 miles to pay him respect, although he twice breakfasted with the great Man, he contrived to pass him without a single word. We are expecting, I think next week, a visit from General Poole, who is just arrived, and who went up with your Uncle to this ungracious Levee.

"We never had a *Courier.* Was it because your Papers never appeared, or that the Editor forgot us?

" I wish to know whether any mortal presumes to dive into the mysteries of diplomacy so far as to guess at what is going on in France, or at any probable result. I feel a very uneasy apprehension that, bad as the French are, the Allies are acting (to say the least) without either vigour or dignity,—and when I think of the universal homage paid to Bonaparte even by our seamen, I am forced to conclude that all national distinctions are melting away. I went to see David's picture of the Corsican, in the hope of finding what I did really find in it, namely, the figure of a very *mean* man, as well as the expression of wickedness. I mean the latest portrait; the one by the same Master, taken years ago, is altogether the likeness of another man.

" If you can prevail with yourself to write, I shall be very glad of a Letter.

" I went to the National School when in Town, and was very highly gratified, but the Master I did not see.

" I have wavered often while writing this note, and at last resolve to say a word of the report which we now suppose had no truth in it. It seemed to come from high authority that you were about to marry, and nothing short of an oracular Voice could have made us listen to the tale, considering your want of means to meet the demands of a family. I am, however, so much entitled, and do really feel so affectionate an interest in your happiness, that I cannot help begging you to let me know your designs, and also to consider well before you trust the mere impulse of feeling, if, as I have but just now heard, the sober judgment of your Friends cannot approve the step. I can abate much of what the world demands in marriage, but I know there are congruities which are indispensable to *you*, which you may overlook in the delusion of fancy, and be forced to see every moment of your life after to be wanting to your comfort, when you are come to yourself.—I am, my dear Thomas, your sincerely affectionate Mother,

"E. QUINCEY.

"Remember that Mr. A.'s privilege of frank is unlimited in weight and number, so do not pay."

By 1818, as we know from the "Confessions," De Quincey had entered fully on the "pains of opium." Though he speaks prior to 1813 of years "set, as it were, and insulated in the gloom and cloudy melancholy of opium," he could still regard himself as having been, on the whole, a happy man till the middle of 1817; and 1818 finds him completely overmastered—helpless to write or produce anything of worth; his affairs in disorder, and the fear of creditors upon him. At length he aroused himself, and had two main points to contend for— the reduction of the opium indulgence, and the discharge of debts that had become pressing. Iu these circumstances, and as a last resource, he made application to his mother. Among his papers we have found the following lengthened statement of his position, difficulties, prospects, and possibilities :—

" When I was a boy I was possessed by that kind of ambition which with most people is the highest that they ever attain. I planned and projected constantly in the ordinary spirit of ordinary minds to raise myself to high stations and honour in the State. With boyhood these purposes forsook me; and I gradually substituted a different ambition (if I may call *that* ambition which in no degree partook of the feelings which belong to vulgar worldly ambition, being wholly disconnected from all love of applause): my ambition was, that by long and painful labour, combining with such faculties as God had given me, I might become the intellectual benefactor of my species. I hoped, and have every year hoped with better grounds, that (if I should be blessed with life sufficient) I should accomplish a great revolution in the intellectual condition of the world,—that I should, both as one cause and as one effect of that revolution, place education upon a new footing throughout all civilised nations, was but one part of this revolution : it was also but a part (though it may seem singly more than enough for a whole) to be the first founder of a true Philosophy: and it was no more than a part that I hoped to be the re-establisher in England (with great accessions) of Mathematics. It would be altogether useless for my purpose to stop here to justify myself for entertaining such hopes, and in fact impossible ; for such hopes can be justified in no other way than by their realisation. In that way I trust that more or less they will be justified. If I fail in the great purposes which I have so long pursued, the failure will be grief enough ; and it cannot add any stings to it that such or such a person has sneered at me : mortification from contempt will be altogether swallowed up in the mortification or (to express it by a fitter word) the sorrow of failure. I mention these hopes now merely as explanations of my past life. It followed naturally that a person who pursued objects so really great, could not have much disposable ambition for the puerile greatness attached to high stations in life. Accordingly for some years my thoughts never wandered in that direction. At length, however, I was compelled to think of some projects for enriching myself. The cause was this : I had received a patrimony of £2600 : being denied by my guardians the sum necessary for my support, I was obliged to contract debts ; and paying a high interest ($17\frac{1}{2}$ per cent.) for money borrowed, I was obliged on coming of age to deduct nearly £600 from my principal to acquit myself of engagements of honour. Then I had about £2000 : from this I deducted in the year 1807 £300 as a gift to Mr. Coleridge. I do not mention this by way of self-applause : it was better to spend money in that way than in self-indulgence, as most young men do : but, in strict morality, I admit that it was wrong : it was an act not for my fortune nor for my situation : nevertheless I did it in a right spirit : for my motive was this : I said to myself—Here is a man of great genius who could accomplish great things for mankind, if he were for a while set above the anxieties and the distractions of immediate necessity : £300 will not only enable him to get rid of any debts that he is likely to have on his scale of living, but will also leave him a surplus which, when added to his present income, may deliver him for two or three years from all necessity of diverting his thoughts to the mere drudgery of getting money, and will thus procure him ease of mind, and will disengage and, I may say, enfranchise his time for a period of duration sufficient for the accomplishment of great works. This was my purpose, and that I could not have had any other will appear from this—that I sent. the money through the hands of Mr. Cottle, and I am uncertain whether Mr. C. to this day has ever learnt to whom he was indebted for the present ; and excepting to yourself and one other person, I have never mentioned the case to this hour—though it is now more than eleven years since it happened.

"In this way my fortune was reduced to £1700 : about £700 or £800 was spent in books : this was almost necessary to the objects I had in view, and so far a duty if I lived in the country : but, as I might have lived in London, and have had the advantage of access to great libraries, it was not necessary, and so far it was wrong. It was done, however, in my boyish days, and I cannot, therefore, have any interest in excusing it more than in defending the composition at my mature age of a school essay or a copy of verses. My fortune was thus reduced much below what could upon any terms support me. It was important, therefore, that I should turn to some mode of raising money. Like all persons who believe themselves in possession of *original* knowledge not derived from books, I was indisposed to sell my knowledge for money, and to commence trading author. I therefore fixed on the law as the only profession which, on many accounts, was now open to me, and I took the necessary steps preliminary to the practice of that profession. My purpose was not to engage in any petty chase after the honours of the profession, to which by that time I was wholly indifferent, and could not regard as fit objects of any but a childish ambition—but simply to get money, of which I purposed to get the greatest possible quantity in the least possible time. The necessity of stopping in the midst of pursuits really great for such a petty purpose as the raising of a fortune was melancholy enough, and I need not say that I designed to get it over in as short a time as possible, and should have thought it to the last point wretched and insane for me, with my views, to make my profession (as most do) the serious business of my life. If I, instead of labouring for years to mature a great scheme of philosophy and education, had pushed myself forward in the path of common vulgar ambition, and had risen to the honours which lie in these paths, I am sensible that I should have experienced a very different treatment from my female relations ; and yet the actual difference between what, on that plan, I should have been and what I now am must be much in my favour : for whosoever gives himself up to law zealously must be very ignorant of most things which it is truly honourable to know. But there are not many minds that are not in a captivity to external things. I do not doubt but that Lord Bacon and Milton were both more respected by their wives for the public offices which they held than for those great endowments which have made them venerable names to posterity. I need not say that I make this reference by way of illustration merely, and not as though their cases were strictly analogous to mine.

" This, however, is digression, and it looks like complaint, but I would beg you to understand that I am not complaining : if there be anything sound in my hopes and projects, they ought to be well able to indemnify me for any losses, slights, mortifications, or injustice to which they have exposed me : they are able to do this, and they so indemnify me beyond the sense of it as any practical misfortune.

" I did, however, pursue the study of the law as zealously as my means would allow me. On that errand it was, as you will remember, that I came down to the South, when I was last at Westhay. Soon after my return I came to the end of my fortune : for you do not seem to be aware that the last penny of it was gone in 1815. Whatever then remained was in Mr. Kelsall's hands. Hence arose a difficulty in the way of my further pursuit of the law. Soon after this, happened an event which increased it. I had long been attached to a young woman, and had visited her: for some time this was undiscovered; but, when it was discovered, I felt myself as much bound in honour as I was inclined by affection to marry her; a connection between a gentleman and the daughter of a 'Statesman [1] would have exposed her to a scandal which she could never have got over. I did marry her, but I did not communicate my marriage to you, believing that, from her station in life and want of fortune, it would give you pain. In justice to my wife, I must say that she is all I could desire, and has in every way dignified the position in which she stands to me.

"Marriage brought with it many expenses:—we have had two children—the elder, a boy, born Nov. 9, 1816, and therefore now more than two years old: as a joint memorial of affection for my brother and schoolfellow and my uncle, I had him baptized by the name of William Penson: the younger, a girl, born on June 5 of this year, and therefore now rather more than six months old: her, as a just expression of affection for my wife, I had baptized by her name—Margaret Simpson. The expense of living, which by two confinements of my wife, and two sicknesses (one a fever, the other a long and painful affection of the breast), by keeping an addi-

[1] 'Statesman—contraction for Estates man = Westmoreland Yeoman.

tional servant, and by the children's clothes, &c., were, of course, much increased, I have hitherto supported by my pen—only that I have received during three years £124, in aid [viz., a loan of £40 from my sister Jane in 1817, and a present of £84 this year, through you, from my uncle]. I should still have been able to get on very well, and gradually have saved a sum sufficient for my law pursuits, but for an unfortunate bad state of health which seized upon me in the latter end of last year, and has not yet left me. In October of last year I was bit three times running by a dog when sitting in a room; and this being followed by some strange and painful sensations some weeks after, I suffered for a long time under fear of *Hydrophobia.* This may or may not have been the first origin of the long illness under which I have languished: be that as it may, it has been sufficient to incapacitate me for all considerable exertions.

"I am now in arrears to various creditors to the amount of £150, which must be paid in part, £50, almost immediately; in the other part about Candlemas (Feb. 14) next.—If this were paid, I have nothing which would enable me to transfer my family to London for the pursuit of the law. On account of my family I would wish to avoid a prison. This is the first request which I ever made for money; and, recollecting that in 1810 you offered to make me a yearly allowance which I have now declined for nine years, I know of no person to whom I can apply except yourself."

In the Memoir we have spoken of the John-Bull element in De Quincey, and endeavoured to emphasise and illustrate it. Here we have an indirect expression of it in De Quincey's views of women. He regarded the female sex with all knightly deference, and was never wanting in courtesy and, in a sense, devotion to them. But he could not be brought to feel that in intellect and in insight in certain directions they were not more markedly limited than men ; more subject to certain inherent prejudices which he regarded as common to the sex as sex. Even in regard to the education of his family, this was felt ; for, though he was as fond of the girls as of the boys, if not more so, he was in a certain way indifferent to points of education in their case, whilst he was assiduously careful with the boys ; losing no opportunity of advancing them, and by every means in his power endeavouring to infect them, when mere children, with a love of study and knowledge for its own sake. He was the sole tutor two of his sons ever had, and they were as students highly successful. But the girls, it must in honesty be said, fared differently. Though he was fond of their company, and did all he could to please and to humour them, he did not feel called on, in the same way, to become exclusive tutor to all or either of them, and in their earlier years (for after they reached womanhood it was different) did not seem inclined to enlist them in sympathy with his own efforts and pursuits. As we shall see by-and-by, his mother was inclined to deal a little too severely with him on this very ground.

Instead, however, of sending the foregoing somewhat over-exhaustive statement, with so many reflections which could hardly have had the effect of conciliating his mother, he contented himself with a simple *résumé* mainly of the latter part of it, dwelling more fully on the character and merits of his wife. And this letter had the desired effect; for we find his mother thus replying to it without loss of time :—

VI.

"WRINGTON, *Dec.* 23rd, 1818.

"MY DEAR THOMAS,—I shall provide the sum of £160 for your use in a week or ten days, and now proceed to explain the terms of this advance, leaving the execution of your part to an after day, not doubting its being done in good faith. I need not explain why I prefer the agency of Mr. Kelsall to any here, but from him you will receive the money in Bills on London; and the whole Loan is from money in Mr. Kelsall's hands belonging to my Brother, for which Mr. K. allows 5 per Ct., and so must you, namely, £8 a year.—I must now speak of myself, before I go on upon the Business, and with a heavy feeling that every word may be taken in another sense from that in which it is spoken. I shall, however, abide in the course which I must take, and ascribe all such misreadings of my real meaning either to my own want of precision or to the terrible irritation which you labour under both from disease and medicine. I hope it will satisfy you, because I think it ought, that I am not unkind or unjust, to know that I have settled my testamentary *division* of that moiety of your father's property which I receive the interest of, exactly as he left it. I have ample power to alter it to any extent among my Children, and I have power to fetter it with conditions as I see occasion, which power I have used as I have seen the necessity; and to this end I have left the whole in the care of Trustees for the use of all my Children, who will receive, on the proportion of Principal allotted by Mr. Quincey, just so much interest as the money brings; those of the Men who leave Children can bequeath the Principal itself which will be paid as their Will directs to the surviving Representatives of my Sons.

" With this arrangement so made, and the views upon which it is made, I am bound to declare that I would not, if I had the liberty, knowingly waste or lessen the amount, but leave it as well as I found it. In addition to this, I can truly affirm that I am not unwilling to assist my Sons by reducing myself within a much smaller way of living, though neither to deprive Jane of a respectable asylum with me, nor to sink myself into so great poverty as my Sons are in, who by marrying, have really made what I could reasonably do quite unavailable.—I· here repeat what I said before, that I offered to leave Westhay, and allow each of you, T. Q., R. Q., and H. Q., £84 a year—that is, £252 a year out of my income of £665, which for single Men, with your share of rent, I reckon at *least* equal to your full proportion at my death with a family; I might say very far beyond it, and, I think, equal to my remaining share to maintain any establishment of comfort and to answer the claims which are upon me. Need I say that the first allowance to Henry has pinched me so much, that I have to maintain a constant struggle to answer those claims and to keep out of debt while I stay here; and as your Uncle made this place solely for our comfort, I thought it my bounden duty to him to give him the choice of setting me at liberty to leave it or to supply my lack of assistance to you. He has taken the latter, and it is as broad as it is long, for I could not do more anywhere without lessening the property, which I will not do; and I am sure your Uncle has spent, and is spending, more upon us by far than he has for himself if he were to come home, which he would now do, being in very bad health at the Cape, if he could fulfil his engagements and live at home. That he and I were sincere in saying we would do what we could to forward your study of the law is certain, though perhaps we had neither of us any precise idea how much would be necessary when your own fortune was gone. Perhaps had he advanced at once as much as your life-interest in £84 a year is worth, that might have been enough as far as money went; but had the scheme failed from your ill-health or any other cause, your affairs would have been worse than now; and I am afraid, from your own account of your deranged health and nerves, though you have many sources opened at your door at Grasmere, it is doubtful whether you will use them. The Paper alone, if it is to be continued and you could go to Kendal, as a sure income I should think preferable to any more promising *speculation,* and surely the too well-known speculations of authors, most justly, are to be called, in your own Words, ' so many romances.' Therefore let me entreat you to hold fast the Kendal certainty, and though I am not sanguine enough to hope that you would or could regularly do all the labour of an Editor which is absolutely necessary, so that you could be without an assistant, I should think a cheaper Drudge might do, leaving you perhaps a hundred a year, with leisure to fulfil any literary engagement which your health and spirits will let you. More than this you cannot do anywhere, and you have really brought to you by your friends or your fortune more than you are able to accomplish. Why, then, go in search of more, and in so doing encounter a thousand evils, not the least of which is the bringing your wife and children away from the place where their natural affinities, tastes, and feelings may best be cherished? We none of us dare recommend you to take the drudgery of the Paper, though we think you could do more and gain more by living at Kendal with a humbler Clerk, but to the proposal of transporting your Wife and Children to London we feel a reluctance insufferably strong and grievous. —And being now at the Threshold, let me at once assure you we all think there can be but one reasonable view taken of the condition in life which you have described your Wife's to be, and that view is the same as yours, that it is a happy and respectable one, and we are greatly rejoiced to find that she has dignified it by her conduct, as well as that she answers your wishes as a Companion and a Wife.

" Henry married a very handsome, well-disposed, and well-mannered Young Woman, the Daughter of a Captain of a trading Vessel from Minehead. They live at Clifton just now, and manage to pay their debts, notwithstanding they have both very bad health and dress like people of fortune; this is wonderful to us, and we think she should be willing to spare a little from her dress to nourish her life by better food; but I assure you, when Mary gave her, lately, a very pretty cambric Muslin Gown, quite new out of the shop, with a narrow blue stripe, such a one as any young Lady would wear in a morning, she said Henry would not let her wear it. Mary begs you will never mention this to Henry. They have no Children, happily. She had not a penny.

" I now go on to state the necessary condition on which I must insist in regard to the Loan, on which alone I could presume to advance it; I mean that you must give the security of your Warehouse share to my Brother. I should recommend you, as you must acknowledge the receipt of the money directly to Mr. Kelsall, at the same time to direct him to send your whole share of Warehouse Rent to me. I will pay your interest to my Brother and remit you the residue with your allowance, or keep it, which would be far better, as a little deposit, to be called for in a time of sickness or any other emergency. Should I have the power by an exemption from sickness or other contingencies myself, I will gladly put to such a deposit any little sum which I may be able to save at the end of a year; a very little it must needs be in the present state of things, and not more in addition to your allowance if they were altered, and so little more if I were dead and your Uncle living at home on his Pension (which drops with him), and any other little means which he may bring with him, that there is nothing to say in any case, but that you must mainly depend upon yourself to meet the exigencies which are created by your Family. To say I wish I could create funds as fast as your occasions is a cheap and fruitless wish, though it be a sincere one.—Mrs. H. More and her only living sister Patty have had a miserable winter so far. —Gen. Mackenzie is in very indifferent health at Weymouth.

" Mary is here, and with Jane unites in love, and so do I join with them, to you and yours. We expect Mr. Serle to-morrow from Oxford. He has taken the United Curacy and Lectureship of Brislington, $2\frac{1}{2}$ Miles from Bristol, going to Bath. He has no House on his Living.—She desires me to say that she will write an account of their Tour, though she thinks she has no talent that way. We are all tolerably well here.

" I certainly do not pretend to any political sagacity, but let me observe, which is an acknowledgment that I do receive the Paper, that I think you admit something now and then like defences of indefensible things, which will lessen the credit of the Paper, and in the long-run tell against the cause of social order.—I am sorry the search into the misapplied funds for schools, &c., has fallen into no better hands than Brougham's, but cheating should never be softened or excused. ' Let the galled jade wince.'—I am, my dear Son, your really affectionate Mother, E. QUINCEY.

" We understand there is a very bad story about an estate in your Quarter belonging to a Charity, but really in the hands of a great Man. Short days and bad eyes, or I would try to write a more legible copy of this."

VII.

" WRINGTON, *Feb.* 25, 1822.

" MY DEAR THOMAS,—I have your letter before me, and a very melancholy one I think it, for I see not at the bottom of your calamities any better hope than that which has ever cheated my unfortunate Children. —I have written to Elton's for the Bill you want of £54 at two months on London in your favor, and if they send it to the Post in time I shall be able to enclose it to-day, if not to-morrow. I write without hope myself, and scarcely know what to say ; for I do know this, that I cannot express what I sincerely think and grieve over but you will call it being angry ; yet I cannot say what I do not think, and if I were to send an enclosure without a word, I should myself feel that at least I acted a cold, unkind part by you, when in truth I do not feel anything like it. You should be aware that with all the flattering accounts which you give me of your literary expectations and successes, and the numerous honourable testimonies which you receive from Men and Journals, and which you think important in proportion as I receive them as you do, I must consider you as not being driven to anticipate what I now send. I do not, however, make any scruple about it, as I have the money. I am greatly troubled at your illness and the opinion of your Doctor as to its tendency, certainly hoping that he is mistaken, though I can easily believe, and cannot but believe, that your stomach is miserably injured by the Opium you have swallowed.

"There is one thing in your Letter which I must take notice of to remonstrate against so far as to show you the impropriety in future of such a measure, and that is your intention of sending expresses hither, and to Westmoreland, I suppose. In the first place, it is doubtful whether any time could be saved; and in the next, to what purpose? For, supposing the emergency the greatest possible, and the end designed completely answered, surely in such circumstances the pain and misery would have been extreme, and I should hope you did not want further security than you have that I should do what is right by your poor Children, without doing wrong by others; and indeed the utmost, if I were dead, must be so little, that the very money spent upon useless Expresses would be missed out of it sadly. I am almost afraid that you have greatly overrated what I have to divide, and therefore I state it here. What has been lost by

Mr. Kelsall I have nearly made up to the estate, so that it may be said to stand in value as it did at first, namely, at £13,000, which will be equally shared in four parts, the surviving Children of my Children to be equal sharers afterwards; but the whole is so tied upon the Children (and yours seem likely to be the only Heirs after their Elders are removed) that none of mine can touch anything but their shares of interest for their lives, with power to settle upon their wives during life as they please. This is in substance my arrangement. . . . I wish you may not be grievously mistaken about the sale of your Library. I can imagine nothing like the amount you expect.—I ought to have said that Jane could not by any means have come to London by herself, if she had been ever so well disposed.

"And now, my dear Thomas, let me say that; knowing how much your spirits are depressed, and that mine being equally so, I hope you will believe me that I feel for you, and as I am continually thinking hour after hour upon your circumstances, and coming for ever to the same sad, hopeless conclusion, you will not wonder that I can offer you little comfort; but if you imagine from this that I do not wish to give it, you do me little justice.—I am, in truth, always your affectionate Mother,   E. QUINCEY.

" I wish you would acknowledge the receipt. Elton's have chosen to draw at a shorter date, I see.

"THOS. QUINCEY, Esq.,
    "Fox Ghyll, near Ambleside, Westmoreland."

VIII.

"WRINGTON, *Jan.* 13, 1825.

" MY DEAR THOMAS,—In answer to your Letter received on Tuesday, I must enter on a few explanations to let you know what I can and will endeavour to do. Things are altered with us, as you may suppose, by your Uncle's return, but not probably just as you may think. I am, however, able, and thankful that I am able, to undertake more than I could before that event; that is to say, I have released him from his former engagement to help any belonging to me, because he is come home with so much less than he wants that he is really the poorest Member of this establishment, with a host of Eastern habits cleaving to him, which we had no notion of, but supposed he would find all that mortal man could desire for comfort and pleasure. But this is far from being the case. He finds himself unable to *live* without things which will cost him a fearful sum to pay for; and the discovery of his unequal means is not a whit more pleasant after I had fairly warned him of the pangs which would lay hold on him when he had relinquished the power and wealth of his appointment. He has been spending £4000 a year for 14 years in India, and has realised very little—so that with his pay he will not have more than £700 a year. He is building a new dining-room in the place of the old Greenhouse—the old dining-room taken to himself, and a new bed-room, bath, &e., attached to it, as his own suite of apartments; a great deal of new stabling and servants' rooms ; the drawing-room enlarged by a bow-window and the west window closed. The house which Mrs. Church calls the Great Babylon is too large for its original character, and much too large for the master's pocket—the alterations must cost him a thousand pounds out of his very moderate principal. He hopes he shall enjoy himself when these works are done and warm weather come ; and it will be well if he be not disappointed, which in my inmost thought I believe he will.—In our present state of confusion we have no delight but what we can pick up out of distant views of order and beauty.

" I have just written to Henry an often-told story, which he either does not or cannot understand, and I here send it to you. It is a statement of my ways and means at present, which, if I live, may be disturbed by various circumstances ; therefore I only say for the present, though, among many others, I mention two things which must set me free in part or make me unable to do what I now mean to do, namely, that your literary productions bring you profit enough or that your Uncle take a Wife, not a more unlikely event than I hope the other is.

" My nominal income, reduced as interest now is, amounts exactly to £600 a year.

I have offered Henry . . .	£100 a year.
I offer you the same . . .	100
I pay to the Westhay Establishment	250
Remainder	150

And this £150 is to meet the following expenditure :—
Cloaths—Journies—Apothecary, this Xmas £35—

Books, Stationery, Charity, little enough, I assure you; and a heavy but uncertain deduction from this £150 in Duckworth's yearly account, both as Agent and Solicitor, though he is a reasonable man—and for allowance to Tenants for repairing from £20 to £40 every year. I believe you will not think I have any great superfluity, but such is Henry's arithmetic and his need together, that he has written to beg of me to help and to lay his circumstances before his Uncle, which, indeed, if I had done, could only have exasperated and made things worse. In the prospect of this rich Uncle's return, Henry actually set up a House and furnished it, not doubting but a Nabob's purse would be open to him. The consequence, as I told him it would be, was that my Brother was so offended with this appropriation of his money, that he has positively refused to see or do anything for the really bewitched Creature, who, hearing of the alterations and many luxuries of the place, cannot comprehend that these expenses dry up the means of liberality, and will not admit that he himself forfeited any claim by his indelicate freedom.

"I have, it may be, convinced him, if not of being in the wrong—for that is impossible—but that his only course is to give up his smart house and sell his furniture down to just enough for a very small cottage; and burning as he is with anger, I do not know what he will do, but he has written such a Letter to me about his Uncle, that if I were to show it, I am sure he would deserve to be blotted out of

T. P.'s Will. Being myself to receive some remuneration from the Commissioners at Manchester for damage done to the Warehouse, which I expect will lessen the rent, and therefore the money ought to go into the Funds—I have promised to furnish £50 towards Henry's foolish debts in July, when I am to receive my recompense. I have no objection to consider your year as beginning the 1st March, but having paid, and having yet to pay for furniture for new rooms, which indeed I did not want and am annoyed to have, I cannot send you more than £20, nor conveniently the remaining till July,—though, if you are in straits, I will send it in part by March, and the whole by May.

" Having lived rent free for 14 years, I could not forbear to save my Brother what I could in furniture Bills, though my convenience is increased by none of these things, nor in anything else except an additional horse to our one, making a pair for the carriage instead of the Wrington Inn Horses.

" We return you our thanks for the promised Novel. On reading the review of it in the *London Mag.* we thought you were the translator. I wish to know, if there is no secret in it, what connection you have with the said Journal in the new series.

" I cannot expect that your literary productions either as a Translator or an Author will rise in moral tone to my point, for I suppose you must please your Readers, and unfortunately little is required, and much will be lauded to the skies, and that by *Churchmen,* sadly at variance with Christianity. I wish I could say that all who hold a purer creed were better people than many men of the world.

"I am sorry for your sicknesses, and felt the irksomeness of writing on the spur of any disagreeable occasion; at the same time believing that you do what you can, I am glad to do what I can, and hope nothing will lessen my means.—I hope your poor Children will not get either of the dreadful fevers.— Do you live at Fox Ghyll?—How many Children have you? Henry heard that you had left Westmoreland and settled in London. I am glad it is not so for the Children's sake.

"Jane has had great trouble with Teeth and Face and nervous affections a long time; she and Mrs. Brotherton are in Bristol, or they would send their love. I am pretty well now, and, I thank God, much better than at my time I could expect.—I am, my dear Son, your affectionate Mother,

"E. QUINCEY.

"THOS. QUINCEY, Esq.,
"4 Eccleston Street, Pimlico, London."

CHAPTER XXIV.

RICHARD DE QUINCEY, having secured a rating in the navy, served in various ships, the *Diomede*, the *Superb*, and the *Prometheus*, and was at least twice in London for a few months at a time, when, in the years 1812 and 1813, he saw something of his family, though it does not appear that he visited Westhay. In 1813 he journeyed to Westmoreland, and spent some time there, though Thomas was then absent from it. The following letters will attest these statements:—

I.

"18 SACKVILLE STREET, PICCADILLY,
14th Feby. 1812.

"DEAR BROTHER,—Having met with a number of unexpected Difficulties and delays in obtaining my Discharge, I did not leave the Ship till the 4th of this Month, and have been in Town a week. Mary and Miss Brotherton have also been the same time, and only left Town for Lincolnshire this Morning. My Time has been so much occupied in attending them, that I have done very little of my own business at present.

"It is so long since I heard from you that I am uncertain whether you may not be in Town at the time I am addressing you at Grasmere. As Mary could give me no information on this point, I went to Murray, the Bookseller, to get Coleridge's address (expecting he might give me some intelligence), but found he was on the point of leaving Town.

" Should you have any intention of visiting London this winter, I hope it will be shortly, as I do not intend, without any particular inducement, to remain here above a Month.

" All were well at Westhay, according to the letter which Mary got yesterday. The Bellman is Ringing.—Yours affectionately,   R. DE QUINCEY.

" Please to write immediately.

"THOS. DE QUINCEY, Esq.,
     " Grasmere, nr. Kendal, Wstmoreland."

II.

"WOOD'S HOTEL, PANTON SQUARE, HAYMARKET,
" *2nd March* 1812.

" DEAR BROTHER,—I think it necessary to apprise you of my having shifted my Lodgings, lest you should happen to address any letters to Sackville St. It is not likely that I shall be able to gain any information on the point you wish, as I am not acquainted with a single person in town, except one or two half-pay Lieutenants. You may conceive I am therefore tolerably dull, especially as I have been rather unwell lately, and confined to the house. I expect to remain in Town all this Month. If you have not engaged any Lodgings you can have a Bedroom here, by which means you will save the expense of a Sitting-Room, as I have one.—After all, however, I do not seriously expect to see you until I am on the point of going away, well knowing how variable you are on these points.

"Jane, in a letter of last week, assures me in a most passionate manner that you had solemnly sworn to Mary to be in Town early in January. I hope I may not have to bring an indictment of a similar nature against you.—Yours affectionately,

"RICH^D DE QUINCEY.

"THOS. DE QUINCEY, Esq.,
    "Grasmere, near Kendal, Westmoreland."

III.

[*From Jane to Thomas de Quincey.*]

"BOSTON, *Thursday, May 6th,* 1813.

"MY DEAR BROTHER,—I had Richard's letter on Monday. If it had come some little time since, I should have made no other arrangement for my journey than the meeting you in London; as it is, I can accomplish this as you propose consistently with an engagement to go with Henry. He wishes to be in Somersetshire for a short time, and in consequence of such an intimation Miss Brotherton has invited him to visit her previously, that we may have a companion for the whole journey. We mean to post, having by an exact calculation ascertained that the difference is trifling for three at the present exorbitant rate of stage-coach travelling. If then you can condescend to take a fourth in a chaise from London, we shall feel ourselves sublimely happy, supremely fortunate, &c. &c.

"Our plan is, shortly, this : we think of leaving Boston, if nothing unforeseen prevents it, on or about the 1st of June, being in London the same night. Later in the evening we must spend two or three hours with a dentist; then, leaving London in the middle of the day, propose to go so far the first night (forty or fifty miles, for instance) as will bring us to Bath in good time the next day to show Miss Hodgson every part of it which is worth a person's notice who has never seen a fine town, and never may again.

If you approve of this plan and can vegetate without much food (two meals a day at most), it will at least be as economical as the generality of coaches, and much pleasanter. Let us hear your mind and where we may write to you in London, finally to adjust all particulars ; but first and chiefly let us know if we cannot come at once to your lodgings and get beds there, supper and breakfast; which would be so much more agreeable, as well as cheaper, than a hotel. If I recollect, the house is not small, and I should think your recommendation could procure us this piece of service, even in the possible event of your changing your London destination, for they *do* say such things have been. Pray make my kindest regards and congratulations to the Wordsworths. Not to mention the pecuniary advantages of a situation (though I don't know what it is) of this kind, I do really think he changes his residence for one even more beautiful. How little to be expected in going from Grasmere! I envy Richard his stormy visit to the Lakes; don't you remember how vainly we languished to see Windermere in a breeze? I dined here in company with a Captain Smith, who professes to be intimately acquainted with the Lakes and all who live near them—Wilson, Lloyd, King, Lough, &c. &c.—and talked with me by the hour about them. I shall have abundance of questions to ask, which I may as well spare now, as we shall, I hope, so soon meet.

"I had a long letter from Mary to-day. She observes very pathetically, 'We *cannot* hear from Thomas.' La! how odd that is!! You will find them, as usual, very busy altering and improving the exterior—in them this is the outward visible sign of the unhappy malady which we have all, I think, agreed reigns in our family. For my part, I yet feel so *sane* in some points that, were I not aware that this species of delusion is common among mad people, I should persuade myself that, by some happy chance, I had escaped the contagion.—Henry's distemper rages violently just now. Take the following instance : instead of following the simple route from Oxford to Huntingdon, and from thence to Boston, he goes to London ; then, without making any stay there, by some truly wonderful contortions, and passing thro' various mail-coaches, he at length writhes himself into Bourn thro' the most uninteresting bits of country, then takes a chaise for a seventeen mile stage to Boston, by which plan he proposes not the smallest pleasure to himself, and succeeds in spending, as I can prove to a demonstration, three times as much money as was necessary. I hope Pink will pursue his intention of being in London with you, and still more that he will at length rest the sole of his foot at Westhay.

"Mr. Leeves has had one letter from Henry,[1] dated Gibraltar. I think he will very probably deliver all your recommendations.

"I wonder to hear of such stormy weather in the north; we have had a beautiful spring, only too hot and dry, and I understand the promise of fruit is everywhere very great—apples especially. Mr. Gee has cut six or seven pines already.

"All desire the kind remembrances to you both. My love to Richard. I am now visiting Miss Brotherton; the young Gees are in London for a short time. I have seen 'Remorse'[2] on the Boston Theatre boards. Pray write an answer to my queries, and believe me ever your affectionate

"JANE DE QUINCEY.

"THOS. DE QUINCEY, Esq.,

"Grasmere, near Ambleside, Westmoreland."

---

[1] Henry Leeves, who, on account of ill-health, had gone to Malta and Spain, &c., and carried letters of introduction procured by De Quincey from Southey and others.

[2] Coleridge's drama. It was published early in 1813.

IV.

On Friday, August the 6th, 1813, we find De Quincey thus writing from Westhay to Miss Wordsworth :—

"MY DEAR MADAM,—I will trouble you or Mrs. Wordsworth, when either of you happen to be in Grasmere, to let Mary Dawson know that I may possibly be at home on Saturday night, August 14. Before that day she need certainly not expect me, and I fear that not even then ; but that I may not, in any case, come upon her by surprise, I think it as well to give her notice that my present purpose is to reach Grasmere about that day, altho' it may happen that I shall be induced to stay a fortnight longer.   But there can be no harm, and much advantage, in having things ready.

"On Sunday last one of my sisters received a letter from my brother Richard, dated London. I believe you know that he is as restless as the sea. So you may guess our astonishment at learning that he had only just left Westmoreland. If he had known that I was here, probably he w^d have communicated more tidings from Grasmere or the neighbourhood ; as it was, his letter communicated nothing except a very short and indistinct mention of Mr. Lloyd's illness in July. This gave us all great concern ; but we collect from the wording of it, that he had recovered before my brother left the north. If Grasmere can be considered a change of scene for Mr. Lloyd, I trust that you will not scruple to make use of my house: even if I return as early as I talk of, you know there is room for us all.

"We have company in the house, and I write in some hurry: else I have matter of one kind or another that might fill a long letter. This must wait till the next chance. Begging you to excuse my brevity, I remain, my dear Madam, yours very sincerely, Thos. de Quincey."

V.

[From Henry to Thomas de Quincey.]

"London, Holyland's Hotel, Strand,
14th Dec. 1813.

"Dear Thomas,—The design of this is purely to be informed whether you really are in existence or not. All parties agree in this, that nothing has either been seen or heard of you since you left Bristol to cross the Severn. Whether you arrived safe on the Cisalpine Side is, to all but yourself, unknown,— but this is certain, that a few nights after your departure my Mother had this extraordinary dream, which, not being superstitious, she treated as a dream, but subsequent events, together with this dream, have contributed to a certain misgiving in my mind. She dreamt that she saw my Uncle's fine watch, consigned to your custody, floating in the tremendous waves of the sea, with its works, of course, completely spoiled. Such was the dream,—you only can prove the fallacy of it, which I most particularly request you will do directly, if possible. If half a sheet be incompatible with your occupations, half a line (just a yes or a no) will satisfy me; but I should like to have a sort of outline of your past, present, and future intentions—whether you are coming to town, and so forth.—All inquiries in Tichfield Street (where I know you have attractions superior to a Hewson) have been unsuccessful.

"I have been in town and out of town so many times this year, that any account of myself would be but a tedious series of locomotions. Richard was confined to his apartments in town for some time with liver complaint and rheumatism. He first lodged at Hewson's; afterwards at 13 George St., Portman Square; and finally removed to Horseman's Hotel, Whitehall, where I was resident with him one fortnight. From thence we both proceeded, per Bristol Mail, to Bath, where he is remaining with one of the girls, for the advantage of warm bathing. I have been introduced, by means of Mrs. Thatcher, to a Mr. Stoakes, a Stock-broker in Throgmorton St., who has promised his services towards procuring me a situation, either in one of the public offices or else in the Bank of England. He is a person of considerable influence, being nearly related to all the *Scots*, East India Directors, a family, you know, very numerous, and, in their way, powerful. I have called once on

Stoakes, when he was in Bath for his health, and he gave me his address in London. In short, Sir, he means to introduce me to one St——, a person of great power in the Treasury, and right-hand man to the Lord Chancellor.

"A new operatic piece called ' Orange ——' is all the fashion at Drury Lane; and another new piece entitled 'Illusion; or, The Trances of Nourjahad' has been performed there 17 times without intermission. It is somewhat prosing, as the design is to show the miseries attending on a visionary and a drunkard, and one who makes pleasure his sole object. The apparatus of it, however, is more splendid than that of the ' Virgin of the Sun.' The Story is taken from a tale of the same nature by the late Mrs. Sheridan.

"I have a free admission for the whole Season to Drury Lane.—I have been rather tedious, and, of course, not very entertaining, as epistolary composition, you know, is not the kind, of all others, in which I excel. I had almost forgot to mention that the new singer at C. Garden, Miss Stevens or Stephens, is quite equal, and I think will be superior, to Mrs. Billington, as is the general opinion.

"Richard is in great distress about his trunk, which he expected from your country.—You, of course, know that Coleridge has been lecturing in Bristol.—And now I hope you will absolve me from any imputation of having diverged from *facts, simple facts*, in this letter, unless indeed dreams be not facts. I only wish to be consistent, which many people are not.

My direction as above, but only for a few days or a week.—Your affectionate   H. DE QUINCEY.

"THOS. DE QUINCEY, Esq.,
     "Grasmere, Ambleside, Westmoreland."

Richard de Quincey, whose life had been thus chequered and eventful, died about the early age of twenty-six, though no exact date could be given for the event. He had been with his ship in Jamaica, and at Port-au-Prince had gone on a sporting expedition to the Blue Mountains. From this expedition, so far as is known, he never returned—probably fell a victim to accident or to wild beasts.

CHAPTER XXV.

HENRY DE QUINCEY.

HENRY, the youngest of the brothers, if he did not, like his elders, run away from school, was constantly in scrapes, which gave his mother and sisters no little concern. He was, as Thomas describes him, "head-strong," but a clever, high-spirited boy, averse to discipline, like the others, but with more of worldly-wisdom and, it may be, of calculation. Of his disposition and character some notion may be derived from the following letters, as well as from stray references to him here and there in other chapters. With all his tutors he was soon at loggerheads, with the exception of the last, the Rev. W. Gambier, from whose school he had, however, to be removed for other reasons, as will be seen. He married the daughter of a sea-captain, a poorly educated girl; but she managed very quickly, as some women of her rank do, to pick up some measure of education and good manners. It is characteristic of Henry that he set up a considerable establishment on the faith of a large allowance from what he regarded as his rich nabob uncle from India, and was disappointed; for Colonel Penson, though he had a fair income of £700 a year on retirement, had learned many expensive habits in India, which he could not wholly give up, and, with the fullest affection and utmost desire to help, had little to spare to his nephews after that time.

I.

"BOSTON, *August* 27, 1807.

"MY DEAR BROTHER,—I was not a little surprised to find by your letter received to-day that you were still at Everton. If I could have supposed that you had been there I should have written before. I believe I told you that Mrs. Pratt and Fanny came to our house (in April, I think) for the health of the latter, who was advised to try the Hot Wells air and Water. After some weeks, poor Fanny continuing to grow worse, Mr. Pratt and the whole of the family came to be with her. My Mother gave up the house in Dowry Parade to them, and Mr. Pratt took Lodgings for us in Princes Buildings. After suffering very greatly, the poor Fanny died about six weeks since. In a short time after the family left for Shaftesbury, Joseph for Cambridge. I came here soon after, and my Mother is now gone to Shaftesbury, where the Pratts took Lodgings for her. She intends to remain there for some weeks. Henry is with her.

"I find I am expected to stay here six months. Whether I shall or not, time must show. I shall return through London, of course, if it were only to see Jane. I called on her as I came. She says you have never written to her. We have not heard anything more of Richard, but his ship is daily expected.

"After having given you an account of myself, I must now beg you will let me know something of your proceedings. Why have you not been to the Lakes? Do you mean (I hope you do) to return to Oxford next term?

"I have not yet been able to get the 'Polish Chieftain.' Did you not tell me that Chalmers' edition of Shakespeare was the best? What is the price? I have ordered Graglia's Italian Grammar. Is Poarretti's Dic. the best? I am afraid you will not have patience to answer all these questions.

"I hope you will come to Oxford, for I shall feel much more happy in the idea of your being so much nearer to me.—Believe me ever your affectionate

"M. Q.

"I hope you have written to my Uncle.

"THOS. DE QUINCEY, Esq.,
　　"At Mrs. Best's, Everton, near Liverpool."

II.

"BOSTON, *Oct. 2nd,* 1807.

"MY DEAR BROTHER,—I believe you are right in supposing that no argument which could be used to Henry would have sufficient weight to inspire him with resolution and constancy enough to form and maintain any plan of conduct. Yet I think it is a pity not to make any exertion. You might write to him and inquire what were his plans for his future life, and, without appearing to persuade, give such a fascinating description of a College life, for instance, as should at least divert his imagination from rioting in the delightful paths of *tare and tret*, as you technically express yourself. If you could get him entered as a student in Christ Church, it would, I think, be an irresistible bribe to all parties; especially as my Mother has not any particular desire to have him a merchant, but acquiesces in it as a means which she expects will be likely to subdue the lofty ideas inherent in the family, and because such a choice requires the least exertion on her own part. If a school could be found such as she would approve, she would, for the present at least, I doubt not, be happy to have him removed there. No one can have a greater objection than myself to his present situation, for there, of all places, his ideas are the least likely to be enlarged, as every boy is intended to occupy the same station to which he aspires. Pray let me hear your further ideas on this subject.—I remain your truly affectionate   M. DE QUINCEY.

"Mr. Thomas Gee arrived from France about a fortnight since. He obtained his passport through the interest of Sir Joseph Banks.

"THOS. DE QUINCEY, Esq.,
    "At Mrs. Best's, Everton, near Liverpool."

III.

"BROCKLEY, *Jan. 26th*, 1810.

"MY DEAR BROTHER,—About two months ago I wrote to you, begging you to send me the books you promised me when you went away. I conclude, as I have heard nothing from you, that it never came to hand.

"I shall, however, be glad if you will send them soon, as I am in great want of them, and I am being continually asked whether you intend to send them or not.

"I suppose you have heard that Richard has had the measles, and the usual concomitant, a bad cough.

"My Mother and Mr. Boak have canvassed over a certain letter which appeared in *The Friend* (signed 'Mathetes') about a dozen times. They both agree that you are the author of it.[1]

"Doctor Bridges asked me the other day what college I was going to. I told him that I believed I was to go to Christ Church, at Oxford, but that I was not certain. He immediately exclaimed what an expensive college it was, and said that nobody but Noblemen's sons went there, and told me that Queen's at Cambridge was by far the best, as there is a very *pious* head there.

"I have been at home for these 5 weeks past, and

---

[1] In this they were wrong, however; "Mathetes" was not De Quincey, but Wilson. Others, and good judges, made the same mistake, so that there may have been a little of De Quincey in "Mathetes" after all (see "Memoir," i. p. 179). We find De Quincey himself, however, writing thus on the point : "Professor Wilson, in conjunction with Mr. (now Dr.) Blair, an early friend then visiting Mr. Wordsworth on Windermere, wrote the letter signed 'Mathetes,' the reply to which came from Mr. Wordsworth " ("Samuel Taylor Coleridge," p. 100 vol. ii. of "Collected Essays," original edition). The letter, along with Mr. Wordsworth's reply, is printed in Wordsworth's "Prose Works," vol. i. pp. 297–308 (and answer, pp. 309–326), without the slightest indication of authorship, so that the unwary reader might easily be led to the idea that "Mathetes" was a mere ruse for Wordsworth, an editorial device to give him the opportunity of reply. But it was not so.

we spent a week at Doctor Bridges'; a most unpleasant week it was, too, for we had nothing at all but discussions of Church preferment, and great and small tithes; how much one man's living amounted to, and what he might make of it, if he would but raise the tithes on cheese and apples. How is your cottage? Have you finished the grand alterations you were making in the shrubbery? Is the sweep made up to the door; for I shall expect to be set down close to your door when I come in my carriage. My Mother and all join in love to you, and I close my letter in hopes that you will condescend to honour me with a letter and a few books which I am much in want of.—Believe me ever your truly affectionate Brother,   H. DE. QUINCEY.

"THOS. DE QUINCEY, Esq.,
   " Grasmere, near Ambleside, Westmoreland."

IV.

       " BROCKLEY, *Dec.* 11*th*, 1810.

" MY DEAR BROTHER,—Having long since given up all hopes of *hearing* from you, I now sit down to *write* to you, though much in doubt whether or not you still enjoy the light of the sun. But though you may not perhaps be absolutely lost to nature, you certainly are to the world in general; for I believe you never use a quire of epistolary paper from January to December. You know, I suppose, that Richard has just now been home, and returns to Portsmouth to-morrow. His health, though lately in a precarious state, is now, I am happy to say, restored. He has not yet got a ship, but expects to, very shortly ; and, what is very probable, a ship that will require to be laid in dock for perhaps a couple of months, which time he may, very comfortably, pass at home.

"I am now going to inform you of a thing by no means either uninteresting or unpleasant to myself. We break up on the 19th inst., and I have now but one tedious week to remain in this place. Never was a reprieved malefactor more extravagantly joyful or more unexpectedly released.

"Where I am to take up my quarters next, time only can discover. But of this I am satisfied, that, wherever it be, it cannot be worse than this place.

"The manner in which I have been calumniated behind my back and reviled to my face is dreadful. It is, however, all comprehended under the sweeping sentence of '*restraining the vicious*' and 'turning one out of many to the fear of the Lord,'—for this is what he includes in his prayer every evening. He takes also every opportunity of cutting me up, by reading particular parts in 'Robinson's Scripture Chapters' and 'Burder's Sermons,' which he thinks applicable to me, pronouncing them with a fiendish pleasure, and frequently enlarging upon them out of his own head. This, he thinks, puts me on the rack ; but, poor ignorant fool, how grievously art thou mistaken !

"I am extremely curious to hear some intelligence of you ; at least whether you are dead or alive. If you think you can possibly make up your mind to dictate your thoughts, and have a scribe to execute the mechanical parts of a letter, it would be very thankfully received. Indeed it is so long since I have seen a letter from you, that I am quite curious to see what sort of a thing it is. Pray send me some account of the Grasmerian affairs, how many hundreds you have received for metaphysical works, &c. &c. My Mother, Mary, Jane, and Richard desire their love.—Believe me your truly affectionate Brother, H. DE QUINCEY."

V.

"LANGLEY, *May* 13*th*, 1811.

"MY DEAR BROTHER,—Here am I in Kent, very much delighted with my situation. The Gambiers are a very pleasant and genteel family, and very kind to me. The only thing I find at all disagreeable is, that people are too lazy to write to me, and so I wait from week to week without receiving a communication from any part of the world. It is, I believe, some seven ages since I heard from you. 'My brethren, these things ought not so to be.' One reason why I now write to you is to request you to send me my certificate of being a member of Brazen Nose, which you know I brought from Oxford with me, and which you, being afraid I should lose it, said you would keep for me. I hope you will not have to tax yourself with the same thing as you suspected me of, viz., having lost it yourself. Another reason why I write is this; *i.e.,* if you could conveniently lend me £2. The reason is, that I have but a very short time ago written home for some money, and they sent me some, commenting at the same time very keenly upon my extravagance, and hoping I should not make another call very soon. Now, from various unforeseen accidents, I am at present reduced to great poverty; nevertheless, I would rather endure to be penniless than let them know I am so soon in want of a fresh supply; so that if you could be good enough to lend me the sum above mentioned, I will return it the first time I have a reinforcement from Westhay. By the bye, I think my Mother and Sisters are by this time at Grasmere. If they are, do not let them know one syllable of my poverty.

"I will now tell you what my studies are. Ever since I came here I have been employing the afternoons in studying Algebra. Mr. G. is a violent lover of Mathematics, and has indeed attended a great deal more to that than to the classics. He was of Sydney Sussex at Cambridge. I have just read with him a most difficult piece of Greek, and, as I am told, the most difficult in the language: I mean the 'Funeral Oration of Pericles,' extracted from Thucydides. At present I am reading 'Longinus de Sublimitate' and Quintilian, previously to which latter I read a good deal in Livy; but finding it too easy to improve myself in the difficulties of the language, I, by the advice of Mr. G., am now reading Quintilian. Mr. G. is a man as different to old

Boak as Nero was from Trajan. He is a perfect Gentleman, being related to several noble families in the Kingdom, and having been accustomed to mix in the higher circles. He permits me to do exactly what I choose, equally as if I was at the University, and on that account never finds his easiness abused. The whole family is perfectly genteel, especially the daughters. They have been brought up in the solid and useful branches of education, without all those vain and contemptible things which are at present thought to be necessary ' *accomplishments.*' Mrs. G. is a woman of good family, and still retains much of her former beauty. Miss G. is about 28, being a complete Mathematician and Latin and Greek scholar. All the others have learnt more or less of Mathematics. There are 4 daughters and 2 sons. By the bye, Mr. G. published a book 2 or 3 years ago entitled 'An Introduction to the Study of Moral Evidence, or of that Species of Reasoning which relates to Matters of Fact and Practice.' It went through two editions. Have you ever met with it? If you have not, you can see mine whenever we meet. It is a book which the *Edinburgh Review* seemed afraid to handle.[1] Price 4s. 6d. Will you let me hear from you as soon as possible?

---

[1] Mr. Gambier's book appears to have met with a considerable success. It was originally published in 1806; a second edition appeared in 1808; and a third and much enlarged edition was issued in 1844. The title is correctly given above, and it contained an Appendix "On Debating for Victory and not for Truth"—certainly not the least wise and practical part of the book. He was incumbent of St. Mary-le-Strand, Westminster, as well as Rector of Langley, Kent.

"If the Westhayians are with you, give my love, and believe me your truly affectionate Brother,

H. DE QUINCEY.

"THOS. DE QUINCEY, Esq.,
    "Grasmere, Ambleside, Westmoreland."

VI.

"LANGLEY, *June 3rd,* 1811.

"MY DEAR BROTHER,—Some time ago I wrote to you for the purpose of requesting you to lend me, if it were convenient to you, £2. As, however, I have not yet had any communication from you, I conclude that my letter never reached the place of its destination. If this should be the case, it will be necessary for me to re-explain, as I did in that letter, the causes which have reduced me to making this request. It was not long since I wrote to my Mother for a supply, which she transmitted me; but it was accompanied with a veto against making another call soon. This call, however, I am under the necessity of making somewhere or other; but I would rather be penniless (as I at present am) than ask my Mother for any more. She would say I am dreadfully extravagant, though, in fact, she is totally unaware that I have to pay every little bill which I incur here, since Mr. G. is not in the habit of paying any small bills for us. So it comes to pass that I have scarcely had any money to spend upon myself. Nay, I have not even wherewith to pay a letter's postage. If, however, you could be good enough, without inconvenience to yourself, to lend me

£2, I should be much obliged to you. I forget whether I told you my direction; but lest I should not, be good enough to direct to me at 'Revd J. E. Gambier's, Langley, Maidstone, Kent.' I will return it, the next instalment I receive from Westhay. I also requested in my last letter (which I suppose to be lost) that you would send at the same time my certificate of being a member of Brazen Nose. If you remember, you told me that, as I might possibly lose it, you would keep it for me. In case, though, you should yourself have lost it (which I should not be greatly surprised to hear, as I suppose it migrated into those bottomless chests of metaphysics 'from which no traveller returns'), I say that in this case it will not, as I should imagine, be of any material consequence to go to Oxford without it. If, however, it should be forthcoming, I will be obliged to you to send it when you write. Let me know also whether my Mother and sisters are with you at this present time. I know that was their intention, but have not heard one syllable from them or from any one else since the 10th of April. '*O tempora! O Mores!*' I wrote to Richard a short time since, but have not heard one word from him yet. I fear that that letter also miscarried. I intended, had my finances permitted, to have made a pedestrian tour from hence to Chatham, and so all along the sea-coast to Dover, during the holidays, which commence on the 20th, but I fear I must relinquish the scheme.

" I have a great wish to know how you stand as to health. Is not your cottage now surrounded with roses, and do you not 'rifle all the breathing spring'? I am fagging hard at Longinus, Quintilian, and Mathematics.

All the family are well. Pray write immediately, if possible.—Believe me your truly affectionate Brother, H. DE QUINCEY.

"THOS. DE QUINCEY, Esq.,
    "Grasmere, Ambleside, Westmoreland."

VII.

"GRASMERE, *Saturday, June 8th,* 1811.

" MY DEAR BROTHER,—Your second letter—respecting the loan of £2—[dated June 3rd], I received late last night : your former letter, dated May 13th, had not [as you suppose] miscarried ; it had reached me duly ; but the truth is that it found me without any money ;—I had therefore, first of all, to write to Manchester for money ; and then a second delay in sending the bill, which I received from Manchester, to Keswick—that it might be discounted. This being effected, I was just purposing to write by the next post, when your last letter arrived. I now enclose you two Bank-of-England notes for one pound each —Nos. 17430 and 18992. I shall be in Town some time next winter ; so that it will be better to repay me then [if you should find it convenient] than at any earlier time ; since, by sending the money in a letter, *double* postage at the least is incurred—which I dislike as an expense out of proportion to the smallness of the sum. I am sorry that it should be necessary for me to say anything about repayment; but my present income is so limited that every shilling is important to me.—I take the liberty of suggesting to you that, if bills are presented to *you* for payment which my mother supposes to be paid by Mr. Gambier, it cannot be necessary to do more than barely to state that fact for your full justification in drawing upon her for more money. Do not suppose, from my saying this, that I feel any reluctance to lend you the money;—on the contrary, I have great pleasure in accommodating you; and beg that, if you should be in any difficulties hereafter, you will at least mention them to me, that I may assist you as far as my means allow. But yet excuse me for reminding you how impossible it is, with your fortune, to live without economy; and yet, *if undilapidated*, what an invaluable freedom as to your choice of profession—and what vast assistance for creating a gentleman's competency in any profession that fortune will secure to you !

" The Westhay party are not yet arrived; nor, I believe, on their road. My last account of them was dated May 3rd, at which time they were waiting to adjust the dispute about the tithes with an agent of Lord Darlington's, who was not expected before the beginning of this month. I shall of course say nothing to them about your application.

" Mr. Gambier's tract I have not read, though I have often heard of it. As to the approbation of the Edinburgh Reviewers—whether expressed, or [more honourably to Mr. G.] implied in their fear to grapple with it,—whether sincere or insincere,—I cannot say that with me it has any weight at all: in whatever numbers of the *Edinburgh Review* I have ever seen, their errors and ignorance in those parts of knowledge which deal with definite and tangible subjects even [as Political Economy, &c.], would alone have been sufficient to convince me that their power is grounded on the weakness of their readers and their opponents. But that on which I chiefly rest my contempt of the *Edinburgh Review* is its utter *feebleness* [not merely *error*, which may often consist with strength] as intellectual power in all those parts of knowledge which are employed about the indefinite [*e.g.*, Moral Philosophy—Æsthetics—Legislation—Metaphysics, in the English latitudinarian use of that word]; on subjects of which class only can any truly great and κατ'εξοχην intellectual power be manifested. Their papers on mathematics, I am told, have gained them much credit; but I must ask *with whom?* What known mathematicians are there at this time in England whose testimony to their merits can be of any value?— These papers, however, I have never examined, and upon them therefore am not entitled to an opinion; [once, indeed, I read a page or two, in their account of a work of La Place's or some other French mathematician, which convinced me that they were utterly unacquainted with the history at least of Continental mathematics and with the claims of the Germans].— I shall, however, go through those articles the next time that the *Edinb. Rev.* falls in my way.—From all this I do not mean to infer that Mr. Gambier's book cannot be a good one because the Ed. Reviewers have happened [whether positively or indirectly] to express their respect for it; for it may be a good book *in spite of* their respect; but simply to remind you [for I think I must have said it to you before] that to me at least such respect is no recommendation of a book.

"To-morrow morning is a post-morning from Ambleside; and, as we have but four post-days in a week from Ambleside, and have also much difficulty in getting our letters conveyed as far as Ambleside [which is between 3 and 4 miles from my house], I think it not right to miss an opportunity which now offers, of sending it thither by a careful person; as I should thus not only miss to-morrow's post—but also be obliged to keep the letter back, several days perhaps, for want of a conveyance to the post-office. I would otherwise have written more at length. —Believe me, dear brother, most affectionately yours, THOS. DE QUINCEY.

" If you write soon to Westhay, you can mention to *them* that you have heard from me, which I shall understand as an intimation that the money reached you.

" I had nearly forgotten to say anything about your certificate of matriculation :—I have it very safe; but, as I never heard of anybody's being required to produce his certificate, I think that I had better return it to you in the winter—when perhaps

you can join me in London for a few days : for it
would add to the postage ; and, if the letter should
be lost, would be irrecoverable. You need have no
doubt of its being safe in my hands ;—I never lose
papers.

"HENRY DE QUINCEY, Esq.,
     "Rev. J. E. Gambier's, Langley, Maidstone, Kent."

VIII.

"ARDWICK, *August* 1811.

"MY DEAR BROTHER,—Last week my Mother received a letter from Mr. Gambier, informing her that,
having discovered the existence of an attachment
between Henry and one of his daughters, and having,
as he said, spoken to both parties on the subject
without success, he must beg her to inform her son
where to go, as he could not keep him any longer
in his house. He regrets to part with him, but
considers himself bound in honour to put a stop to
anything of this kind which concerns one of his
pupils. My Mother has written to endeavour to
prevail on Mr. G. to keep him till October, when he
goes to Oxford, hinting to him that violent measures
were not likely to produce the effect he desired.
This being done, she informed us that if Mr. Gambier
would not keep him, it would be necessary to return
home and receive him there. Jane and I were at
that moment going out to dine with Mrs. Elsdale,
and had therefore no time to combat this plan, but
contented ourselves with thinking it too monstrous

to be put in execution. The next morning, however, she got up, having determined that it was more advisable to go on to you, and endeavour to procure a lodging for him at Grasmere. But as she had told Mr. G. she would await his answer here, and none having arrived this morning, I am under the grievous necessity of informing you that we are not to set off till Thursday. If we do not arrive at your door on Friday Evening just as the Kettle boils over, conclude we are dead, dying, or mad. The valuables you enquire after were put into a box containing books, which was sent off three weeks since in the waggon. My Mother's illness has been of the same nature as mine, and was probably hastened on by her attendance upon me. She is still weak and unable to bear company. Northern air, our Doctor says, is the best thing in the world for both of us.

"After dinner :—Mrs. Kelsall waiting for my letter. I am very sorry that you will not receive this till Wednesday. Notwithstanding the checks which I have received by these continual delays, my spirits have risen to such an extraordinary height in the near prospect of seeing you that I am hardly like a civilised creature. Once more adieu till we meet.—Your affectionate   M. DE QUINCEY.

"THOS. DE QUINCEY,
     "Grasmere, Ambleside, Westmoreland."

IX.

"LONDON, 13 COVENTRY ST.,
"*29th August* 1814.

"DEAR THOMAS,—After calling at Townend at 6 or 7 different periods, and remaining there latterly the whole of 22nd and 23rd inst., I at length 'gave up the ghost,' for I perceived that at least nothing more than your ghost made its appearance, and not even that to my waking visions.—After visiting the Scotch Lakes and the Clyde falls, I stepped down to the English Lakes—all which, as well as Lowther Castle, I saw in $4\frac{1}{2}$ days, to my full satisfaction, for with most of them I was much disappointed. From thence I went to Liverpool, where I stayed 4 days, and then departed for Whitehaven. With the help of 4 horses, I reached it just as the mail was going on board.—Went on board and cleared the harbour at 11 at night; and after a dreadful passage of 40 hours (during which nothing but puking was heard on the gale) we arrived in Douglas Harbour, Isle of Man. Next Day but one, hired the packet, and sailed from Peeltown, and after a passage of 18 hours (during which we were driven 30 miles down Channel) landed at Ardglass, county of Down. Hence I procured a carr (*i.e.*, a common cart) as far as Downpatrick, 8 miles, from which place I proceeded in chaises to Newry, Co. of Armagh, arriving there at 9 in the evening. The Dublin Mail being quite full that night, I was content to sleep there, and in the morning proceeded in chaises to Dublin, 50 miles

(64 English); and owing to bad driving did not pass Santry Wood (the nest of Collyer and his Satellites, and the place where the Belfast mail was stopped) till 10 that night. The post-boys drove past it at full speed, being much more alarmed than I was, as they said they never had passed it so late in their lives.

" We arrived, however, safely at Prince of Wales's Hotel, Sackville St., where I stayed 5 days, for the sake of viewing Dublin and being present at the grand musical festival, attended by Catalani, M^{dme} Bianchi Lacy, and M^{dme} Ferlendio, as also Signor Chiodi, a very fine Bass singer. It was Sunday evening when I got to Dublin, and on Monday morning heard the 'Messiah' very finely performed. Catalani exerted all her powers. As soon as the Lord Lieutenant and Duchess of Dorset entered, the whole orchestra struck up 'God save the King,' which was most divinely sung by Catalani solo.— The following day I attended a concert at the Rotunda —at which was a very crowded, though rather *mixed* company. Madame Gerbini on the violin and Lindley on the violoncello astonished without pleasing. But a performer who accompanied Catalani on the Oboe was most enchanting. On the following Friday was exhibited a very grand display of Fireworks given by Lord Whitworth—but at these I did not think it worth while to be present, so departed the day previous for Limerick, thence to Killarney, Cork, Cove of Cork, Clonmell, Waterford, Wexford, and Wicklow, back to Dublin; thence to Belfast, which is the most beautiful brick-built town in the 3

Kingdoms, and contains 40 thousand inhabitants. Proceeding to Donaghadee, I crossed in Packet to Port Patrick, arriving there at 12 night of Saturday 20th August, where I found to my joy that, the mail for Carlisle not starting till next morning, I might enjoy 6 hours' sleep, having travelled 108 hours without closing my eyes.—Monday at 4 A.M. arrived at Carlisle, and went by chaises to Grasmere, where I stayed two days—then proceeded to Bolton Abbey and Leeds, whence the Mail brought me to London. As I did not think it worth while to stop till morning for Rockingham, the fare in which is raised as high as Mail fare, *i.e.*, 4 guineas; but I was sorry I did not take the Rockingham, as it is only one night on the road, and the Mail 2 nights. Nothing should induce me to set foot in Ireland again, as I may safely affirm it to be in all respects the most detestable country in the world—with not one beautiful spot but Killarney, and even there the air is poisoned with Roman Catholics.—Excuse this abrupt ending, but truly a Roman Catholic is to me so detestable, that if I thought one of them could go to Heaven, I should prefer the other World.

"The two Theatres are coming out in a fortnight with such magnificent alterations as cannot till seen be conceived. In a fortnight or so I think of going to Bath.—Your affectionate

"HENRY DE QUINCEY.

"When last in Kendal I had no money, but a bill on London, which Kelsall had sent me. On presenting it for cash at the bank there, they did not much like changing it, as the two first names of indorsement were scratched out; and they would not have it without I could mention some respectable name about Kendal. I therefore mentioned that you were my Brother. If, therefore, they send the bill back to you, be so kind as to pay it for me (15 pounds), and I will immediately enclose you the money, on receiving the bill enclosed from you, as in that case I must return it to Kelsall.

> "THOS. DE QUINCEY, Esq.,
> "Wrington, Bristol."

Henry de Quincey, who, on attaining manhood, developed very decided marks of phthisis, died at the early age of twenty-seven, at Bristol.

CHAPTER XXVI.

"*Feb.* 23, 1 CHURCH ST., BATHWICK,
"BATH, 1829.

"MY DEAR SON,—I am so exceedingly anxious for some further Tidings that I can no longer endure the feverish watching of the post-hour day by day; not only Margaret's state, but your whole condition I would know, if I possibly could; for you may remember that you not only left very fearful apprehensions alive as to the twofold evils of your wife's affliction, but also made me feel that your own health and spirits were much broken, as well as, by implication at least, to draw something very like a conclusion that on the 14th of this month your resources would be closed up. Now, the whole account, so much beyond most former grievous communications, has left an abiding foreboding with me on all and every part of your trouble. And as I feel much, I must also say, having no intention of standing aloof from your family in distress, I wrote to my Brother after your first letter, and have received more than one enquiry from him, and on Friday could no longer delay telling him that I heard no more; so I suppose he may think all things restored to their usual state, though I told him I did not, but, on the contrary, was entirely occupied in preparing my mind to meet a difficult and painful development of affairs.

" Your Uncle is a kind Man, with some peculiarities, but none which bring his good qualities into question; and though he will not come here to meet Jane, with whom he is sadly offended, certainly not without reason, he expressed a wish to meet me, and that to discuss the means of giving help in case your poor Children should be left without the care of a Mother, though he would on no account appear in the matter. When I was staying at Mr. Roworth's in July, this really kind Man came down to Bristol privately to meet me for one day at an Hotel, when, though I neither could nor would attempt to persuade him to live with us again, I thought I might have brought him nearer, but failed utterly :—so that (as I cannot but say my good Brother's infirmity is *suspicion,* where there is the least appearance of reserve, of something in the background) I cannot but wish myself more in possession of the whole truth of your condition, quite as much, I am sure, on account of your family as for any other reason; I may certainly say for no reason which is not combined with that one paramount interest.

" Mr. Serle and Jane have both thought that an Indian family, who have laid themselves down to serve and please my Brother, have crooked ends to secure. I do not, however, lend myself to that thought; first, because I think well of these friends; and, secondly, I believe my Brother to be a Man of the strictest justice; and although he will not encounter Jane, he offered in her suffering state to take her to Cheltenham, that is, to find the money, if medical men advised the trial, so that his kindness is no more extinguished than his integrity.

"Strictly, I believe I am not quite right in saying this much, but surely you will see what impels me to say it.—I am now ever your affectionate Mother,

E. Quincey.

"Thos. Quincey, Esq.,
  "Porteous's Lodgings, 18 Duncan Street, Edinburgh."

II.

"*April* 18, 1829, Bath,
" 1 Church Street, Bathwick.

"My dear Son,—Doubly pressed to write by my anxiety to hear of you and by my intelligence yesterday that my Brother will be here on Thursday next, 23rd, from whom I have had several enquiries which I could only answer by saying 'no letter.' Yesterday he says, 'I wish I could hear anything good of poor Mr. Quincey's wife.' Oh then, good or bad, do not let your Uncle think you scorn his really kindly excited interest for Margaret. I wonder it does not occur to you that I can hardly help fearing, since what you said of William and your promise of a letter in 4 days on 28th March, that something dreadful may have occurred about William—or as you were sick with grief then (though that is a slow-killing malady), you may now by more channels than one be drinking deeply of sorrow. I do sincerely advise you to write immediately, for your Uncle makes only a flying visit in his road elsewhere, and must needs think affairs not so bad which are not worth communicating to anxious friends. Surely at the worst you could use another pen to say a few words.

"I will say no more on this subject, and only, in answer to other parts of your last letter, tell you, if you knew how my mind has been disturbed by the Catholic business, you would easily believe that I require no apology for the like effect on others, and though I do not feel exactly with you, I see enough to make me tremble. I have had long misgivings of any judgment I could form about it. Had the time, and spirit of the time, been more favourable for enquiry, I felt that my scanty knowledge and mere common sense (as I saw in others) might sooner make me a Babbler than a Judge, so that, at the utmost, on the direct point at issue, I only said my feelings are not satisfied that the Bill should pass, neither could I repose myself on the integrity of anti-Christian Rulers to legislate for us in this great affair. After saying this much, I can now add that I do not think emancipation the worst thing now before us: it comes of our wicked misrule of Ireland, and could not perhaps be long delayed; and being convinced that a large proportion of the best men, and very able ones too, have long been of that opinion, not only that we could not help it, but that the measure is absolutely a right and a duty owing; though *few*,

I presume, think the Catholics will desist from the prosecution of all their objects. The College of Maynooth, and our thereby providing an idolatrous Priesthood, this long-since committed transgression, still continued, is most grievous. I fully expect that, sooner or later, the bitter trial will come upon our Church and nation which both good and bad men have seen from far. It is but too clear that infidelity holds one-half of our Houses of Parliament fast, and formality or indifference the rest. The best hope is that there is a spirit in the people at large, not yet extinct, of religious feeling, and a zealous application is now being made to that feeling by hundreds of good men not to disturb the country, but to submit to the laws, and to turn to God in earnest care for their souls : these men are the true friends of all, though equally hated by the High Churchmen and Infidels. Lords Eldon and Lansdown, I fancy, like Herod and Pilate, would be good friends if they could effect the laudable service of extirpating the Evangelicals.

"On the Catholic question, the letter of Dr. Wilson met the floating, confused thoughts which had taken possession of my mind—indeed I had the thoughts, but knew not how to turn them to any use ; but his letter has at least given me the conviction that so it must be, and I seem to perceive a light springing up in the gloom, of a revival of religion : to use Mr. Serle's words now before me, ' I consider the Duke of Wellington as an instrument to work for higher and better ends than any he has proposed or ever dreamed of.' You need not, however, fancy that I subscribe to Mr. Wilson's sanguine hopes without a fiery purification. The truth is, as to my feelings, that a Church like ours, arrived at such overgrown wealth, filled with the profligate sons or relations of the nobility, wants pulling down.

" I now finish as I began, begging for a letter by Friday Morning, and am ever your affectionate Mother,   E. QUINCEY.

" THOS. QUINCEY, Esq.,
     " Porteous's Lodgings, 18 Duncan Street, Edinburgh."

III.

" WESTON LEA, *July* 30, 1835.

" MY DEAR SON,—We are now about to send off the Chest containing your Uncle's Wardrobe, plate, and household linen, devised to you.   I should now only be rejoicing to think of its comfort to you all, but I must now append to this announcement some uneasy thoughts which are busy to disturb my complacency, for I cannot help recollecting that when, in a time past, you were contriving one of your migrations, you spoke of selling your Goods and Chattels as an agreeable expedient! Now, as I may truly say we have not kept to the amount *named* in the will, in plate and linen, and have sent the Chest fuller and closer packed than it was received, it would add to my bitter regrets, both to think of my folly and your scorn, of our goodwill in the surrender of our rights and your disrespect to your Uncle's memory ; and I need hardly add you would sell for a small sum,

plated things for nothing, what you could not buy
for a large one.

"I have sent also, packed at the bottom of the
Chest, the Books promised, namely, Scott's Bible and
Commentary, with the manuscript Prayers, and also
a small vol. of printed prayers, which with all the
Scotch words, or, I should say, combinations of words
which do not always suit my ear, I think much better
than my labours have produced; that is to say, breathing a higher, purer air than mine ; so you may see I
do not, like you and Mr. Ord, contemn all Scotch
things : of English things, men, and manners I have
not much good to say at present. The exposure of
popery as it ever was and must be has just given
a shake to English sleepers, but I fear they will soon
go to sleep again. This City [Bath] is perfectly
entranced and in love with Dr. Baines' popery and
music : I mean its gentry, and two-thirds of the
whole population, if not more, thoroughly Radical.—
I have a good hope young Margaret will like Charlotte Elizabeth's 'Siege of Derry,' which I send her
with a Grandmother's love. My poor Brother was
listening to the conclusion of this story, the tears
falling down his furrowed checks, at the moment of
his seizure, which in 16 hours ended the mortal
strife.

"The Cheltenham Executor has been here, and
is now in London, with the other acting Executor.
When they have proved the Will and wound up the
affairs, I suppose you will receive your first payment;
but, lest you should be deceiving yourself about the

amount of your Uncle's property, I can, with sufficient precision, assure you it is little, though quite as much as I expected it could be. His income as Senior Col. in the service, with off reckonings, Batta, and other outlandish things, were altogether considerable, but died with him; and his disposable property, all very *honestly obtained,* when the various legacies, debts, and last expenses are discharged, over and above your £100 a year, will be to me for my life as residuary Annuitant, and probably at the utmost may amount to £400 per an.—£200 of which I have received from my Brother ever since Westhay was sold, which he gave me in place of the £6000 which it sold for; so that my *addition* will be about more or less than £200. At my death this divides between you and Jane; I mean the whole £400 divides between you *as income.* While I live I shall pay you £100 a year, and conditionally something more. But I must now enter on some very painful subjects: 1st. I have heard and noticed before, though you replied not, that you are still an Opium-Eater, and this dreadful Drug, as it is its nature to ruin the unhappy recipient, thus acts on you, destroying alike both the will and the power to discharge all bounden duties, to the full extent which the more common forms of intoxication effect! Well, with all you wrote *so well* before me, of poor Coleridge's dying opium misery, I am lost in the saddest wonder, and what I have further to say, however grievous, can be no wonder at all. That you write, in a disreputable Magazine, on subjects and in a spirit afflicting, as I hear too, to your real friends, I suppose may be accounted for in this way, that to the last moment of opium delirium, you will not write where you might with honor and no compromise of your professed principles; money being spent, and no choice left, you take up with Mr. Tait! Another report I rejected as quite incredible, namely, that your Children's education is neglected.

"I am so overcome with the great heat of the weather that I find it difficult to write at all, being by reflection, I believe, from Jane's afflicting malady, almost as nervous as she, poor creature! is; but I am so touched with your Children's misfortune, that I am ready to help them, if I may be permitted. I therefore propose that you shall procure and enforce the instruction which I will pay for; but observe, I must and will only pay the School Bills, or if, as is here the case, a day Governess is to be had who gives a certain set time, which the Pupils are diligently to work upon, so as to produce the expected results to the Teacher the next day. I mention this mode, if to be had, as the best; but you may conclude that this is an object close upon my best affections, and for nothing else will I advance the money. I have long been too certain that you were bringing up your Sons in idleness, but hoping they were to be made scholars and their minds taught to work, I supposed they would be kept from falling necessarily into profligacy, and live by literature, but I know not where or what now to hope; and O my son, if they are all brought up in idle ignorance, what but the worst can be expected? I am sure of this, that a Parent with your means who does this is utterly unworthy of Children; but still, in the present time, where must the wages of this bad work fall the heaviest?—In this time, bad as it is in many points, to bring up girls in idle ignorance is only to make them victims, not prepared to take their place among industrious people labouring for bread, yet too ignorant to be received elsewhere!! I cannot express my feelings as I ought; I can only proffer my help; and if you can possibly be angry to hear the truth, I too well remember what you said touching my respect for the lowly virtues to be surprised, though not shaken in my well-assured convictions."

[It is all too evident from this letter that De Quincey's mother was the recipient of mischievous gossip on many points; and her very formal and severe condemnation of Mr. Tait and his magazine would suffice to show how little she was fitted to judge or to advise in such matters, while the very spirit and tone of her letter was only too likely to rob it of any such effect as she intended and honestly meant that it should have. As to the education of the children, though in their more youthful years it was perhaps more fitful and irregular than it might have been, it was always attended to; and not only so, but many lessons in generosity and self-denial towards each other enforced in the most winning and touching ways. As to the sons, as they grew up their education was made a special care; and the positions they secured and maintained with honour is the best witness for their father's carefulness in this respect, for he was the only tutor they ever had. But in this letter of his mother's, as in many others, it is evident at once how anxious and tender was her concern for the welfare of her children and her children's children, and how apt, by too strong expressions and too ready acceptance of other people's opinions, she was to undo all the effects which otherwise she might have produced.]

CHAPTER XXVII.

AMONG the letters for the years 1836–8, we find the following three, which may be given here—the first for the illustration it gives of Mrs. de Quincey's resolution and self-denial; for it tells that she rose from her bed in her last illness—(she died in August 1837)—to serve the interests of her children. In explanation of the letter, it may be mentioned that Francis, De Quincey's son, had been sent, for change of air and scene, to a place near Penrith :—

I.

" Postage Paid.   Keep this letter.   Half-a-crown for it.

" Wednesday, March 2, 1836.

" MY DEAR FRANCIS,—Here is *your* money; namely, One *Five-Pound Note* of Sir Wm Forbes's Bank, N° $4 \cdot \frac{19}{212}$, 2 May 1829. To-morrow comes *Anne's* money ; namely, *Twenty Pounds* in 2 Ten-Pound Notes of the same Bank.

" Now then, as to the use and application of this money :—First of all, order your clothes after your own fancy : only, do not get any long coat—

but a *jacket* of any form you like.—In to-morrow's letter I will say everything about your journey; and I will *advise* you about the day: but observe—I will leave you free to do as you please as to the *time*. Only, you must attend to my direction about the mode of coming.

"Farewell till to-morrow. Your Mama sends you a thousand kisses: and much you are indebted to her in this very matter of the money. For had she not got out of her bed, though very ill, to go before the Lord Provost and sign various Deeds, no money could have been got for you. — Your affectionate father,   Thomas de Quincey."

II.

The next letter, which must belong to 1837 or 1838 (it is wholly without date), shows the annoyances De Quincey received from the liberties taken by sub-editors and printers' readers with his proofs, as they are very apt to do with the proofs of other people. Here is De Quincey's protest—thoroughly characteristic :—

"Mr. de Quincey presents his Compliments to Mr. Hughes, and would beg the favour of his interfering, before it is too late, to recover for him either the MS. or the Proof of—

"1. The *close* of his paper on Maynooth:

"2. A note on the speech of Mr. Macaulay.

"At the same time he would observe that some unknown person at the Press is constantly doing him the most serious injuries. He has a list of some 15 to 25 cases, where capricious and generally most injurious changes have been made *after* the whole press arrangements—Proofs, Revises, &c.—had been closed; never with any application to himself for a sanction of these changes; and, if the changes happened to be by omissions, never with the slight courtesy of transmitting a copy to himself.

"A striking instance of the rashness with which such changes are made occurred last month. The unknown persecutor, who follows in Mr. de Quincey's steps doing secretly whatever mischief he can, took upon himself to make the two following changes :—

"1. A note upon the word *Transcendental*, absolutely indispensable to liberate the word from the grossest pedantry, he struck out :

"2. But, which was worse (as totally perverting the sense) he altered—'The *dust to dust* ascended'—into 'The *dust to dust* descended.' If this had been right, he, the unknown corrector, might have relied on it that Mr. de Quincey's eye is too accurate to have neglected it. His mistake arose from understanding the *dust to dust* of the *thing*, whereas it was the *word* [viz., in English Burial Service] which was really meant. The *thing* descended ; but the *words* ascended.

"In the papers on *Ricardo* it was probably the same person who substituted for the correct word

Calendar, and 3 times over, the monster of a word *Calenderer*: which evidently grew out of the following blunder:—It is a local peculiarity of Edinburgh to call a 'mangle' a *calender*: which arose originally on the same principle as the term 'Dumb-waiter;' *i.e.*, the name of a person, indicating an office, transferred to a thing. The calender of Edinb., though expressing a thing, does so under the idea of a *person*. But this unknown critic, not aware of *this*, supposing a *calender* always to indicate a thing, and seeing that in the *Ric.* papers a person was meant, fancied he would make it a person by adding the syll. *er*, which made up such a monster of a word as was never heard of before."

And it is evident that he suffered evils of the same kind later. Here is one of his protests :—

III.

"Mr. Troup is quite unaware of the injury he has already done me.

"1. Who is answerable for the beauty, for the grandeur, for the effect of my papers? Can he pretend to say I will be so? He cannot. He might as well say: You shall act as I think morally right, and I become answerable for the result. It is impossible. Every man must answer for himself. He cuts away one-half from Michael Angelo's Sistine Chapel, and says I will be responsible. He sends for a house-painter to coat with paint the Transfiguration of Raphael, and holds that if he bears the blame, no harm is done.

" 2. But where or how does he bear the blame? My name is there : *his* is not."

IV.

The fourth is a funny little note to one of his best friends of that period, Miss Elizabeth Miller :—

" *Wednesday, May* 9, 1838.

" MY DEAR MISS ELIZABETH,—You see what a very little shred I have left of note-paper; from which follows one consequence that you will and must approve, if you should find nothing else to approve, in this billet—viz., its brevity : brief, you perceive, it must be ; that is its necessity.   But I shall endeavour to turn this necessity into a merit :—and how? —simply by substituting for this brevity of pure negation [viz., the *not* saying much] a positive and meritorious brevity, the difficult Spartan brevity, which *does* say much and even piques itself on saying much, but—within a very little compass.

" Well : having thus spent one side of my paper, one page out of two, upon mere preface, how hard I must work to fetch up the lost ground !   And how can I be so absurd as to go on wasting more of my narrow space in idle regrets for having already wasted so much ?   How indeed ?   Vastly I should admire the man that could throw any light upon that problem : but I have a notion that much of this absurdity is due to the steel pen with which I am now writing ; for I find that these metallic pens are always leading me astray. However, if I ever am to come to business, let it be whilst I still have a little relique of space at my disposal.

"*First*, then, and this (be it known to you, fair lady !) formed the original and the sole purpose of my billet, the one only reason for writing at all,— I am uneasy to-day, and in fact very uneasy under an apprehension that last night by what I meant for the most inoffensive and playful raillery nevertheless and in fact you were sometimes annoyed or even hurt. What reason have I for this apprehension? Little or none, I must admit, beyond your having once or twice suddenly looked grave : and that is not much undoubtedly : but a little reason becomes a strong one, you know, where the thing feared would — being realised — inflict more than usual pain ; as upon me it would to have caused even a moment's annoyance to any member of your family.—*Secondly*, but that, being the most interesting article of my note, its Spartan gem, I shall [after the example of your sex generally, unless they are grievously belied] throw into a *Postscript*. Meantime I remain ever, my dear Miss Eliz., your faithful servant.

CHAPTER XXVIII.

LATER LETTERS FROM AND TO DE QUINCEY.

THE fact that so many letters of De Quincey's were already used in the Memoir gave little hope of any fresh " finds " from his hands ; but, from various sources, a few belonging to the years 1854 and 1856 have come to our hands ; and these we shall present here, just stitched together, as we may say, with a thread or two of comment. The first is a playful diatribe against a friend for failing to date his letters, a fault from which, as De Quincey recognises, he was not himself by any means exempt. He was prone not only to substitute the day of the week, written at full, instead of day of month or the year, and, what is still worse (particularly in view of autographs, and their increased value by age), he was prone to give no signature at all, as if *his* sign-manual lay so indubitably dispersed through the whole tenor of the letter that there was no necessity to gather it up in full-beaming individuality at the end. To his daughters, indeed, he hardly ever signed himself one way or another, and would sometimes despatch his missives with no winding-up whatever, as though his correspondence was meant to be continuous, and one

epistle just to be tacked on to the end of the other.
But here is the letter :—

I.

"Mavis Bush Cottage, *March* 30, 1854.

"My dear Sir,—This morning I received, and
with very great pleasure, your letter dated—not at all ;
that is, not dated by yourself, but by the motherly
old Post Office [whose dilapidated roof, you know,
finds itself of late clothed in purple and gold as a

'*national grievance*'] dated thus <table><tr><td>GLASGOW
MAR. 29 H
4</td></tr></table>. I am

sure it must be a secret spiritual consolation to
every gentleman who in his race and strife with
Brandy knows how easily he may be *overtaken* by
the dreadful potentate, that in such a case his own
errata and oversights will be corrected and supplied by the benign old lady in Glassford Street.
A good creature she really is—but also a mysterious
creature. For mark those deep cryptical symbols,
held aloft like blazing cressets to some distant
corresponding scoundrel—H close after the 29,—
and underneath the whole, as the basis of some
inconceivable knavery, that tetragonic numeral or
digit 4. What is the first impulse on finding
oneself *under*written [as they say at Lloyd's], and
*over*written [as they say—in no rational place that I
am aware of], and round-about-written [as they never
will say]—in short, *super*scribed, *subter*scribed, *cir*-

*cum*scribed—what, I ask, is the first, the earliest impulse ? Why, this—Like the faithful slave in the *Forty Thieves* [what is her name—is it Margiana ?], one seeks to indorse H and 4 upon all the letters of one's friends ; so that, if one has no chance of being symbolic anywhere else, he might indulge it here, and rely on the motherly old Post Office to be more specific as it suits her. How much we of these later days have to be thankful for; not Mercury, swift-footed of the olden time, would or could have attempted to do so much, though one half of his mission was to mend the helpless failures of heroic strugglers." . . .

The next two letters of the many addressed to him by Professor J. P. Nichol of Glasgow are all we can recover. They sufficiently explain themselves :—

II.

"OBSERVATORY, *Glasgow, Feb.* [1854].

" MY DEAR DE QUINCEY,—We have read your second volume with increasing pleasure as we turned over every successive page. But I now write for business, not compliment. The Students here publish an Album or Miscellany every two years. This year it happens to be edited by my son. He wants to insert ' The Elder Coleridge,' by Thomas de Quincey. Would you object ? If not, don't answer me until you are otherwise disposed. Recollect you promised to stay at the Observatory on your progress to

Ireland : I do trust that Florence and Emily will count on us as a half-way house.—Would you further oblige by telling me Mrs. Craig's real address ?—Ever faithfully yours, J. P. NICHOL."[1]

III.

"OBSERVATORY, *Glasgow, 16th April* 1854.

"MY DEAR DE QUINCEY,—I fear I must solicit you to make my respectful apologies to Miss Florence because of a crime of whose stain you, of course, know nothing—my defect of correspondence. I did not infer, however, from what she wrote that an immediate reply was absolutely requisite, nor did I know, until Lushington told me a few days ago, that you felt anxious about that Nebula. Certainly you can get a copy of it taken if you desire it, and my brother James, bookseller of Bank Street, will indicate the article. I think an aquatint plate would cost only about 30s. But I must use this great liberty to ask you to reconsider about the paper. It may seem presumptuous in me to say so ; but I recollect that I did state at the time that your resolution of the Nebula into something very different from Matter

---

[1] John Pringle Nichol, LL.D., was born in 1804 at Brechin, in Forfarshire, Scotland. He was a licensed preacher of the Scottish Church, but early turned his attention to astronomy, to which science he made valuable contributions : making an end of the nebular hypotheses of La Place. In 1836 he was appointed Professor of Astronomy in Glasgow University. He wrote many books, the chief of which are " The Architecture of the Heavens " and " Contemplations of the Solar System." He died in 1859.

was hardly so effective as might have been ; indeed, notwithstanding its singular and undeniable power. And the reason perhaps is that our other and real ideas are so firmly *nailed* to such things, that it is next to *impossible,* if not altogether impossible, to detach them, and substitute anything else.

"But this first reason of mine may not be a good one, or go farther than indicate the inveteracy of my own materialism. Secondly, however, the Nebula, as known now, is wholly different from what it seemed then. Its form is not the same—thanks to the great telescopes, which have revealed so much more of it ; and its composition is not now a mystery. All which goes to render your way difficult, or, as one might say (if one had been born in Tipperary), yet *more impossible* for even your genius to accomplish the resolution aforesaid. You must pardon me for writing that : nay, you cannot help it ; because you thoroughly know how eagerly I have read everything from your pen within my reach, and how heartily I wish that you would turn out a real Almansor, and that your pen would write on for ever !

"As to John's Album : he had many thanks to offer you for your kindness. But he felt from the first that he could not ask you to take any specific trouble on his account, and the publication, besides, could not wait. He will send you a copy one of these days. His productions are signed J. N., Σ, and Basalt. He was obliged to put in more from his own pen than he cared to acknowledge. Pray read them and tell me what you think of them. I rather like Iris, Psammanitus, and the Ode from Catullus. You will find in the same volume a brief appeal to yourself concerning Kant. Don't imagine that *I* have any pretensions to enter on controversy with *you* on such a matter. But I think it would be well if so important a matter in philosophical history were set at rest. Do, therefore, take up the question again, and by authorities set it at rest.[1] ·

"Are you coming to Glasgow? If so, you will not forget the Observatory. Say to Miss Florence and Miss Emily that Mrs. Nichol and I should be very glad if they could find occasion to make this a resting-place on their way to Tipperary.—Ever very affectionately yours, J. P. NICHOL."

IV.

The next is addressed to his daughter Florence, and tells of an escape which it almost looks as though he had from personal violence by taking a round-about; for doubtless the villains who assailed and beat the muscular carpenter would have found it an easier matter to deal with him :—

" *Wednesday, September 26, 1854.*

" MY DEAR FLORENCE,—This day week, under coercion of the Press, I was obliged to go away—not an hour, I believe, before you returned : and strangely

----

[1] See Appendices iii. and iv.

enough, having gone a roundabout road by Pentland and Morningside, I missed by one 30 minutes (it was just dusk) a couple of villains who attacked—robbed—and left almost for dead—a master carpenter well known to Mrs. Wilson of this house. He is still lying ill in bed.

"On Friday or Sat., roaming along the Queen's Ferry road, I met the two Misses Todd driving home; which home is Cramond House. Their Papa has been very seriously ill. I promised to go over. Yesterday I dined in George Square with Mr. Findlay and Mr. Russel (editors of *The Scotsman*).

"To-morrow or next day I will come over. The 4th vol. is about 200 pp. on its road to completion. Yesterday, Mr. Findlay tells me, a London daily paper (*Globe*, I think) had some large extracts from the 3rd vol.: it is well that the book is thus kept alive in men's remembrance. Forgive this egotism —Ever yours, dear F."

The next letter, the original of which is in the possession of Mr. Alfred Mudie, is interesting as anew showing the keen interest he took in all the great questions of the day, and the delight he found in throwing off his thoughts in letters to his daughters, if no other channel opened. Mr. Mudie, in kindly transmitting a copy of the letter, said : "The original exactly fills the sheets of paper, leaving no room for a signature. Miss de Quincey, in kindly sending me the autograph, said that he seldom wrote letters, and very seldom signed them. She offered a beautifully written *signature* which, she suggested, might possibly have belonged to it. But I think the letter is complete as it is. The signature was probably written much earlier : the paper, pen, ink, and mental state were all different : "—

V.

"*Tuesday, Dec.* 12 [1854].

"MY DEAR EMILY,—Parliament is at this moment [½ past 2] opening its sittings, unless some new Guy Fawkes should kindly have endeavoured to warm its damp cushions, squabs, and woolsacks, with a few hogsheads of gunpowder. But what good will their assembly do ? They will remove certain technical hindrances to the free interchange of men and fire-locks between one service and another. A militia-man will be authorized to volunteer into the line. But, when all is done, here comes the inevitable result. Three months ago, when our people were gathering at Varna—' frequent and full '—for a run over to the Crimea, I [and doubtless thousands beside] said—' Within 2 months you, that now play the *rôle* of Besiegers, will have become the Besieged.' Well, *that* happened : the storm was a killing one ; but we pulled through it by means of divine self-devotion such as never ought to be looked for at the price of 1 shilling a day. What follows ? Why, this—that possibly during the winter state of the roads *out-side* of the Crimea, and altogether in consequence of that state,—we, the Allies, may so far obtain the upper hand as to master the august fortress [Σεβαστος, Sebastos, is the Greek version of the Roman *Augustus*]. Suppose this to happen on some day bet. St Valentine [Feb. 14—is it not?] and Lady-Day (March 25)—which day, until the learned Ld Macclesfield interfered about 1752, ecclesiastically *opened* the year. Good. The Park and Tower guns will be fired; Clonmell, perhaps even Tipperary, will be illuminated; and Eva[1] will crow exultingly—a little too early in the morning. And in Paris or London there will be published by some great *Artiste des Modes* the *Sebastople* for ladies, whether a bonnet —mantle—or new variety of *Chaussure*, my prophetic telescope does not enable me to decide. But wait a little : in less than 2 months comes May-Day, viz., May 12 O. Style; on which morning I fancy that through my glass I descry the haughty standards of Eng. and France flying above the ruins of the Citadel, but outside the walls a girdle of 150,000 RUSSIANS. It is true, we shall still have the advantage of an open communication by sea. But the enormous cost of a permanent defence against Russia is what we never can support. Not to speak of feuds that will too probably arise bet. the Allied Armies, either through drunken rows among the privates, or disgusts bet. officers, or jealousies in the division of advantages and spoils. Now this special case unhappily is the universal case. Nowhere has

---

[1] De Quincey's first grandchild, a few months old.

Russia a *Vulnerable* point; no heel of Achilles. Or, if she had, and it were in the extremities and outermost limbus of her mighty disk, of what avail would it be? This we can do: we can mount guard upon the Black, the White, and the Baltic Seas. That is something. And if besides, in conjunction with the Sultan, we can keep the Danube open, we shall have improved our own position, and also that of our client Turkey.—The sword of the assassin, as you know, is always hanging over the Czar, when his foreign policy thwarts the interest of his nobility. Tallow is good: but Tallow, that will not sell for English candles, stenches in the nostrils of Asia. Neither will Europe abide it. Hemp is good: good for hanging people that you and I know: but, if Hemp hangs nobody, and only *hangs* on hand, wasting its sweet powers of suffocation upon the desert air, then 'be hang'd to it'—say all the grandees of Russia. And therefore through the commerce of Russia always we can reach the Czar; but in a painful way; for surely none of us wishes the Czar to be strangled; which really *was* the fate of Paul—the last Russian Emperor that ranged himself steadily against England. Alex. might do so theatrically, but seriously all was understood to be nonsense. Here then is my profession of faith :—All is Vanity. We shall fail—yes, as much as if we fought the sea, or fought the air. Sea and Air is Russia. 'Well,' you say, 'here is a long polit. lecture that I didn't want.' Didn't you? Well, then you can make it over to Eva, who certainly *does* want it."

VI.

The next letter has to do with Dr. Samuel Brown, and the estimate his friends formed of him, and the more sober estimate of the world and of posterity :—

> "*Tuesday night, Sept.* 23, 1856.

"MY DEAR EMILY,—By this morning's newspaper I learned for the first time the DEATH OF Dʷ SAMUEL BROWN. Not that I might not have learned it by the same paper [*Daily Express*] of yesterday's date. But it so happens that every morning, just as the good old clock [which, by the way, Mrs. Wilson and her sister generally call the *knock*] gives its 4 minutes' warning—that very soon it will reveal the hour of 9 A.M., I send off my daily penny newspaper to the other [viz., the Northern] side of the entrance hall— where sojourneth an English family named *Worry*,[1] pronounced not, as by the ill-disposed it will calumniously be pronounced, but as the noble word WAR would be pronounced with the addition of an affix *ee;* in fact, as the two first syllables of the word *warrior.* They have been co-lodgers for a full week ; and every morning of this week I, the undersigned, have duly forwarded the said *Daily Express,* price one penny for each several publication. Consequence of which is—that yesterday I did not observe at the very head of the *Obituary* the following notice :—

---

[1] I have since found it to be *Warry.*

"'Deaths.

"'At Canaan Grove, Morningside, on the 20th inst., Dr. Samuel Brown, after a severe and protracted illness of eight years.'

"But on this morning, viz., Tuesday, it was not possible to escape the notification; seeing that there is an enormous art. from the Editor, clearly an extravagant admirer, an outrageous adulator in fact, calling himself by the vague name of *friend*—which sort of person it is that has so much mystified and perplexed the whole atmosphere investing Dr. B., that finally no plain and honest judge, seeking neither to disparage nor hyperbolically to exalt, has known what to think of him. This night, for example, for the first time my co-tenant, Dr. Worry, called upon me; and naturally, as an Englishman who had never heard till this morning so much as the name of Samuel Brown, he applied to me for some information on the subject. 'It is hard for me,' he said, 'to go along with such raptures as these of the Editor, who says glibly that S. B. '*mounted by a single leap far over the heads of Dalton, Davy, Faraday, and all the foreign chemical celebrities.*' Faraday, Dr. W. went on to say, that personally he knew, and it was, to *his* knowledge, not quite so easy a thing to take a flying leap over *him*, or over Dalton and Liebig. I told Dr. W. all that I knew,—that Dr. Samuel Brown was a very ingenious and able man, but doubtless, in the eyes of practical chemists, floored himself, to use a vulgarism, by aspiring too high and aiming at too much; and, like Icarus, had his wings singed, though he could walk well enough on the solid earth, and deserved more credit for work which his friends and admirers did not deign to consider or in any way commemorate. And all that comes, my dear Florence, of people erring through extravagance and exaggeration, even with the most amiable intentions. Dr. S. Brown had many good and amiable traits, and was a man of penetrating and powerful intellect, but his real claims are left in the background, or overshadowed by crazy excessive adulation, at which discerning people, as you see, can only shrug their shoulders and laugh consumedly.

"Comes there any more of it? Yes, just such another half, which, when found, I'll take a note of—and forward.

"ANTELOPE, [By this you will agnize the correspond^g Half when found]."

VII.

The sixth and last letter of this sheaf conveys something of De Quincey's estimate of the Brontë family, whose genius he admired, more especially that of Charlotte and Emily, but whose defects of character he duly notes :—

"Do you hear much about Miss Madeleine Smith of Glasgow? What a strange case, when the sole possible accuser, so far as *I* know, is in his grave. Have you seen Miss Brontë's posthumous novel, *The Professor?* The Brontës, meaning the girls, had some very *noble* features in their characters, but not many that were *amiable.* The males of the family were scamps. Think of this—the elder scamp (*Papa,* I mean) always dined alone, like the Savages in so many regions, and even Mahometan Barbarians, whose wives eat apart (or perhaps *after*) their tyrants. Now what excuse did the "leathery Herr Papa" make for this practice? Why (says Mrs. Gaskell), his stomach being peculiarly delicate, it became requisite that he should not be tempted away by a wider and miscellaneous choice from his own simple diet. Simple! —So then his daughters no doubt had a luxurious— a *tempting*—table! Now elsewhere it comes out— that these poor girls, who through life were models of self-denying abstinence, had mere plain potatoes for dinner, without any animal accompaniment, and I believe without any seasoning or sauce. *Condiment* is pedantic. One after one, in regular succession, the 3 younger girls—1. Charlotte, 2. Emily, 3. Anne— were turned out of doors to get their own bread in a far worse service, to my thinking, than that of a housemaid: for surely it is better by much to go down on one's knees to scour the front door-steps, with the prospect at night of creeping to an undisturbed bed, in humble respectability, than to make *one* in a crowd of most vulgar Belgian girls; generally vicious, inquisitive, scandalous, spiteful, silly, and ignoble, gathered into one huge dormitory.

" Write to me, please, some short answer to my questions. As to the loan, if you cannot conveniently, never mind it. By the way,—you must not suppose that I am still holding the relation of *Debtor* to the Inc. Tax Commissioners, as possibly you might f^m the sums being the same. I settled *that* at once. No tick *there*, unless Tic douloureux.—Yours affectionately."

CHAPTER XXIX.

THE following letter from the Rev. Thomas Grinfield, Rector of Clifton, frequently referred to in the
" Memoir," may find a place at this point :—

"CLIFTON, *Feb.* 4, 1847.

" MY DEAR SIR,—Happening only yesterday to
glance over, 'Notes on Landor, by Thomas de Quincey,'
in the January No. of *Tait's Magizine*, the brilliant
Writer's name, like a spell, wakened up such a train
of early recollections, that I resolved (unwisely perhaps) to intrude on your ever-bright and busy mind
in this form of a few dull lines, and thus allow myself
the chance of a few, certain to interest me, from
your pen.   Just 20 years ago, recovering from illness, I read with admiring interest (like others) your
'Confessions of an Opium-Eater,' afterwards your
'Autobiography,' and *both*, with the same revival of
young days and feelings, which prompts me now at
last to trouble you with this hasty and most unexpected letter."

[Here follows much information of a private kind concerning his life and family during a quarter of a century, and then he proceeds.]

"As though I had not enough tired you already, I have taken (you see) another formidable sheet, as the old Puritan divines sometimes turned the hour-glass at the middle of their homilies, and announced another glass! The truth is, I rather recoil from these *last* probably, as well as *first* words, with you, to whom I must have long been an *unknown* rather than *unforgotten* Stranger. You have redde your history in the nation's eyes. Mine has been quite the obscure and '*fallentis semita vitæ.*' But I have never ceased to be '*Musis Amicus!*' My elder daughter was united last summer to a literary and a gifted person, whose name *may* have reached you, *Francis Barham*, who has published the political works of Cicero in his own Version, and re-edited Collier's 'Eccles. Hist.' He has also printed a tragedy of his own called 'Socrates,' and a Version of Grotius's remarkable poem, 'Adamus Exul,' the supposed germ of the 'Paradise Lost.'[1] He resides with me, where I have passed the principal part of my days; now retired from the long-practised duty of a parochial clergyman, for which declining health

---

[1] Mr. Francis Barham, who was born in 1808 and died in 1871, was the son of Thomas Foster Barham, a musician of some note. He was a most voluminous writer and a man of most active mind. He was the author of some nineteen works besides those mentioned, among them being "The Alist or Divine," and was the founder of the Society of Alists and of a Syneretic Society. He left behind him a very large number of manuscripts.

would often disqualify me. I can remember your very intelligent Mother and your Sisters, whom I have met in an evening (*many* years ago) at the late *Mrs. Ford's* house, of Clifton. It may interest you to know that I enjoyed the acquaintance of those two variously admirable men who adorned this neighbourhood, *Robert Hall* and *John Foster*, the latter of whom you must have specially liked to converse with, and (so far as you might) explore the hidden treasures of his so deeply meditative and reflective mind. But let me have mercy and regard to your use of time. I hope that you are still favoured with the blessing of nearly unimpaired health and vigour, —physical, as well as intellectual :—and, *assured* that you will excuse this friendly, however otherwise unwelcome, invasion of your leisure, I remain, with sincere best wishes for your happiness, your Winkfield Schoolfellow and Friend,

"Thomas Grinfield."

This letter was addressed, "Thomas de Quincey, Esq., College Post Office, Edinburgh," and is endorsed in De Quincey's neat handwriting: "Received on this day, Friday, April 30, 1847, 3 P.M."—the delay doubtless having been caused by its lying at the University Post-Office till some friend told him of it.

CHAPTER XXX.

LETTERS FROM STRANGERS.

IN a vast sheaf of letters and papers from strangers connected with the later years, there are some peculiar requests and confessions. That people in the Western States of America should write gushing letters merely to tell the " Opium-Eater " how much they had been interested in his works; that others should write asking where such-and-such an article they had heard spoken of would be found; that others should write urging him to do what he was just then doing—collect his works; and that some should inquire whether he had ever written anything on Moral Philosophy (!) and where, and should confuse " Walladmor " with " Vladimir," is only perhaps what might have been expected, as well as urge requests for autographs, demands for opinions on scraps of poetry, little essays, handsomely copied out or privately printed; and that young folks should ask for counsel about embarking on a literary career. Medical men in foreign countries seem to have been particularly anxious to cultivate his acquaintance by correspondence. It is most characteristic of him that he struggled to answer these letters, and that many of them were answered; and that in the case of almost each one he has noted on the back when received, even to the hour of the day, and also the nature of the contents. In this mass, however, there were some bits of interesting and characteristic quality, and most of all those in which the writers, with that wonderful demand for comprehension and sympathy which lies so deep in human nature, confess themselves to him, and though hardly expecting an answer, seem to find a satisfactory relief in having thus unbosomed themselves, though in some cases desirous of preserving the veil of anonymity or pseudonymity. Here is one of that class, which he has docketed and endorsed, " Received this morning, May 3, 1853,"—with such exactitude and care as important or business communications too frequently failed to secure from him :—

" PROVIDENCE, R. I., *April 19th,* 1853.

" Who is this presuming to sit down and write a letter to Thomas de Quincey, a man more honoured by all who are capable of appreciating him than any other English writer dead or living? Indeed I hardly dare tell him, for it is a lady, a young lady who is confessing herself the vainest of her sex by this simple act. And she will not tell him how many sheets she has covered with her illegible hieroglyphics, and then sent them to enliven and enlighten the dark heaps of sea-coal and anthracite, in her humiliation at the thought of her presumption.

Yet I am very sure he would forgive her if he knew the homage her heart has been so long rendering him, an homage far surpassing anything he could have felt for the idol of his young affections. For the man he loved had no soul,—a splendid intellect he had, which I could equally admire, but I should never dream of loving him. How could you? But you were better able to appreciate that intellect in all its length and breadth and depth, and not being a woman, the heart perhaps was not of quite so much consequence.

"This young lady will honestly confess that Mr. de Quincey is too profound for her woman's understanding and woman's education in his learned essays, though he has not written a word that she has not attempted to interpret. The 'Confessions' was the first book from his pen that she read, and she fell in love with the boy, with his noble soul, his fearless pursuit of what he thought right, and his manly defence of all whom he loved. And perhaps it was her love that blinded her to all his faults and foibles, and made the sins, that many think almost heinous, only little compared to the beams that should obscure the eyes of those who criticise and condemn. But when he went to live in Grasmere, and she wandered with him for the thousandth and ten thousandth time through all its woods and dells and sunny vales, he would almost pity her if he could see the tears she shed, such as no fiction ever wrung from her eyes. And her woman's heart has yearned to tell him of its fulness and its gratitude to one who

could retain through so many trials a soul as pure
and young and warm and fresh as it was in boyhood's days. Often and often she takes up the book
and lays it down to weep—for his sorrows have
been in some respects like her sorrows, and her
intellect, like his, though not in degree or in proportion, has been quickened and expanded by almost
unparalleled physical sufferings, and her heart has
been wrung and wrung with agony, while she has,
to all appearance, remained as blithe and joyous as
if a shadow had never crossed her path.

" Before she had heard of Mr. de Quincey, when
only a little girl, she had read all Prof. Wilson's
stories, and loved them and loved him with no
ordinary effection, but she never thought of writing
him a letter, never was in danger of ' falling down
and worshipping him,' as she would be if she should
see the author of ' The Household Wreck' and the
' Spanish Nun ; ' and had she the means, she would
cross the ocean for no other purpose than to sit at
his feet, not to learn wisdom, feast though indeed
it would be, but to pour out her heart, with all its
deep and strong enthusiasm, to one who could understand her, and would not only counsel wisely, but
chide gently. She would visit Grasmere, oh yes !
and pluck one rose or blade of grass, more hallowed
in her eyes than moss or ivy from castle, hall, or
tower ; but nothing else could turn aside her steps
till she was in the city where he dwells, and she
had listened to the sound of his voice, and looked
upon a countenance in which, to her imagination,

is blended the expression of all that is great and noble and good.

"He must be now *nearly* an old man, with sons and daughters grown up around him; and if he is what he seems, and also in this respect like others who have grown old, it is more pleasant to be remembered with affection than with admiration; and a *man* who is not ashamed to confess that he *feels* as well as *thinks*, will pardon this expression of her love in one who is a stranger, and must ever be, to him who is so wise that she would be afraid to speak in his presence, and yet so unpretending and so good that she might feel the confidence of a little child and scarcely fear to caress him.

"Sometimes when persons have been reading what he has written in my presence, they have exclaimed, 'Indeed you are very like him—this sounds exactly like *you*,' but only in those places where there is some heart and soul revelation—some proof of the peculiar effect of sorrow in the influence of some great joy, which others would never make known. I have often wished there could be given to us more *true* heart histories, that those who are capable of deep and holy enthusiasm would speak what they feel. It is for this sympathy, to know how others love and hate, that the young resort to novels, where they find so much that is false and wicked, that they are corrupted and unfitted for real life. When a Biography is written, everything that ordinary people care to know is left out. The heart is treated as if it were an 'accursed thing,' and anything concerning the affections as they really exist, as if it would be pollution to portray them. Until History and Biography tell us the *truth*, fiction will feed the most readers, and in some respects it is really more true and more beneficial than the prosy stuff which prosy people recommend in its stead !

"How I would like to introduce you to my mountain home in one of the most beautiful of New England valleys ! How you would love its wild woods, dells, and dingles, its canny brooks and silver streams. Why will you not come ? Perhaps you have a daughter whom I should love as a sister, and there are many, many homes in our bonny land to which you and yours would be welcome.

"I am one of those ladies whom you so often commend for preferring to be wed to my pen and books than to a heart which could not appreciate mine, but I have never given my *name* to be bandied about by heartless critics, and do not think I shall ever acquire the amount of courage and resolution necessary for this sacrifice. So I have not become famous, and should not, even if I were worthy to be. I never had a single aspiration for notoriety, and should not trouble my head about learning or literature if my heart had something to satisfy its yearnings; but your advice in your allusions to Miss Wordsworth has done me good. I will cultivate letters as a resource when I am old and there is nothing living left for the lone heart to love.

"It would gratify me more than any words can express to know that this reaches you safely, and that you smile, not with ridicule but with approbation, at my girlish frankness and unsophisticated trust.

"A line directed to M. M., care of *A. G. Johnson*, Editor, Troy Daily Post, *Troy, New York*, would find me. I give my *nom de plume*, confessing it is not polite or respectful to conceal my own, after such an epistle, lest you will believe it is from pure timidity and conscious unworthiness. If you pardon me this I am not sure but I shall tell you all I am and all I know!   M. M.

"I have the impression that you do not reside permanently in Edinburgh, so I direct to Care of Prof. Wilson, who will, of course, know where you are. You cannot think how I blush at the thought of what I am doing."

It was told by Miss de Quincey in her father's Memoir that he received many letters from the Brontës while yet they were merely to the world Currer, Ellis, and Acton Bell, as well as afterwards with copies of their works. These letters, unfortunately, have been lost or given to autograph collectors, with the sole exception of the first, which we print below—a letter which will be admitted to be very characteristic :—

"SIR,—My relations, Ellis and Acton Bell, and myself, heedless of the repeated warnings of various respectable publishers, have committed the rash act of printing a volume of poems.

"The consequences predicted have, of course, over-taken us; our book is found to be a drug; no man needs it or heeds it; in the space of a year our publisher has disposed but of two copies, and by what painful efforts he succeeded in getting rid of those two, himself only knows.

"Before transferring the edition to the trunk-makers we have decided on distributing as presents a few copies of what we cannot sell : and we beg to offer you one in acknowledgment of the pleasure and profit we have often and long derived from your works.—I am, Sir, yours very respectfully,

"CURRER BELL.

"*June 16th,* '47.
　　"T. DE QUINCEY, Esq."

That remarkable brother, Patrick Branwell Brontë, a genius, but in his last days, at all events, a mournful wreck, round whom, as we know from Charlotte's letters, the thoughts and anxieties of the sisters so long painfully circled, seems also to have written frequently to the Opium-Eater—letters which, so far as they can now be remembered, were full of confessions, of regrets, of hopes, and aspirations mingled together in the most affecting and striking manner. That correspondence has left token of itself in some copies of poems, which, as we are not aware that they have been preserved elsewhere, we here venture partially to give, in memory of that weak, wayward, unfortunate man, but singular genius—so singular that Mr. Leyland,[1] indeed, essays to prove that the leading idea of one at least of the sisters' stories was due to him; and that, in fact, he had written a novel with the same plot, characters, and incidents as " Wuthering Heights," quoting Mr. Grundy[2] to this effect : " Patrick declared to me, and what his sister said bore out the assertion, that he wrote a great portion of ' Wuthering Heights' himself."   Mr. Leyland, with full knowledge and refined sympathy, abundantly establishes the fact that much misknowledge and exaggeration characterised the writing of Mrs. Gaskell in her Memoir of Charlotte Brontë, so far as it related to Patrick, and that she has been only too closely followed in many of her misrepresentations by Mr. Swinburne, Miss Mary F. Robinson, and other writers of more recent date.   Patrick Brontë has enough to bear in his inherited constitution, his tendency to disease, his morbid predisposition to melancholy, and the reactions from it favouring outbursts of excess in many directions, without having fables fathered upon him.   " The defects of faith, and taints of blood," of which the Laureate sings, were very strong in him ; and great allowance should be made for a man of such a temperament and such inheritances.   But it is clear, from Mr. Leyland's volumes, that there must have been great exaggeration with regard to many things in the career of

---

[1] "The Brontë Family, with special reference to Patrick Branwell Brontë."   By Francis A. Leyland.   Hurst & Blackett, vol. ii.

[2] " Pictures of the Past."

Patrick Brontë.   Mr. Leyland, in his picture up to the last few years, would have us to regard him as a shy, sensitive, fanciful, excitable creature, with high aspirings, but without steadiness or will to adhere to fixed resolutions, and finally losing his balance, and surrendering himself to hallucinations of many kinds. This, at all events, is at once the more charitable and the more grateful view to take; and certainly in Mr. Leyland, Patrick Brontë has found a very thoughtful and well-informed apologist, if not a defender.   His portrait of Branwell, at all events, is not that of a half-madman, half-fiend, half-poet, half-reprobate; rather that of a man with many fine impulses, but without ballast, and finally surrendering himself to indulgences that did much to wreck his career and shorten his life.

While disproving wholly the truth of the assertion of Miss Mary Robinson that Patrick Brontë was an opium-eater at twenty, he goes on to speak of the attraction of De Quincey's writings for the whole family, and is fain to admit that when, later, Branwell betook himself to opium, he may have *in some degree* been led thereto by study of De Quincey's "Confessions."   He writes :—

" There is no reliable evidence whatever that Branwell at this period of his life [his twentieth year] was an opium-eater; and, considering the fact that the biographer of Emily has assigned the art-practice at Bradford to a period subsequent to his tutorship at Broughton-in-Furness, one may, perhaps, be permitted to suspect that she is equally in error in her assertions as to his opium-eating so young. Branwell did, indeed, later fall into the baneful habit, and suffered at times in consequence; but there is no reason to believe that he became wholly subject to it, or was greatly injured by the practice either in mind or body. We can only surmise as to the original cause of his use of opium; but, when we consider the extraordinary fascination which De Quincey's wonderful book had for the younger generation of literary men of his day, we shall recognise that Branwell, who read the book, in all probability fell under its influence. Let us remember, moreover, that the young man's two sisters had died of consumption, and that De Quincey declares the use of the drug had saved him from the fate of his father, who had fallen a victim to the same scourge. De Quincey had used the drug intermittently, and we have reason to believe that Branwell, who followed him, did the same. Let us, then, imagine the young Brontë revelling in the realm of the dreamy and impassioned, and hoping fondly that consumption might be driven away, resolving to try the effect of the 'dread agent of unimaginable pleasure and pain,' a proceeding from which many less brave would have shrunk. Branwell had doubtless read in the 'Confessions of an English Opium-Eater' that the drug does not disorder the system, but gives tone, a sort of health, that might be natural, if it were not for the means by which it is procured."

Mr. Leyland has devoted a good deal of space to Patrick Brontë's poetical efforts, and cites extracts from many of them, but of those which are before us it does not seem that he had any knowledge. Probably they were written at a time when neither he nor his friends were in personal association or correspondence with Brontë—and it is certain that they reached De Quincey at a time of sickness and great prostration, which may account for their having been swallowed up in his vast piles of papers and never recovered till his death. We give the most striking passages of the poem—together with the translations of Horace's Odes, which accompanied it :—

SIR HENRY TUNSTALL.

'Tis only afternoon—but midnight's gloom
Could scarce seem stiller, in the darkest room,
Than does this ancient mansion's strange repose,
So long ere common cares of daylight close.
I hear the clock slow ticking in the Hall ;
And—far away—the woodland waterfall
Sounds, lost, like stars from out the noon-day skies—
And seldom heard until those stars arise.
　The parlour group are seated all together,
With long looks turned toward the threat'ning weather,
Whose grey clouds, gathering o'er the moveless trees,
Nor break nor brighten with the passing breeze.
　Why seems that group attired with such a care ?
And who's the visitor they watch for there ?
The aged Father, on his customed seat,
With cushioned stool to prop his crippled feet,
Averting from the rest his forehead high
To hide the drop that quivers in his eye ;
And strange the pang which bids that drop to start ;
For hope and sadness mingle in his heart ;

A trembling hope for what may come to-day—
A sadness sent from what has passed away !
Fast by the window sits his daughter fair;
Who, gazing earnest on the clouded air,
Clasps close her mother's hand, and paler grows
With every leaf that falls, or breeze that blows:
Sickened with long hope bursting into morn
Too bright for her, with longer pining worn !
Even those young children o'er the table bent;
And on that map with childish eyes intent,
Are guiding fancied ships through ocean's foam,
And wondering—" what he's like "—and " when he'll come."

  .   .   .   .

But long that house has lost all trace of him,
Whose very form in memory waxes dim.
Long since his childhood's chosen friends have died;
The shaggy pony he was wont to ride—
The dog, so faithful to its Master's side—
The rooks and doves that hover round the door
Are not the same his young hand fed of yore;
The flowers he planted many seasons past
Have drooped and died and disappeared at last;
For him afar, tempestuous seas had torn,
Before the children round that map were born:
And, since, so many years have passed between
The voiceless farewells of that parting scene,
That scarce they saw it then through gathering tears
So dim as now through intervening years.
" But still "—said Mary—" still I think I see
The Soldier's plumèd helmet bent o'er me,
The arm that raised me to a last embrace,
The calmness settled o'er his youthful face,
Save when I asked ' how soon he'd come again '—
And all that calm was lost a moment then !—
Our Father shook his hand, but could not speak,
Our weeping Mother kissed his sunny cheek,

Our Sisters spoke not—'twas a mute farewell,
And yet no voice could speak it half so well.
We saw our *Henry* on his charger spring,
We heard his swift hoofs o'er the pavement ring,
There—long we stopped—as if he still was there—
Hand clasped in hand, and full eyes fixed on air :
He scarce seemed gone so long as we beheld
The chequered sunshine and the open field,
But—when we turned within—when closed the door
On that bright Heaven—we felt that *all* was o'er ;
That never more those rooms should hear his call,
That never more his step should cross that Hall.
We sat together till the twilight dim,
But all the world to us seemed gone with him.
We gathered close, but could not drive away
The dreary solitude that o'er us lay.
We felt when *one* has left the home fireside
It matters not though all be there beside,
For still all hearts will wander with that one,
And gladness stays not when the heart is gone,
And—where no gladness is a crowd may feel alone.

.   .   .   .

"Since then how oft we've sat together here
With windows opening on the twilight air,
Silently thinking of the climes afar
Beneath the shining of that evening star,
Dear as a friend unto our loneliness
Because it seemed to link those lands with us.
He saw it, perhaps, whom time's and ocean's tide
So many years had sundered from our side,
And 'twas the same he used to look upon
While all beside so different had grown.
Our woods, our house, ourselves, were not the same
As those that floated through his boyhood's dream.
Is he too changed ?—Alas ! the cannons' roar,
The storms and summers of that burning shore,

May have made the last great change!—Too well I know
Even *our* calm words cannot escape *that* blow!
We cannot greet him if again he come
With the same group that made his ancient home—
The Heart that he loved best is clad in clay—
She is laid in lasting rest—she is far away!"

So Mary spoke—but she said nothing now,
Turning so earnestly her pallid brow
On the dull Heavens to which they all were turning
With looks that could not clear the shade of mourning
Worn far too constantly upon each face
For that one day of feverish hope to chase;
That day, determined from Madeira's shore,
When they their wanderer might behold once more;
Not now the boyish ensign he had gone,
But full of honours from his foes o'erthrown.
Time after time fresh tidings of his fame
Had roused to life his aged Father's frame,
When the old Man would raise his gushing eye,
And lose his sighs of grief in smiles of joy.
At last, that letter with *Sir Henry's* crest
The tidings of his swift approach expressed,
A Victor General to his England's shore—
At last—that sixteen years' suspense seemed o'er.
At last—the fresh-rolled walks, the shaven lawn
That long a look of such neglect had worn,
The rooms so fairly decked—the expectant calm
O'er all things brooding like a magic charm,
At last, proclaimed the mighty moment come
When hope and doubt should both give place to doom.
Stay—what was that which broke the hush profound?—
Like rapid wheels I heard its murmur sound.
Why are the servants' footsteps heard within
So sudden intermixed with hasty din?
What pales each cheek—what lights each swimming eye
Through the close circle of that company?

.   .   .   .

I cannot paint the start of mute surprise,
The tears that flashed in scarce-believing eyes,
The long embrace—the silence eloquent
Of more than language ever could give vent;
The Father's face that said, "Thy will be done—
Take me if fit since Thou hast given my son;"
The Mother's look, too fond to turn above
Her Son beholding with a mother's love;
The Sister's eyes that shone in youth's o'erflow
Of feelings such as age could never know,
With whom this world was not the earth it seems,
But all surrounded by the light of dreams,
With whom even Sorrow took a heavenly die,
Since where it darkened Hope seemed shining by;
So thus, while, speechless, held in *His* embrace,
She saw, she knew, her long-lost Henry's face,
She let past times part—hurrying down the wind,
And years of vain repinings leave her mind.
    Not so Old Age—for Sorrow breaks it in,
And—used to harness—it can ill begin
Existence o'er again.   Dissolved in tears
Of heartfelt gratitude, the head of years
Was bowed before that Soldier—but in vain
Each parent strove to shake off Sorrow's chain,
Their eyes were dim to present joys—yet still
Past joys to them were far more visible.
They saw their first-born's golden locks appear
Shining behind the cloud of memories dear;
They looked—and was this war-worn warrior Him?—
Ah! how the golden locks waned dark and dim!
Their innocence destroyed—for India's clime
Had touched him with the iron hoar of time;
Wast him?—They gazed again—a look, a tone
Can sometimes bring the past—'twas Henry—'twas their
      own!
They did not mark his restless glances roam
As if he sought but could not find his home;

They did not mark the sternness of his cheek
Even if to smiles its muscles chose to break ;
They only saw the stately Soldier's form
Confirmed, not altered by the battle's storm ;
They only saw the long-lost face again,
Darkened by climate, not by crime or pain.
    But what *He* thought it would be hard to tell,
Since worldly life can mask the heart so well,
Can hide with smiles a sorrow-eaten cheek,
Can bitter thoughts in cheerful accents speak,
Can give to icy minds heart-eloquence,
And " clothe no meaning in the words of sense "—
Words he poured forth of warm and welcome greeting,
For—" Heaven," he said, " smiled in this happy meeting."—
By turns he wandered o'er each long-lost face—
By turns he held them in a fast embrace—
Then Mary saw—though nought her parents knew—
For youthful love has eyes of eagle view—
She saw his features in a moment alter,
Their rapture vanish and their fondness falter ;
And—in that moment—Oh how cold seemed all
The mind that lurked beneath that passion's pall !
A corse beneath a gilded shroud—the corse
Of him who left them on his battle-horse
Sixteen long years ago !—
                        —Sir Henry broke
A sudden pause where only glances spoke,
With a request for one half-hour alone
To call his spirits to a steadier tone
And moderate their swell.   He left them then
To spend that time in calling back again
The ancient image to their wildered view,
To mark the difference 'twixt the old and new :
But—strange—whene'er they strove to realise
The form erewhile enshrinèd in their eyes,
The visioned Idol of each vanished year—
How *like* a vision did it now appear !

They could not bear to see it shrink from view,
Like a vain dream—but ever came the new
Before the old—thus on a sudden faded
When by life's stern realities invaded.
    Changed—like life's dreary paths from youth to years,
And dull as age. The twilight hour appears,
The hour ordained by God for man's repose,
Yet often made by man an hour of woes,
A summing-up of daylight's toils and grief,
Of moody musing, not of mild relief.

    .   .   .   .

    That dull hour darkened in the boding sky,
And bore the breeze in mournful murmurs by,
With promise of a storm.   Within the room
No cheerful candle shone to cheat its gloom,
Nor cheerful countenance smiled—for only one
Lone tenant held it, seated still as stone—
Sir Henry Tunstall—with a vacant gaze,
As if his mind were wandering through a maze
Of alien thoughts, though on that very bed
Long years ago had lain his infant head
In sleep unstained by sorrow.   Still there hung—
Wrecks of a time when all the world looked young—
His guns—his rods—wherewith he'd often trod
The breezy hills or wandered by the flood,
And breasted mountain winds, and felt within
The first bold stirrings of the Man begin.
There, pictured as of yore, the self-same wall
Showed England's victory, and her Hero's fall
On cold Canadian hills.   With strange delight,
In other days the child would fix his sight,
Whene'er he wakened, on that time-dimmed view,
And inly burn to be a hero too;
Would fill his spirit with the thoughts divine
Of the loud cannon, and the charging line,
And Wolfe, departing 'mid commingling cries
To join immortal spirits in the skies!

'Twas that dim print that over Indian seas
First led his feet and fixed his destinies.
So why on what was childhood's chief delight
Will manhood hardly deign to bend his sight?
The old print remains—but does the *old mind* remain?
Ah World!—why wilt thou break enchantment's chain!—

    Bending his brows, at last Sir Henry said—
"Well, *now* I know that Time has *really* sped
Since last my head has in that chamber lain—
That nothing has my *Now* to do with *Then!*
Yes—now at last I've reached my native home,
And all who loved me joy to see me come,
And memory of departed love is nigh
To cast a holier halo round their joy.
I have seen my Father full of honoured days,
Whom last I saw adorned with manhood's grace,
Who has lived since then long winters but to see
Once more—his first-born—world-divided me.
I have seen those eyes rekindle, that have mourned
For me.   I have seen those grey locks that have turned
From raven black for me.   I have seen Her too—
The first I loved on earth—the first I knew—
She who was wont above that very bed
To bend with blessings o'er my helpless head;
I have seen my Sister—I have seen them all—
All but myself.   They have lost *me* past recall,
As I have them.   And vainly have I come
These thousand leagues—my Home is not my Home.
   Yet—let me recollect myself—for strange
And vision-like appears this sudden change;
In what consists it?   I am still the same
In flesh and blood, and lineaments and name.
Still wave the boughs of my ancestral trees,
Still these old gables front the western breeze,
Still hang these relics round this chamber lone,
I still can see—can call them still my own.

   .   .   .   .

"They fancied, when they saw me home returning,
That all my soul to meet with them was yearning,
That every wave I'd bless which bore me hither;
They thought my spring of life could never wither,
That in the dry the green leaf I could keep,
As pliable as youth to laugh or weep;
They did not think how oft my eyesight turned
Toward the skies where Indian sunshine burned,
That I had perhaps left an associate band,
That I had farewells even for that wild Land;
They did not think my head and heart were older,
My strength more broken, and my feelings colder,
That spring was hastening into autumn sere—
And leafless trees make loveliest prospects drear—
That sixteen years the same ground travel o'er
Till each wears out the mark which each has left before.

"So—old affection is an empty name
When nothing that we loved remains the same,
But while we gaze upon the vapour gay,
The light that gave it glory fades away.
And—Home Affection—where have we a home?
For ever doomed in thought or deed to roam,
To lay our parents in their narrow rest
Or leave their hearthstones when we love them best;
Nay, sometimes scarce to know we love at all,
Till o'er love's object Death has spread his pall!—
I feel 'tis sad to live without a Heart,
But sadder still to feel dart after dart
Rankling within it—sad to see the dead,
But worse to see the sick man's tortured bed.
    "Well I have talked of change—but oh how changed
Am I from him who o'er those dim hills ranged
With trusty dog—poor Rover!—where art thou?
I seem to see thee looking upward now
To thy young Master's face, with honest eye
Shining all over with no selfish joy.

He paused with heavy eye, and round the room
Looked, through the shadows of descending gloom,
Like one heart-sick, for 'twas a bitter task
The hollowness of spirit to unmask
And show the wreck of years.   To change his mind
He took a book lying by, in which to find
Some other course for thought—and, turning o'er
Its leaves, he thought he'd known that book before;
And on one page some hand had lightly traced
These lines, by Time's dim finger half-effaced :—

" My Father and my childhood's guide,
    If oft I've wandered far from Thee,
  Even though Thine only Son has died
    To save from death a child like me,

  Oh ! still, to Thee when turns my heart
    In hours of sadness—*frequent now !*
  Be still the God that once Thou wert,
    And calm my breast and clear my brow.

  I am now no more a guileless child
    O'ershadowed by Thine angel wing,
  For even my dreams are far more wild
    Than those my slumbers used to bring;

  I farther see, I deeper feel,
    With hopes more warm, but heart less mild,
  And ancient things new forms reveal,
    All strangely brightened or despoiled;

  I am entering on life's open tide,
    So fare ye well, lost shores divine !
  And, O my Father !—deign to guide
    Through its wild waters—CAROLINE !"

.   .   .   .

Long o'er that dark'ning page Sir Henry pondered,
Nor from its time-worn words his eyesight wandered;
Yet scarce he comprehended what they were,
For other words were sounding in his ear—
Sent to him from the grave far-off and dim,
As if from Heaven a spirit spoke to him,
That bade the shadows of past time glide by
Till present times were hidden from his eye
By their strange pictured veil—scene after scene
Sailing around him of what once had been.—
He saw a Drawing-room revealed in light
From the red fireside of a winter night,
With two fair beings seated side by side,
The one arrayed in all a soldier's pride,
The other sadly pale, with angel eyes,
O'er whose fair orbs a gushing gleam would rise
Whenever, tremblingly, she strove to speak,
Though scarce a sound the voiceless calm would break,
So silent seemed despair.—He took her hand
And told her something of a distant land
Soon to be won with fame, and soon again
Of his return victorious o'er the main.

"Oh no!"—at last she said—" I feel too well
The hollow vanity of all you tell.
You'll go, you'll join the ranks by Ganges' flood,
You'll perhaps survive through many a field of blood,
You'll perhaps gain fame's rewards—but nevermore
Those far-off climes *my* Henry shall restore
To England's hills again.   Another mind—
Another heart than that he left behind—
And other hopes he'll bring—if hope at all
Can outlive fancy's flight and feeling's fall
To flourish on an iron-hardened brow.—
The Soldier may return—but *never Thou!*
And, further, know, our meeting must not be,
For even thyself wilt not be changed like me.
I shall be changed, my Love, to change no more;

I shall be landed on a farther shore
Than Indian Isles—a wider sea shall sever
My form from thine—a longer time—*For ever !*
   Oh ! when I am dead and mouldering in my grave,
Of me at least some dim remembrance have,—
Saved from the sunken wrecks of ancient time,
Even if to float o'er thoughts of strife and crime :
Then on the grave of Her who died for thee
Cast one short look—and, oh ! Remember Me ! "

   " Alas, Lost Shade ! why should I look upon
The mouldering letters of thy burial-stone !
Why should I strive thine image to recall,
And love thy beauty's flower and weep its fall ?
It cannot be—for far too well I know
The narrow house where thou art laid below.
I know its lifeless chill, its rayless gloom,
Its voiceless silence, and its changless doom.
I know that if from weeds I cleared thy name
And gazed till memories crowding round me came
Of all that made the sunshine of my home,
'Twould be of no avail—*Thou* couldst not come
That I might almost think I saw thee stand
Beside me—almost feel thy fairy hand.
Still would that form be pressed 'neath earth and stones.
And still that hand would rest in dust and bones.
   No, Caroline—the hours are long gone by
When I could call a shade reality,
Or make a world of dreams, or think that one
Was present with me who, I knew, was gone.
No—if the sapling *bends* to every breeze,
Their force shall rather *break* the full-grown trees.
If Infancy will catch at every toy,
Pursuits more solid must the Man employ.
He feels what *is*, and nought can charm away
The rough realities of present day.

Thou art dead—I am living—my word is not thine,
So keep thy sleep—and, Farewell, Caroline!

.   .   .   .

"Yet—while I think so, while I speak farewell,
'Tis not in words the dreariness to tell
Which sweeps across my spirit—for my soul
Feels such a midnight o'er its musings roll
At losing—though it be a vapour vain—
What *once* was rest to toil and ease to pain.
I knew not, while afar, how utterly
These memories of youth were past from me.
It seemed as if, though business warped my mind,
I could assume them when I felt inclined;
That though like dreams they fled my wakened brain,
I, if I liked, could dream them o'er again.
I did not think I *could* be seated here,
After the lapse of many a toilsome year
Once more returning to accustomed places
Amid the smiles of ' old familiar faces;'
Yet shrinking from them—hiding in the gloom
Of this dull evening and secluded room,
Not to recall the spirit of the boy,
But all my world-worn energies to employ
In pondering o'er some artifice to gain
A seat in council or command in Spain.

"Well—world, oh world!—as I have bowed to thee,
I must consent to suffer thy decree ;
I asked—Thou'st given me my destiny ;
I asked—when gazing on that pictured wall,
Like England's Hero to command or fall ;
I asked when wandering over mountains lone,
Some day to wander over lands unknown ;
I asked for gain and glory—place and power ;
Thou gavest them all—I have them all this hour ;
But I forgot to ask for youthful blood,
The thrill divine of feelings unsubdued,

The nerves that quivered to the sound of fame,
The tongue that trembled o'er a lover's name,
The eye that glistened with delightful tears,
The Hope that gladdened past and gilded future years;
So—I have rigid nerves and ready tongue,
Fit to subdue the weak and serve the strong;
And eyes that look on all things as the same,
And Hope—no, callousness, that thinks all things *a name!*
　　So, Caroline—I'll bid farewell once more,
Nor mourn, lost shade; for though thou'rt gone before,
Gone is *thy* Henry too—and didst not thou,
While just departing from this world below,
Say thou no longer wert a guileless child,
That all old things were altered or despoiled?—
And—hadst thou lived—thine angel heart, like mine,
Would soon have hardened with thy youth's decline—
Cold, perhaps, to me, if beating, as when laid
Beneath its grave-stone 'neath the churchyard shade.

.　　　.　　　.　　　.　　　.　　　.　　　.

　　"I home returned for rest—but feel to-day
Home is no rest—and long to be away,
To play life's game out where my soldiers are,
Returned from India to a wilder war
Upon the hills of Spain—again to ride
Before their bayonets at Wellesley's side,
Again to sleep with horses trampling round,
In watch-cloak wrapped, and on a battle-ground;
To waken with the loud commencing gun,
And feed life's failing flame and drive the moments on—
There is our aim—to *that* our labours tend—
Strange we should love to hurry on our end!
But so it is, and nowhere can I speed
So swift through life as on my battle-steed!"

　　He ceased—unconsciously declined his head,
And stealingly the sense of waking fled,
Wafting his spirit into weeping Spain:

Till—starting momently—he gazed again,
But all looked strange to his beclouded brain:
And all was strange—for, though the scenes were known,
The thoughts that should have cherished them were gone,
Gone like the sunshine—and none others came
To shake the encroaching slumbers from his frame.
So, while he lay there, twilight deepened fast,
And silent, but resistless, hours swept past,
Till chairs and pictures lost themselves in gloom,
And but a window glimmered through the room,
With one pale star above the sombre trees,
Listening from Heaven to earth's repining breeze.

That Star looked down with cold and quiet eye,
While all else darkened, brightening up the sky,
And though his eye scarce saw it, yet his mind,
As, half awake and half to dreams resigned,
Could scarce help feeling in its holy shine
The solemn look of sainted Caroline,
With mute reproachfulness reminding him
That faith and fondness were not all a dream;
That form, not feeling, should be changed by clime;
That looks, not love, should suffer hurt by time;
That o'er life's waters, guiding us from far,
And brightening with life's night, should glisten Memory's
  Star.   P. B. B.

Broughton-in-Furness, *April* 15, 1840.

HORACE.

ODE XV.   BOOK I.

'Twas when the treacherous shepherd bore
 His Royal prize away,
In Phrygian ship—from Spartan shore—
 Across the Ægean Sea,

That Nereus raised his awful brow,
   And hushed each favouring breeze,
Till not a ship its path could plough
   Upon the slumbering seas;

And thus did that old Sea-god sing
   His prophecy of doom—
" Vain Man! ill-omened thou dost bring
   Thine hostess to thy home,

Whom Greece shall seek with mighty host,
   Conjured to overwhelm
Thy pleasures, bought at such a cost,
   And thy ancestral realm.

Alas! what strife round Xanthus' wave
   Thy treachery shall bring!
What fiery funerals o'er the grave
   Of Ilion and her king!

Now Pallas lays her olive by,
   And grasps her shield and spear,
And mounts her chariot in the sky,
   And wakes her rage for war.

In vain thy guardian goddess' care
   Thy spirit may inspire;
In vain thou comb'st thy curling hair,
   Or wakest thy wanton lyre;

In vain the shouts—the lances' thrust—
   Or Ajax,—thou may'st fly,
For, with thy long locks trailed in dust,
   Adulterer! thou shalt die!

Ulysses see, and Nestor grave—
   Thy hapless people scourge;
And Sthenelus and Teucer brave
   Thy flying footsteps urge:

'Tis Sthenelus the reins can guide,
    While noble Diomede,
Greater than Tydeus, at his side
    Hunts for the adulterer's head;

Whom thou shalt fly as flies the wind
    In vale or woodland lone,
From the deep death-bark, heard behind,
    Of wild wolf hastening on;

With beating heart and bated breath,
    O'er mountain and through grove—
Was this the victory—this the death
    Thou promisedst thy love?

Pelides' ships, Pelides' arm
    O'er Phrygia's fated shore
For these thy deeds, the avenging storm
    Resistlessly shall pour;

And after years of weary wars,
    Shall wrap in funeral flame,
Unquenched by all her blood and tears,
    My Ilion's very name."

BOOK I.   ODE XI.

LEUCONÆ, seek no more
    By magic arts t' explore
How long a life our God has given to thee or me.
    If we've winters yet in store;
    Or if this whose tempests roar
Across the Tyrrhene deep, is the *last* that we shall see.

Be cheerful wisdom thine;
My goblet fill with wine;
And shape thy hopes to suit the hour that hastes away;
For while we speak, that hour
Is past beyond our power;
So do not trust to-morrow, *but seize upon to-day.*

BOOK I.   ODE IX.

See'st thou not amid the skies
White with snow Soracte rise;
While the forests on the plain
Scarce their hoary weight sustain;
And congealed the waters stand
'Neath the frost's arresting hand.

Drive away the winter wild;
On the hearths be fuel piled;
And from out its sacred cell—
Kept in Sabine vase so well—
Generous—bring thy four years' wine,
Wakener of the song divine.
Wisely leave the rest to Heaven,
Who, when warring winds have striven
With the forests or the main,
Bids their raging rest again.
Be not ever pondering
Over what the morn may bring.
Whether it be joy or pain
Wisely count it all as gain,
And, while age upon thy brow
Shall forbear to shed his snow,
Do not shun the dancers' feet,
Nor thy loved one's dear retreat.

Hasten to the plain or square;
List the whisper, telling where,
When the calm night rules above,
Thou may'st meet thy dearest love:
When the laugh round corner sly
Shall instruct thee where to spy:
When the wanton's feigned retreating
Still shall leave some pledge of meeting:
Perhaps a ring or bracelet bright,
Snatched from arm or finger white.

BOOK I.   ODE X.

FOR what does the poet to Phœbus pray—
　With new wine from his vessels flowing?
Not for the flocks o'er Calabria that stray;
　Nor for corn in Sardinia growing;

Nor prays he for ivory, or gold, or land
　Which the Liris, gently gliding,
Would crumble away into fugitive sand
　Down its silent waters sliding.

Let *him* gather the grapes who has planted the vine;
　Let the Merchant whom Jupiter favours,
His Syrian treasures exchange for wine
　Which a golden goblet flavours:

Thrice in a season o'erpassing the sea,
　Nor by waters or winds prevented,
While olives and mallows shall satisfy me,
　With the lot fortune gives me contented.

Son of Satona ! oh grant me to taste
  The goods thou hast placed before me;
And a spirit undimmed, and an age undisgraced,
  And a Harp with whose strains to adore thee !

BOOK I. ODE XIX.

THE mother of love and the father of wine
  And passion resuming its throne,
Backward command me my mind to incline
  And kindle the flame that seemed gone.
     For Glycera warms
     My heart with her charms
Whiter than Parian stone.

Her sweet arts inflame me, her countenance beams
  Too bright to be gazed upon,
Till Venus, departing from Cyprus, seems
  To rush upon me alone :
     And no longer my verse
     The deeds can rehearse
By Scythian or Parthian done.

Raise me an altar of living sod,
  And crown it with garlands and bear
Wine undiluted, a drink for a god,
  That Glycera, hearing my prayer,
     May know I adore,
     And be cruel no more,
But an answering passion declare.

There are doubtless many mistakes of sense and language—except
the first. I had not, when I translated them, a Horace at hand, so was
forced to rely on memory.—P. B. BRONTË.

The following is a note from Robert Montgomery —"Satan" Montgomery—with whom De Quincey had had some intimacy :—

> "LINCOLN COLLEGE, OXFORD,
> "*March* 1831.

"MY DEAR DE QUINCEY,—You will do me a great favour in accepting a copy of 'Oxford' and my free and unaffected confession of the pleasure and pride I feel in being acquainted with the author of the 'Opium-Eater.'

"May I venture to anticipate a line from you in the course of a week? How happy I should be— could I fancy any page in 'Oxford' calculated to touch or thrill a chord of memory in your heart, linked with associations that reach back into other years when you were (as Wordsworth says)—

> 'An eager Novice robed in fluttering gown !'

At all events, ever believe me, my dear De Quincey, with great admiration, your very obliged

"R. MONTGOMERY.

" With a copy of 'Oxford,' Blackwood's Parcel.

"TH. DE QUINCEY, Esq.,
"7 Great Queen [King] Street, Edinburgh."

In later years, names still more familiar appear. Here is one instance :—

"BALLYSHANNON, IRELAND,
"*11th of March '51.*

"SIR,—Will you oblige me by accepting the accompanying volume? And pray allow me to use the opportunity of saying that I have associated respect and admiration with your name ever since I became acquainted with it—for it is delightful to me to give so much expression, however unimportant to you, of that feeling.

"I wish it were in my power to send (but the thing is not in *esse*, but in *posse*) a copy of a Second Edition of the Verses, 'thoroughly revised,' for the experience of the short time, during which they have been standing in the market-place and remarked upon by a few cobblers and others, has opened my eyes to many things; an effect caused partly too, I hope, by regular advance in my own mind.

"I am a young man, not regularly educated, living without personal intellectual intercourse in this corner of Ireland, anxious to be sincere and to improve. Should you think it worth while to send me any observations of yours on my first literary publication (I fear, too hastily put forth), it would please me greatly.—Believe me sincerely and respectfully yours,

"WILLIAM ALLINGHAM, Junr.

"To THOS. DE QUINCEY, Esq."

And here is another :—

"KNELLER HALL, ISLEWORTH,
"*5th Dec.* 1853.

"MY DEAR SIR,—I forward you with this a short Review on the ' Autobiography ' inserted on the first of this month in a little magazine named the *Educational Expositor.*   It is a liberty, I know, to criticize any man's writings : a liberty to blame them, and a still greater liberty to give them commendation. The utmost apologies are therefore in this case what I am bound to offer :—but by a few words at the close of your Preface I am encouraged to hope that you will not look unkindly on any attempt, however imperfect, to express sympathy not only with the aim and the result, but with the mind that has directed them in your writings.

"May I be allowed the additional liberty of expressing the high interest and expectation with which many besides myself look forward to the appearance of the second volume, and the Chapter entitled *Laxton?*—I have the honour to be, dear Sir, yr. obedt. Servant,   F. T. PALGRAVE.

"T. DE QUINCEY, Esq."

The following is from an American gentleman who had visited De Quincey at Lasswade :—

"MANCHESTER STREET, MANCHESTER SQUARE,
"LONDON, *Dec.* 4, 1853.

"MY DEAR SIR,—When at Lasswade I promised to write you, but have neglected it so long that it is now hard to write at all. If neglect has been long, remembrance has also been long; so, late acknowledgment carries in its heart its own apology.

"Since my blessed visit to you, I have travelled through the more interesting portions of Ireland, Wales, and Central England. During the past few weeks in London, I have been translating M. Cousin's lectures on the True, the Beautiful, and the Good, so have been abroad but little. The book will be published in two or three weeks by Messrs. Clark, in Edinborough. Shall do myself the pleasure and honor of sending the author of the 'Cæsars' a copy.

"Met Carlyle the other day by appointment, and walked with him an hour or more. He was in a merry humor. The lion was gentle enough, allowed his terrible mane to be stroked with some pleasantries about those 'eighteen millions of bores,' the long nails of satire were withdrawn and his tread was sweetly soft. In fact, I love Carlyle, have read him thoroughly, and I think understand him well. Two or three times I mischievously repeated to him one of his own great sayings. He immediately said the same thing in other words, adding humorously enough, 'As you say.'

"I shall go to Paris in about two weeks. You remarked to me that you should be there some time during the winter. If I can be of any service to you there, please command me.

"Give my regards to your daughters. Please

remind one of them of that perverted quotation that she showed me in Sir William Hamilton's book.—Very truly yours,   O. W. WIGHT.

"THOS. DE QUINCEY, ESQ."

Knowing Mr. de Quincey's aversion to travel, I was in doubt whether, in reading the above letter, I was right in making the word which occurs in it *Paris.* But so it was. Mrs. Baird Smith informs me that it was one of the childlike foibles of her father to allow himself to be interestedly enlisted in the talk of his guests about visits to foreign places, and that he would often advance to the point of speaking as though it were possible for him to join his friends in their excursions on the Continent—many of the historical places and scenes in which he much wished to see. He had actually at one time made up his mind to go with Mr. Wight—who was himself a literary man—to Paris, just as he had made up his mind to accompany Mr. J. T. Fields to many places; but he never actually set out on any of these excursions.

As an illustration of the pains De Quincey took to satisfy these various correspondents by polite replies, the following note may be given, a copy of which was found docketed beside the letters to which it related :—

"*July* 8, 1854.

" The gentleman, who has waited so long for an Autograph, expresses by his patience a compliment to myself far greater than any which I can flatter myself with deserving. For this I thank him sincerely. At the same time I am painfully sensible how little I can seem to have met this courtesy on his part by any corresponding expressions of courtesy on my own. My delays must have appeared unaccountable. Yet they are not so, but have real grounds of palliation in facts notorious to my friends. The first is this—that through some accidental oversight in the boyish stage of my education I was never taught to make (or consequently to mend) a pen.

" The second is this :—I suffer now, and have long suffered, from such a shattering of the nervous system as causes a sense of distraction, and even of horror, to connect itself with the manual act of writing—or indeed with any act requiring a close effort of attention. Hence it has arisen that, for some years, I have transferred—in all cases where the circumstances allowed it—all my duties of letter-writing to one of my daughters ; that it is mainly accounts for the delay and appearance of discourtesy, but with this I trust any impression of wilful discourtesy will be removed. Thomas de Quincey."

CHAPTER XXXI.

OUT of a considerable sheaf of letters written to the family immediately after Mr. de Quincey's death—letters sympathetic, grateful, and consoling—from almost all parts of the world, from the United States, from Canada, from British India and the West Indies, we here limit ourselves to presenting two, because both of the writers are well known, and had enjoyed intimate intercourse with him, and both remained on the most friendly terms with the family. The first is Professor Lushington, who at the time of Mr. de Quincey's death and burial was in the midst of his most pressing labours of the session connected with the Greek Chair in Glasgow. He wrote as follows:—

"GLASGOW COLLEGE, *Dec.* 13, '59.

"MY DEAR MRS. CRAIG,—I am much obliged and gratified by your kind letter in many ways. I thank you very heartily for your wish that I sh^d choose one of your dear Father's books, and for what you say of his regard for me, which I shall always remember with gratitude, while I must feel that the commendation you quote is far more than I merit. I do not at present particularly recollect any book that I should wish to have, but any one referring to the subjects we used so often to talk about, mental philosophy or the old English writers, would be a highly prized memorial of him—all the more if there happened to be any notes by himself scattered about the pages. There has been for some years in my keeping here a box which belonged to him, filled, I believe, mainly with books, among which one of mine is included. What steps would you like me to take about forwarding this box? If you will let me know I will do accordingly. I shall be in Edinbro' for a few hours on Saturday, when I shall try to see you. Thanks also for the details about the place of his burial, which I shall look on with deep interest. As yet I have not seen the notice of Dr. Begbie which was to appear in the *Scotsman*—perhaps it is deferred for a day or two. I did not see the letter you mention of Mr. Grinfield.—With kindest regards to Mr. Craig and your sisters, believe me ever yrs. most sincerely, E. L. LUSHINGTON."

The second was Mr. James T. Fields of Boston, who was then in London :—

"LONDON, *June 3rd,* 1860.

"MY DEAR MRS. BAIRD SMITH,—Thank you very sincerely for your most kind letter of May 30th. It is now our intention to leave town to-morrow, thankful to get away from the fatigues of a London month during the season. We shall go first to the Lakes, and then find our way to Edinburgh for a day or two. My wife will drop a note telling you *when* we shall probably have the pleasure of meeting you and your sisters at Lasswade. One of our most cherished prospects on leaving home was the hope of offering our hands for a hearty shake with the De Quinceys. To find *you* at home is a great surprise, but it greatly rejoices us that we are in Europe while you are not in India. Miss Emily too we shall be so glad to see. Mrs. Craig we would go a long way to greet, but Ireland is too far off for our very limited time. I had always looked forward to hearing the sound of your father's voice again. In my whole life I have never met a man of genius who won upon my *affectionate* interest more. He was so great a man, and yet so gentle and kind! As I walked with him to Roslin he talked with an eloquence I have never heard surpassed of the men he had lived among and the scenes of his early days, till it seemed as if it were sinful not to note down his wonderful sentences. I hope some one has made a record of his daily talk, for since Plato I cannot believe a mortal has equalled him. You know how deeply his writings have impressed the world, especially our American side of it, but I think his conversation quite equal to his printed pages. I can never forget my day at Lasswade when I met you all at your own little table in that pleasant cottage. Your father, when we parted under the misty Scotch hills, spoke of you, his children, with an affection I well remember as most touching. Dear old man! Some of the best moments of my life I owe to him, the great Master of English Prose.

" My wife joins me in most sincere regards to you and your sister, and anticipates much pleasure in making your acquaintance. I think of you as old friends always, and long to see you again.—Very faithfully yours, JAMES T. FIELDS."

APPENDIX.

APPENDIX.

I.

THE "DE" IN DE FOE AND DE QUINCEY.

SOME very interesting points arise in the case of De Foe and his adoption of the "De" in the name. In Mr. Lee's valuable "Life and Uncollected Writings of De Foe" we read :—

"Daniel Foe, or De Foe, as he chose afterwards to call himself, was born in the Parish of St. Giles's, Cripplegate, in the year 1661.

"The assertions of Oldmixon and Browne, and the conjectures of biographers, as to De Foe's reasons for altering his name, appear to be without foundation. He was called De Foe several years before the death of his venerated father, who never used any other name than that of Foe. The son was not a man to be ashamed of the surname of his living parent, nor the True-born Englishman likely to have been actuated by the vanity of assuming a Norman prefix. His practice disproves the assertion, and shows rather that the form of his signature was a matter of personal indifference, which continued to the end of his life. It is true that he used the surname of De Foe, but I am inclined to think that it began accidentally, or was adopted for convenience, about 1703, to distinguish him from his father. The latter from his age and experience, and the former from his commanding ability, were both influential members of the Dissenting interest in the City. They would respectively be spoken of and addressed orally as Mr. Foe and Mr. D. Foe. The name, as spoken, would in writing become Mr. De Foe, and thus what originated in accident, might be used for convenience, and become more or less fixed and settled by time. The simple explanation is favoured by the following proofs of De Foe's indifference in the matter. His initials and name appear in various forms in his works, subscribed to dedications, prefaces, &c., and this may be presumed to have been done by himself. Before 1703 I find only D. F. In that year Mr. De Foe and Daniel De Foe. In the following year D. D. F., De Foe, and Daniel De Foe. In 1705, D. F., and three autograph letters, all addressed within a few months to the Earl of Halifax, are successively signed D. Foe, De Foe, Daniel De Foe. In 1709, D. F., De Foe, Daniel De Foe. In 1710, a letter to Dyer signed De Foe. Two autograph signatures by himself, in 1723 and 1727, and two of the same dates by his daughter Hannah, are Daniel De Foe and Hannah De Foe. Yet in 1729 a letter to his printer is signed D. Foe, and the one to his son-in-law in 1730 is D. F."

It is, however, odd that the inconvenience out of which Mr. Lee says the difference of the names arose did not suggest itself or, at all events, find a practical remedy till Daniel Defoe was forty-two years of age, having already been in trade under the name of Foe both as hosier in Cornhill, and as brick and tile maker at Tilbury; and just as odd that after his brick and tile business was brought to an end in 1703, with the greatest loss to himself, he should begin to use the form De Foe. It was when his father was in business and he was in business within a short distance of each other in the City of London that inconvenient mistakes were most likely to arise, not after De Foe had launched into the sea of public life and pamphlet writing and authorship, and was not in such near neighbourhood to his father. Mr. Lee's explanation, therefore, loses all its force when facts and dates are carefully attended to; and it is certain as anything can be that the accidental transference of the " D "—initial for Daniel—into

"De" of the surname would sooner have had effect, if its origin had been such as Mr. Lee is inclined to hold.

We read that De Foe's grandfather was a man of means in Northamptonshire, a landowner, who himself cultivated a part, if not the whole, of his land ; and that he actually kept a pack of hounds. My idea would be that in earlier times the "De" had been used by the family, just as in the case of "De" in De Quincey; and that in the stormy times of the Commonwealth it was dropped, and not revived again while the male members of the family were mostly engaged in trade—butchers, hosiers, &c.; and the assumption of the "De" by De Foe just at the moment when he escaped from association with trade has certainly its own significance.

But it would appear that De Foe suffered insinuations and insults on the ground of his Normanised name too. For when he chanced to have a quarrel with journalists, notably so in the case of *Read's Journal*, they declined to write his name De Foe, as he now did himself, and dubbed him Foe. This is the way in which one series of attacks is wound up :—

" *N.B.*—Foe is desired to declare whether he did not authorise a certain publisher, not long ago, to come to Mr. Read, to desire a Cessation of all Personal Hostilities. If so, why he treacherously breaks the articles," &c. (Lee, vol. i. p. 300).

Mr. Lee proves that there was no treaty whose articles could be broken, and that De Foe was not guilty of using the phrases found in *Mist's Journal* which had roused anew the ire of Read.

Now, this insult was given to De Foe on the 10th October 1719, by which time the name of De Foe was in many ways famous. The first volume of " Robinson Crusoe " had been published on the 25th April of that same year, and was at once exhausted ; and a second published only seventeen days after ; a third followed only twenty-five days later ; and a fourth on the 8th of August. But still to *Read's Journal* he is Foe; " Mist's Author," " Mist's Man " (as the leading writer of *Mist's Journal*), in one breath, abundantly showing the animus; for why else should it be only enemies who persisted in using the Foe unless it was a term that might in the reader's mind carry some latent sting, after he had become so well and widely known as De Foe? This style of thing exactly reproduces and recalls to us Dr. Maginn's "Quin Daisy," &c., &c., as well as the somewhat spiteful and vulgar hints of some of his followers with respect to the use of the "De" by De Quincey. So history repeats itself even in so small a matter as this—a matter in which every man, if he has no dishonourable intention, is free to do as he pleases.

II.

MR. DE QUINCEY AND POETRY, MORE ESPECIALLY THE POETRY OF POPE.

A recent writer on De Quincey has said: "I doubt whether De Quincey really cared much for poetry as poetry; he liked philosophical poets: Milton, Wordsworth, Shakespeare (inasmuch as Shakespeare was, as he said, the greatest of philosophical poets), *Pope even in a certain way*" (the italics are our own).

Now this, we confess, surprised, and even somewhat shocked us, as being at once most erroneous and perverse. Assuredly, as regards Pope, the words "in a certain way," should have been "in an *uncertain* way," as we shall conclusively show in a moment. But meanwhile, let us ask, what of the Greek dramatists, Æschylus, Sophocles, Euripides? what of Homer? Did De Quincey not relish his hexameters? And yet more emphatically, what of Chaucer? Was he, under any construction, a philosophical poet, and did not De Quincey "like" him? Why, he even preferred him to Homer, declaring this preference in terms so strong as to be unmistakable, and to seem exaggerated. "Show me a piece of Homer's handiwork," he says, "that comes within a hundred leagues of that divine Prologue to the Canterbury Tales, or of the Knight's Tale, or of the Man of Law's Tale, or of the Tale of the patient Griselda ?"

And then as to Milton: was it the *philosophy* on which he laid stress when he wished to convict Dr. Johnson of error and malice when the practical-minded Doctor declared that the "Paradise Lost" was *tedious?* No; it was the scenery; the incidents, the processions of majestic imaginations; the pictures from near and far, from all the high places of history and mythology—from the "grandeur that was Greece and the glory that was Rome;" from India, Syria, Babylon the great, Persia in its prime, Phœnicia in its zenith. This is from one of the notes he added to his article on Milton in defence of his position as a poet tedious or little read, any more than the monumental work of any other great classic is necessarily so :—

"In the older and larger poem ["Paradise Lost"], the scenical opportunities are more colossal and more various. Heaven opening to eject her rebellious children; the unvoyageable depths of ancient Chaos, with its 'anarch old,' and its eternal war of wrecks; these traversed by that great leading angel that drew after him the third part of the heavenly host; earliest paradise dawning upon the warrior-angel out of this far-distant 'sea without shore' of chaos; the dreadful phantoms of sin and death, prompted by secret sympathy, and snuffing the distant scent of 'mortal change on earth,' chasing the steps of their great progenitor and sultan; finally, the heart-freezing visions, shown and narrated to Adam, of human misery, through vast successions of shadowy generations;—all these scenical opportunities offered in the 'Paradise Lost' become in the hands of the mighty artist elements of undying grandeur not matched on earth. The compass being so much narrower in the 'Paradise Regained,' if no other reason operated, inevitably the splendours are sown more thinly. But the great vision of the temptation, the banquet in the wilderness, the wilderness itself, the terrific pathos of the ruined archangel's speech, ' 'Tis true I am that spirit unfortunate,' &c. (the effect of which, when connected with the stern unpitying answer, is painfully to shock the reader); all these proclaim the ancient skill and the ancient power. And, as regards the skill naturally brightened by long practice, that succession of great friezes which the Archangel unrolls in the pictures of Athens, Rome, and Parthia, besides their native and intrinsic beauty, have an unrivalled beauty of position through the reflex illustration which reciprocally they give and take."

Are these the words of a man who liked only philosophical poets and did not care for poetry as poetry?

Again, in the article on Roscoe's "Pope," when illustrating the difference between the literature of *knowledge* and the literature of *power*, he writes: "What do you learn from 'Paradise Lost'? Nothing at all. What do you learn from a cookery-book? Something that you did not know before in every paragraph. But would you therefore put the wretched cookery-book on a higher level of estimation than the divine poem? What you owe to Milton is not any knowledge, of which a million separate items are still but a million of advancing steps on the same earthly level; what you owe is *power*, that is, exercise and expansion to your latent capacity of sympathy with the infinite, where every pulse and each separate influx is a long step upwards—a step ascending as upon a Jacob's ladder from earth to mysterious altitudes above the earth: *All* the steps of knowledge, from first to last, carry you further on the same plane, but could never raise you one foot above your ancient level of earth; whereas, the very first step in *power* is a flight—is an ascending into another element where earth is forgotten.

"The very highest work that has ever existed in the literature of knowledge (say Sir Isaac Newton's *Principia* or Kant's *Kritique*) is but a *provisional* work: a book upon trial and sufferance; whereas the feeblest works in the literature of power, surviving at all, survive as finished and unalterable among men. . . . The great moral, the last result of the 'Paradise Lost' is once formally announced; but it teaches itself only by diffusing its lesson through the entire poem in the total succession of events and purposes ; and even this succession teaches it only when the whole is gathered into a unity by a reflex act of meditation ; just as the pulsation of the physical heart can exist only when all the parts in an animal system are locked into one organisation. To address the *insulated* understanding is to lay aside the Prospero's robe of poetry."

And then as to Coleridge : it is, of course, open to any critic to declare his opinion that it was the *residuum* of philosophical thought in Coleridge's verse that De Quincey admired, and that he never efficiently separated between the poetry as poetry of Coleridge and the poetry *plus* philosophy of Coleridge. But it has to be remembered that De Quincey's conviction of the appearance of a great poet was based simply on " The Ancient Mariner," published in Wordsworth's volume as the work of an anonymous friend, and that he deeply regretted that opium, in Coleridge's as in his own case, had stimulated the metaphysical faculties at the expense of the imaginative or poetical. Here are his own words :—

" Nobody is happy under opium except for a very short term of years. But in what way did that operate upon his exertions as a writer ? We are of opinion that it killed Coleridge as a poet. The ' harp of Quantock ' was silenced for ever by the torment of opium ; but proportionately it roused and stung by misery his metaphysical instincts into more spasmodic life. Poetry can flourish only in the atmosphere of happiness. But subtle and perplexed investigations of difficult problems are amongst the commonest resources for beguiling the sense of misery, and for this we have the direct authority of Coleridge himself speculating on his own case. In the beautiful though unequal ode entitled ' Dejection,' stanza six, occurs the following passage :—

> ' For not to think of what I needs must feel,
> But to be still and patient all I can,
> *And haply by abstruse research to steal*
> *From my own nature all the natural man,—*

> This was my sole resource, my only plan,
> Till that which suits a part infects the whole,
> And now is almost grown the habit of my soul.'

" Considering the exquisite quality of some poems which Coleridge has composed, nobody can grieve (or *has* grieved) more than ourselves at seeing so beautiful a fountain choked up with weeds. But had Coleridge been a happier man, it is our fixed belief that we should have had far less of his philosophy, and perhaps, but not certainly, might have had more of his general literature."

And this suggests a point about De Quincey himself— that he, despite the opium, should have preserved so clear a perception of poetry as poetry, and to the end was enabled not only to dream his dream, but to record his phantasies in such pieces as " The Daughter of Lebanon " and " The Three Ladies of Sorrow," while all the time his intellect was preternaturally active in logic, metaphysics, and political economy, and most of the speculations that have at once enticed and vexed the mind of man from the beginning.

It might, of course, be argued that De Quincey, in the above-quoted passage, lays too much stress on " happiness," as the only atmosphere in which poetry can flourish. And De Quincey's opponent here might cite Wordsworth's famous verse :—

> " We poets in our youth begin in gladness,
> But thereof comes in the end despondency and madness."

But Wordsworth is there speaking for the class whose high-strung nervous phantasy had done something to undo them ; for certainly this was not Wordsworth's own case, and that very stanza also contains these lines :—

> " Of him who walked in glory and *in joy*
> Behind his plough upon the mountain-side."

Possibly, too, the case of Milton might be cited here, rolling his majestic metres in the midst of his personal trials and his domestic miseries, when all seemed against him—national events, household jarrings, his blindness, and so much else. But Milton's muse, for all that, made an atmosphere of joy for him in the very heart of life, and in spite of his saddened *circumstances*. The fact that he could sing remained; and just as the darkened bowers, which the trainers of the Harz find so essential in training, teach the birds to concentrate themselves in their notes, and find gladness in the sweet sounds they make when all is dark around them, so it is with the poet; and he *is* a poet or singer because he can make this gladness for himself in the fact that he can sing. If it had not been so, how could Milton have sustained himself in his work and constructed his grand oratorios? He had no hope of reward in coin of the realm; publishers were not besieging him for " copy " and for copyright, nor did it seem as if the nation were waiting hushed for his numbers. What sustained him then in his work? It was the joy he had in the doing of it—the sense of youthful power and impulse, the consciousness of creative fervour, the grand imaginings that were their own reward, and made a glorious world of his own around him, wherein he walked apart, if not lonely as a star, like a star dwelling in its own radiance and glad in the light it shed, whether men were ready to witness it or not. It was this inward " light of joy " that De Quincey meant—this consciousness of power to interpret and to express, in a word, to create the beautiful and minister to the good and true; for we cannot for one moment think of De Quincey dwelling on a merely coarse, outward, sensible happiness—if such there can be, at such a moment, and in such a connection; but even if he did, whilst we should then be compelled to range ourselves against him, his position would still be in our favour as against the critic with whom we are concerned; for either form of happiness is opposed to the metaphysical or abstractive temper. Opium, we may add, taken in excess, disturbs the sense of creative function at its very roots, annihilates the capacity of continuous and joyous exertion; and translates the very abstractive functions, which it preternaturally quickens, into a mere mode of fitful escape from a misery which it has itself created. In this sense, too, Milton's words are true: " *To be weak is to be miserable."*   Probably also George Eliot's lines in " Armgart" may have, in the eyes of most readers, a very close illustrative bearing here,—we mean when she makes one speak thus of her heroine :—

> " For herself,
> She often wonders what her life had been
> Without that voice for channel of her soul ;
> She says it must have leaped through all her limbs,
> Made her a Mœnad—made her snatch a brand
> And fire some forest that her rage might mount
> In crashing roaring flames through half a land,
> Leaving her still and patient for a while.
> ' Poor wretch !' she says of any murderess,
> ' The world was cruel, and she could not sing ;'
> I carry my revenges in my throat,
> I love in singing and am loved again."

Coleridge himself was decisively of this opinion, if we may judge from the fifth stanza of the ode on " Dejection : "—

> " This light, this glory, this fair, luminous mist,
> This beautiful and beauty-making power,
>   Joy, virtuous Lady ! joy that ne'er was given
> Save to the pure, and in their purest hour ;
> Life and life's effluence, cloud at once and shower,
> Joy, Lady ! is the spirit and the power
> Which wedding Nature to us, gives in dower
>   A new earth and new heaven,
> Undreamt of by the sensual and the proud—
> Joy is the sweet voice, joy the luminous cloud.
>   We in ourselves rejoice !
> And thence flows all that charms or ear or sight,
>   All melodies the echoes of that voice,
> All colours or suffusion from that light.
> *There was a time when, though my path was rough,*
>   *This joy within me dallied with distress,*
> *And all misfortunes were but as the stuff*
>   *Whence fancy made me dreams of happiness ;*
> For hope grew round me, like the twining vine,
> And fruits and foliage not my own seemed mine.
> But now afflictions bow me down to earth,
> Nor care I that they rob me of my mirth ;
>   But oh ! each visitation
> Suspends what Nature gave me at my birth,
>   My shaping spirit of imagination."

And then follow the lines which De Quincey has quoted,

which are imperfect and less emphatic without these pre-
ceding ones.

Then as to Wordsworth: it is certainly not the philosophy
qua philosophy that De Quincey admires in "The Excursion." That dissatisfies him. He finds fault with the episode
of Margaret because it has been so overlaid by the Solitary's
philosophy, and so also with the Sceptic. "Indirectly, besides, it ought not to be overlooked that, as regards the
French Revolution, the whole college of philosophy in 'The
Excursion' makes the same mistake that he [the Sceptic]
does. . . . It is not easy to see how the Laureate can avoid
making some change in the constitution of his poem, were it
only to rescue his philosophers, and therefore his own philosophy, from the imputation of precipitancy of judgment."
On account of the philosophy in "The Excursion" operating
to break up and disconnect, it was laid down that "The
Excursion" would live only as a series of fragments; followed by this most telling passage:—"Not therefore in
'The Excursion' must we look for that reversionary influence which awaits Wordsworth with posterity. It is the
vulgar superstition in behalf of big books and sounding
titles; it is the weakness of supposing no book entitled
to be considered a power in the literature of the land, unless
physically it is weighty, that must have prevailed upon
Coleridge and others to undervalue, by comparison with the
direct philosophic poetry of Wordsworth, those minor poems
which are all short, but generally scintillating with gems
of far profounder truth. Let the reader understand, however, that by 'truth' I understand not merely that truth
which takes the shape of a formal proposition, reducible to
'mood' and 'figure,' but truth which suddenly strengthens
into solemnity an impression very feebly acknowledged
previously, or truth which suddenly unveils a connection
between objects always before regarded as irrelate and
independent." How then could it be said that De Quincey
preferred the philosophical to the purely imaginative poems
of Wordsworth? In truth, De Quincey admired "The Excursion" in spite of its philosophy, and not because of it. It

was not merely that it was wrong, but that it was there, as one might say in chemical phrase, unprecipitated. No; what De Quincey admired and liked in Wordsworth were these four things : (1.) an eye for new aspects and new meanings in Nature's shows and pomps, especially in the forms of cloud architecture; (2.) his hold on, and interpretation of, certain sentiments which poetry had heretofore greatly overlooked or inadequately and perversely treated; (3.) his hold on the permanent in human feeling; and (4.) the depth of his sympathy. "The great distinction of Wordsworth," he says, "and the pledge of his increasing popularity, is the extent of his sympathy with what is *really* permanent in human feelings, and also the depth of his sympathy." De Quincey therefore based his liking for Wordsworth, and his conviction of his profound influence, on elements that are opposed to *philosophy*, though they may be allied with *meditative* moods, and may sometimes draw effect from them.

But even as to Pope, it was not as the philosophical poet, moralist, or satirist that De Quincey liked or admired him, but rather as the fanciful and inventive artist in such things as "The Rape of the Lock," especially in the final form, with its machinery of sylphs and gnomes, or as the painter of human nature in emotive crises, as in the "Abelard and Heloise." Let the writer from whom we quoted at the outset, and those who are inclined to swear by him, read that portion of "Lord Carlisle on Pope," pp. 22 to 32 (author's original edition), and they will see how little, when De Quincey was free to wield his critical weapon and give verge to personal opinion (which he hardly was in writing for the "Encyclopædia Britannica," though even there he takes care to rebuke those who have very unreasonably fancied the "Essay on Criticism" Pope's best performance, which he there decides to be "The Rape of the Lock"), he gave countenance to this statement, and certainly no support could be found for it in the essay on Roscoe's "Pope."

"Pope valued upon that scale [as an original philosopher or philosophic moralist] is nobody; or, in Newmarket language, if ranked against Chrysippus, or Plato, or Aristotle,

or Epicurus, he would be found 'nowhere.' He is therefore reduced at one blow to the level of a pulpit moralist.
. . . And in a function so exceedingly humble, philosophi-
cally considered, how could he pretend to precedency in
respect of anybody, unless it were the Amen Clerk or the
Sexton ?

"In reality, however, the case is worse. . . . . Whatever
service Pope may have meditated to the philosophy of morals,
he has certainly performed none. The direct contributions
which he offered to this philosophy in his 'Essay on Man,'
are not of a nature to satisfy any party; because at present
the whole system may be read into different, and sometimes
into opposing meanings, according to the quality of the
integrations supplied for filling up the chasm in the chain
of development. The sort of service, however, expected
from Pope in such a field falls in better with the style of
his satires and moral epistles than of a work professedly
metaphysical. Here, however, most eminently it is that
the falseness and hypocrisy which besieged his satirical
career have made themselves manifest. . . . Untruly, therefore, was it ever fancied of Pope that he belonged, by his
classification, to the family of the Drydens. Dryden had
within him a principle of continuity, which was not satisfied
without lingering upon his own thoughts, brooding over
them, and oftentimes pursuing them through their unlinkings
with the *sequaciousness* (pardon a Coleridgean word) that
belongs to some process of creative nature, such as the unfolding of a flower. But Pope was all jets and tongues of
flame; all showers of scintillation and sparkle. Dryden
followed, genially, an impulse of his healthy nature. Pope
obeyed, spasmodically, an overmastering febrile paroxysm.
. . . Pope was habitually false in the quality of his thoughts,
always insincere, never by accident in earnest, and consequently many times caught in ruinous self-contradiction.
The satires offend against philosophical truth more heavily
than the 'Essay on Man,' but not in the same way. . . .
The two brilliant poets [Horace and Pope] fluttered on
butterfly wings to the right and to the left, obeying no

guidance but that of some instant and fugitive sensibility to some momentary phases of beauty. In this dream of drunken eclecticism, and in the original possibility of such an eclecticism, lay the ground of that enormous falsehood which Pope practised from youth to age."

It was, therefore, not "in a certain way" that De Quincey admired Pope as a philosophical poet, but "in a most uncertain way," far more "in a certain way" does he admire Pope in "The Rape of the Lock," &c., when Pope tried to write poetry as poetry; so that this critic is doubly wrong—wrong in what he positively asserts; wrong in what he omits; wrong alike in what he sees and signalises and in what he omits to see and to signalise; wrong as to the fact and wrong as to the criticism; wrong both before and behind, as one might say, and this surely is a sad plight to put oneself in!

Thus, putting aside the point about Shakespeare— ("Shakespeare, inasmuch as Shakespeare was, as he said, the greatest of philosophical poets")—on which much might be said, we have advanced quite enough to show that this writer's statement is not to be implicitly accepted, and is likely to be misleading if accepted as an accurate, faithful, or discriminating interpretation of Thomas de Quincey's views of poets and poetry.

This same writer is wrong on one other point, and contradictory on a second. He is wrong when he says that De Quincey shifted his lodgings after his pecuniary troubles had ceased. He did not; and that is the very reason why the cottage at Lasswade and 42 Lothian Street, Edinburgh, are now so familiar to us. Then (2), while we are told that "nobody can be held to have known De Quincey during his later years" [were then Mr. Hill Burton, Professor Lushington, Mr. J. R. Findlay nobodies? not to speak of the want of gallantry in so ignoring De Quincey's daughters, or in relegating them to the same rank], in another page we are told this: "Indeed what we do hear [about De Quincey] dates almost entirely from the last days of his life ”—the legitimate inference from which, in the light of the other statement, is not very complimentary to all or to any of those who have told us anything regarding him.

III.

THE SCEPTICISM OF KANT.

The last clause of Professor J. P. Nichol's letter on page 186 would be very obscure without some explanation. In the second volume of De Quincey's “ Collected Works ” appeared the Reminiscences of “ Samuel Taylor Coleridge,” in which De Quincey took occasion to make some remarks on the inconsistencies of points in Coleridge's philosophy with the tenets of Unitarianism with which Coleridge was credited ; and he passes on to illustrate the contradictions that befall philosophers by citing the case of Kant, who, in spite of much in his published works, was yet, he asserts, apt in private conversation to express doubts as to the inspiration of the Bible and the immortality of the soul. Professor J. P. Nichol contributed to the *Glasgow University Album* for 1854 a few pages, calling in question the assertions of De Quincey on this point, though in the friendliest spirit, and asking him to give authorities and set the matter thoroughly at rest. The following is Professor Nichol's little paper, to which he has directed De Quincey's attention in the letter :—

Mr. de Quincey versus *Immanuel Kant.*

No reader of this Miscellany can require to be informed that Mr. de Quincey is now engaged in revising and superintending the publication of his principal writings. Nor is it needful that—in sympathy with the whole literary world—we add our expression of congratulation, that this admirable Writer and most interesting Man has found leisure and opportunity to complete and perfect a Monument which will certainly be as enduring as any other that has been erected by Genius in the present age. In the second volume of the Selections, however, there is a paragraph to which we venture to take grave exception,—a paragraph so very important that we feel persuaded Mr. de Quincey will not be the last to recognise the propriety of this formal and public request for his renewed attention to the statement it contains. In pages 162, 163 is recorded as follows :—

" Who can read without indignation of Kant, that at his own table, in social sincerity and confidential talk, let him say what he would in his books, he exulted in the prospect of absolute and ultimate annihilation; that he planted his glory in the grave, and was ambitious of rotting for ever! The King of Prussia, though a personal friend of Kant's, found himself obliged to level his state-thunders at some of his doctrines and terrified him in his advance: else, I am persuaded that Kant would have formally delivered atheism from the Professor's Chair, and would have enthroned the horrid Ghoulish creed (which privately he professed) in the University of Königsberg. It required the artillery of a great King to make him pause; his menacing or warning letter to Kant is extant. The general notion is, that the royal logic, applied so austerely to the public conduct of Kant in the Professor's Chair, was of the kind which rests its strength ' upon thirty legions.' My own belief is, that the King had private information of Kant's ultimate tendencies, as revealed in his table-talk."

It is very evident that an imputation so serious on the memory of one of the greatest Thinkers in modern Europe ought not to be sent abroad unless the grounds of it are definite and above question. Now, we take leave to say that, in the current and open literature of Germany nothing authorising that imputation has up to the present moment found a place. We have several biographies of Kant; and his metaphysical system was, from the hour of its birth, subjected to much and even angry criticism; but neither in any reputable biography, nor in any decent criticism known to us, have we been able to detect the vestige of such a charge. The Critical Philosophy could not escape, indeed, much vehement denunciation. It met the fate of all grand innovations,—being quite unacceptable at first to a party in the German Churches. Pamphlets, nothing tolerant either of Philosophy or philosophers, but very fiery and furious, came in hordes from the press; we have sufficient experience, however, of the weight and worth of such things, even in our own comparatively quiet country, to deem it a matter of much consequence, although sundry Pamphleteers of that cast may be known to have associated Kant with Apollyon himself. A serious statement by Mr. de Quincey is confessedly an affair of a different order; and we submit that he owes it to himself as well as to Kant, and all the ·young minds whose opinions his genius will yet influence—*to examine and* PRODUCE *his* Authorities. Will he forgive our recording our own strong impression that the whole story of the Ghoulish table-talk, and of the King of Prussia's letter, may be found to have a certain undeniable family resemblance to the famous " *Three black crows* " ?

This conviction of ours rests not merely on what is accepted in his own land regarding Kant personally, but also on the nature of the Critical Philosophy, and the character of the high intellect that evolved it. An impression, indeed, was once afloat in this country that Kant's system is, in so far, an *Ideal* one—tending towards the denial of Ontological Realities ; but that has waned in exact proportion as our insular Metaphysicians have ceased to despise German Literature, and to refrain from understanding [? undervaluing] courses of thought originating elsewhere than in some Scottish preserve. The mistake arose in this wise. After achieving that memorable task, for the accomplishment of which all modern Speculation must ever be indebted to him,—the task, namely, of vindicating the authority of Absolute Truths by tracing them to a dynamic force inherent in Mind itself,—we asked how, from the platform of *Subjective* KNOWLEDGE, can we reach the height of *objective* BEING ? How from PSYCHOLOGY pass to ONTOLOGY ? And, in discussing this—the most thorny and arduous problem within reach of the Human Reason—we showed that, while there is one way by which the transition can be effected, there is another by which it *cannot.* By the speculative faculty, Kant said, we *cannot* construct a requisite bridge ; it does not follow, because we have a *speculative* longing for Unity that there must be an *objective* unchangeable Substance corresponding to that notion of Unity. The Speculative Faculty has merely to recognise those controlling notions, as *its own absolute Laws ;* and it is, in itself, complete and adequate to itself, irrespective of Externality. Now, this memorable Critique at once discredited multitudes of paralogisms popularly current and held by as satisfactory ; and as lack of ability to think is usually accompanied by lack of courage, the terror went abroad that " the foundations of Ontology " were being quite removed by this remorseless destroyer of Königsberg. Terror blinds alike Intellect and Conscience. It was not observed that Kant had really proposed and established for evermore the surest foundation of Ontology. It may be, that even *he* has not seen deep enough among the capacities of the Speculative Faculty. It is not improbable that a clearer view of certain Intuitions would remove a portion of the difficulties which confronted him. But two averments may be hazarded. *First,* the difficulties in question were not removed in his time, and still stand where he found them—stern as ever. And, *secondly,* there is a strong *à priori* probability that we shall discern the Realities of Ontology—*easiest* at least—by aid of that portion of our complex Nature on which these dread Realities the most directly act ; viz., our MORAL NATURE, or, as it was named by Kant, the PRACTICAL REASON. It has been alleged that Kant, either shrinking from the consequences of his former conclusions, or desirous to conciliate popular belief, *sought* this outlet; and that he proposed it, although it is clearly discredited by the very considerations which swayed him in the previous case. An averment of Irreflection or Ignorance. The cases bear no resemblance. The Speculative Faculty, acting in obedience to its own Laws, is, as we have said, complete in itself; wherefore, it demands no supplementing through Externality. The Practical Reason, on the other hand, is essentially *extra-regardant*. It cannot act at all, unless in relationship with other Minds, equal and superior: its Laws *presuppose* an Ontology; and thus constrain our Belief in Ontology. Whether this reasoning be sound or not, assuredly it was earnestly put; and we have yet to learn that it has been overthrown.

In further exercise of that frankness any departure from which Mr. de Quincey would consider the reverse of complimentary, we protest also against the content of the expression, "*let him say what he would in his books.*" Kant's confidence in God and Immortality, in the Moral Attributes and Responsibility of Man, was not, as presented by himself, the result of any questionable Speculation. It forms, on the contrary, in its various modes, the ground of a fair half of all his philosophic labours,—witness the *Critique of the Practical Reason*, the *Metaphysic of Ethics*, and his essay on *Religion*. Were works like these nothing but an "organised hypocrisy"? Observe the amount involved in so monstrous a charge! Not merely the character of Kant—a great man who, through much worthy service, has left on the world an obligation to protect his name; but *this* further,—the untenable—the impossible proposition, that any illustrious Thinker, any human Spirit gifted with the ability to explore new regions of Moral Truth, can be tainted by the mean vice of *insincerity*. On the Socratic doctrine in its broadest sense—that Knowledge is identical with Virtue—we shall not at present dilate; but we aver that this vice of Insincerity is utterly inconsistent with the power to advance one hair's-breadth among untrodden districts of the Moral World. There is not an instance in History that goes to contradict our averment; nor is the ground of it remote;—*no man can discover new Moral Truth who does not know Truth, and love it.* A maxim at the root of all the Teaching of Socrates as well as at that of One higher still: let it be written with Pen of Iron on the heart of every young Man who longs for insight and desires a guide! Mr. de Quincey assuredly will not quote against us the venerable name of BACON. Research, honestly undertaken and unremittingly pursued, is fast clearing away the falsehoods that—to the disgrace of what is called History—have so long obscured the lustre of one of England's proudest possessions; to us, *à priori* considerations ever seemed sufficient. . . .

The Author of these exquisite Essays, which—now that they are being collected—we shall henceforth frequently enjoy, cannot feel surprised at our express claim of justice at his hands on behalf of so marked a leader of European Thought, or that we are unwilling to resign the character of Kant. And yet further. Of Prejudice, inane Terror, and the poorest Appreciation regarding Teutonic Philosophy, there is still enough and to spare amongst us; nor are there wanting persons—in the garb of Truth-seekers—who, instead of grieving lest imputations like the foregoing should have even a shadow of foundation, receive them gladly, and—for the purpose of discrediting the Philosophy—are prepared eagerly to diffuse them. Now, without meaning to stand answerable either for the whole or any special part of the result of recent Continental Speculation, we hold it a heavy misfortune that a course of Thought so remarkable continues virtually disregarded among young Men who aspire to be Teachers of the next generation; that, while History must describe it as a memorable phase in the intellectual and moral unfolding of Humanity, they consider it safe very nearly to ignore it. Alas! it is not thus that influence over the future may now be attained: even Scotland is insular no longer. He who would sway *Scotchmen* henceforward must be able to sway *Men;* and no combatant ambitious to do service for Truth need persuade himself that he can correct error merely by resolving not to comprehend it. With the counsel implied in these sentences, and respectfully but earnestly as well as affectionately commended, it is perhaps not unfitting that one volume of the *University Album* should close.   J. P. N.

This passage which Professor J. P. Nichol animadverts upon in the section of the " Literary Reminiscences " headed " Samuel Taylor Coleridge," follows a paragraph in which De Quincey contrasts the great constructive powers of Coleridge with those of the same order which were so weak, as he holds, in Kant. With that weakness De Quincey connects a tendency to scepticism, allied with a lack of love, faith, humility, self-distrust, child-like docility, so pronouncedly features of Coleridge's character ; and then follows the paragraph quoted by Professor Nichol. But in the article on " Kant in his Miscellaneous Essays," originally published in *Blackwood's Magazine* in August 1830, in the form of a letter to Christopher North, he had written :—

" It must not be concealed that Kant is an enemy to Christianity. Not content with the privilege of speaking in an infidel tone, and with philosophic liberty, he manifestly thinks of Christianity with enmity—nay, with spite. *I will never believe that Kant was capable (as some have represented him) of ridiculing in conversation the hopes of immortality ; for that is both incredible for itself, and in contradiction to many passages in his writings.* But that he was mean and little-minded in his hatred to Christianity is certain. Nor is it at all unintelligible that, philosopher as he was, and compelled to do homage, therefore, unwilling homage, to the purity and holiness which so transcendently belong to the Christian morals (a subject which he could not decline or evade, having himself treated that part of philosophy with such emphatic truth and grandeur), after confessing, as, in fact, he did, its superiority to the Stoic morality, which certainly approaches nearest to the Christian in uncompromising rigour of principle, it is still not unintelligible that he should harbour enmity to Christianity

as an entire scheme of religious philosophy. Though at
first sight startling, I repeat that this coexistence of two
opposite states of feeling with regard to Christianity is no
inexplicable phenomenon."

But the letter of the King of Prussia and Kant's reply
to it were real enough, and in this article De Quincey gives
a translation of the former and a kind of *résumé* of the
latter; so that Professor J. P. Nichol was quite wrong
when he expressed the conviction that they would be found
of the same order as the "Three Black Crows." It is clear
that Kant's relation to Christianity was not exactly what
Professor Nichol would fain have made it out to be. And
it would seem that, whereas in August 1830 De Quincey
was inclined to doubt what had been said of Kant's disbelief in immortality as expressed in his table-talk, by
1854 he had convinced himself that it was well attested:
hence there was no necessity for further investigation or
further argument. So far as we are aware, he did not
publicly take any notice of Professor J. P. Nichol's paper;
nor did he *himself* reprint in his "Collected Works"
the paper on "Kant in his Miscellaneous Essays" from
Blackwood for August 1830, else probably he would in
notes to that essay have made some reply to the stric-
tures of Professor Nichol in the *Glasgow University Album*
for 1854.

IV.

PROFESSOR JOHN NICHOL'S EARLY WRITINGS.

The contributions of Professor John Nichol, then a
student in Glasgow, to which his father refers in the
letter directing De Quincey's attention to them, are certainly remarkable alike as regards originality and felicity
of form for so young a man. Both under his initials and
under the pseudonyms of "Isis" and "Basalt" he con-

tributed, and in each of the contributions we detect traces of great promise—such traces as would lead one to expect later such a work as " Hannibal."

" Psammenitus," indeed, is, in our opinion, a poem of considerable finish and fancy. It is in blank verse, with perhaps a suggestion of Tennyson's influence, yet is original and happy in phrase here and there. It tells the story of of the descent of Cambyses, the son of Cyrus, on Psammenitus, to wrest from him the throne of Egypt. The poem opens with some fine lines on Egypt :—

> " Deep-shrouded Egypt, lone, mysterious land ;
> A land of mingled shrines and palaces,
> Where the stern shades of Death o'ershadowing,
> Subdues the pillar and the pomp of life,
> And mellows all things to a dreadful calm :
> There greatness moulders slow—the tombs of kings
> Are their own most enduring monument.
> Still Ammon rules across the desert sands
> That melt away beyond the dreary waste,
> But all the empire of the land has passed.
> No longer do the shafts of triumph speed
> From conquering chariots of avenging chiefs ;
> And now no more the sound of Memnon's voice
> Wakes up the far glad music of the Vale ;
> No more ascending from the hills of Thebes
> Is incense curling upwards to the Gods,
> No longer now from congregated crowds
> The clang of symbols unto Isis sounds ;
> Silent the hum of worshippers, and low
> In crumbling ruins, stately temples rest."

V.

"DIRE NECESSITY" LED TO WRITING FOR THE PRESS.

When severe or satirical remarks are made on the lack of practicality in De Quincey, and on the constant scrapes and embarrassments in which he found himself, some lack of insight is shown into the whole bearings of the case.

Had De Quincey *been* practical, and careful to invest even his small fortune with skill, not to speak of judicious calculation, instead of making gifts and spending injudiciously, he would in all probability have passed through life a very amiable and respected gentleman, famed for his extensive knowledge, his power in conversation, and his out-of-the-way reading. But he would not have troubled the world with any of his lucubrations. He had none of the itch of writing which pursues some people. He was content to live and to enjoy. His intellectual faculties and sympathies would at all times have found exercise, as well as his quaint and gentle humour; but he would never probably have joined the army of writers for the press. Possibly his superabundant thought and fancy and felicity of expression might have found some scope in letters to his friends and acquaintances; and possibly these might have been gathered together by some intimate or admirer; the world would have laughed over the extravagances, the paradoxes, and the gentle raillery which thus he would have fired off; but his fame would only have been short-lived. Unless, indeed, he had met with some friend who had had the sagacity to become his *alter ego*, and treasure up his table-talk—Boswell-like—more especially in those early hours when, if in congenial and appreciative society, his discourse was said to be brilliant and novel beyond expression. He himself repeatedly confesses that he wrote only under the spur of necessity. "Failing which case of dire necessity," he confesses at one place, "I believe that I should never have written a line for the press." To the necessities, therefore, we owe what we have.

———————

VI.

EARLY DOUBTS OF DE QUINCEY'S STRICT ADHERENCE TO FACT.

It would appear that doubts of a similar tenor to those recently expressed were cast on sundry points in the " Confessions " when first published—doubts which, it may be, De Quincey had in his mind when he replied to James Montgomery's remarks ; but he made no particular reference to *them* then. Five-and-twenty years after, however, in the third instalment of the " Suspiria de Profundis " in *Blackwood's Magazine* for July 1845, p. 49, he referred to them at some length and with some humour also. He writes :—

" I saw in one journal an intimation that the incidents in the preliminary narrative were possibly without foundation. To such an expression of mere gratuitous malignity, as it happened to be supported by no one argument except a remark, apparently absurd, but certainly false, I did not condescend to answer. In reality the possibility had never occurred to me that any person of judgment would seriously suspect me of taking liberties with that part of the work, since, though no one of the parties concerned but myself stood in so central a position to the circumstances as to be acquainted with *all* of them, many were acquainted with each separate section of the Memoir. Relays of witnesses might have been summoned to mount guard, as it were, upon the accuracy of each particular in the whole succession of incidents ; and some of these people had an interest, more or less strong, in exposing any deviation from the strictest *letter* of the truth, had it been in their power to do so. It is now (1845) twenty-two years since I saw the objection here alluded to ; and, in saying that I did not condescend to notice it, the reader must not find any reason for taxing me with a blameable haughtiness. But every man is entitled to be haughty when his veracity is impeached, and, still more, when it is impeached by a dishonest objection, or, if not *that*, by an objection which argues a carelessness of attention almost amounting to dishonesty, in a case where it was meant to sustain an imputation of falsehood. Let a man read carelessly, if he will, but not when he is meaning to use his reading for a purpose of wounding another man's honour. Having thus, by twenty-two years' silence, sufficiently expressed my contempt for the slander, I now feel myself at liberty to draw it into notice for the sake, *inter alia*, of showing in how rash a spirit malignity often works."

And then he proceeds to show that certain of the features in his description of the house in the street off Oxford Street where lived the shady attorney who allowed him a gratuitous lodging there had been missed, and this made the ground of fastening on him a charge that he had said the house was in Oxford Street, and that no house answering to the description could be found in Oxford Street.

"Meantime, it happens," he goes on, "that, although the true house was most obscurely indicated, *any* house whatever in Oxford Street was most luminously excluded. In all the immensity of London there was but one single street could be challenged by an attentive reader of the Confessions as peremptorily *not* the street of the attorney's house —and *that* one was Oxford Street; for, in speaking of my own renewed acquaintance with the outside of this house, I used some expression implying that, in order to make such a visit of reconnaissance, I had turned aside from Oxford Street. The matter is a perfect trifle in itself, but it is no trifle in a question affecting a writer's accuracy. . . . I may now mention—the Herod being dead whose persecutions I have reason to fear—that the house in question stands in Greek Street, on the west, and is the house on that side nearest to Soho Square, but without looking into the square. This it was hardly safe to mention at the date of the published Confessions. It was my private opinion, indeed, that there were twenty-five chances to one of my friend the attorney having been by that time hanged. But

then this argued inversely: one chance to twenty-five that
my friend might be unhanged, and knocking about the
streets of London; in which case it would have been a
perfect God-send to him that here lay an opening (of *my*
contrivance, not *his*) for requesting the opinion of a jury
on the amount of *solatium* due to his wounded feelings
in an action on the passage in the Confessions. To have
indicated even the street would have been enough.
Because there could surely be but one such Grecian in
Greek Street, or but one that realised the conditions of
that unknown quantity. There was also a separate danger,
not absolutely so laughable as it sounds. Me there was
little chance that the attorney should meet; but my book he
might easily have met (supposing always that the warrant
of *Sus. per coll.* had not yet on *his* own account travelled
down to Newgate). For he was literary, admired literature; and, as a lawyer, he wrote on some subjects fluently:
might he not publish *his* Confessions? Or, which would
be worse, a supplement to mine—printed so as exactly
to match? In which case I should have had the same
affliction that Gibbon the historian dreaded so much, viz.,
that of seeing a refutation of himself, and his own answer
to the refutation, all bound up in one and the same self-
combating volume. Besides, he would have cross-examined
me before the public in Old Bailey style: no story, the
most straightforward that ever was told, could be sure to
stand that. And my readers might be left in a state of
painful doubt whether he might not, after all, have been a
model of suffering innocence—I (to say the kindest thing
possible) plagued with the natural treacheries of a school-
boy's memory. . . . I never succeeded in tracing his steps
through the wilderness of London until some years back,
when I ascertained that he was dead."

The letters we have been able to give in this volume,
indeed, are decisive on the points with which they deal;
and the presumption is, that, had complete collections of
letters existed, every point in detail—however strange—
would have been confirmed by contemporary testimony.

VII.

REFERENCES TO LORD SLIGO'S LETTERS IN THE "CONFESSIONS."

The letters printed in the first volume from the Marquis of Sligo have an interest for students of literature and lovers of De Quincey over and above the testimony they afford of his truthfulness in narration. They form a part of that very parcel of letters which he tells us in the "Confessions" he carried about with him, during his sad novitiate in London, and presented to the money-lending Jews and their attorneys as proofs of his identity. The passage in which he states these facts we may here reproduce :—

"To this Jew [Dell] and to other advertising money-lenders [some of whom were, I believe, also Jews] I had introduced myself with an account of my expectations, which account, on examining my father's will at Doctor's Commons, they had ascertained to be correct. The person there mentioned as the second son of —— was found to have all the claims [or more than all] that I had stated, but one question still remained which the faces of the Jews pretty significantly suggested—was I that person ? This doubt had never occurred to me as a possible one ; I had rather feared whenever my Jewish friends scrutinised me keenly that I might be too well known to be that person, and that some scheme might be passing in their minds for entrapping me, and selling me to my guardians. It was strange to me to find my own self, *materialiter* considered (so I expressed it, for I doated on logical accuracy of distinctions), accused, or at least suspected, of counterfeiting my own self *formaliter* considered. However, to satisfy their scruples, I took the only course in my power. Whilst I was in Wales I had received various letters from young friends ; these I produced, for I carried them constantly in my pocket, being, indeed, by this time almost the only relics of my personal incumbrances (excepting the clothes I wore, which I had not in one way or other disposed of. Most of these letters were from the Earl of [Altamont], who was at that time my chief (or rather only) confidential friend. These letters were dated from Eton. I had also some from the Marquis of [Sligo], his father, who, though absorbed in agricultural pursuits, yet having been an Etonian himself, and as good a scholar as a nobleman needs to be, still retained an affection for classical studies and for youthful scholars. *He had, accordingly, from the time that I was fifteen, corresponded with me ; sometimes upon the great improvements which he had made or was meditating in the counties of M—— and Sl—— since I had been there ; sometimes upon the merits of a Latin poet, at other times suggesting subjects on which he wished me to write verses.*"

CORRIGENDA ON THE MEMOIR OF DE QUINCEY.

The perusal 'of letters in this later " find " of materials has led to correction of two errors in the Memoir, which, so far as we are aware, have passed unnoticed :—

1. At p. 37 of Revised Edition, line 2 from top, " Ballinasloe " should be " Ballinrobe."
2. At p. 76 of Revised Edition, lines 7 and 10 from bottom, " contempt " should be " contemplation."

And a *printer's error* :—

3. At p. 426, line 5 from top, " scientific " should be " simple."

(Ballinasloe is twice referred to in the former page, and

repeated at top of p. 37 would imply going backward instead of forward to breakfast.)

The Mr. Oliver White referred to at p. 293 of Memoir is the same person as Mr. O. W. Wight from whom a letter is quoted on pp. 238–240 of vol. ii. of this work. And the latter is the correct designation.

THE END.

PRINTED BY BALLANTYNE, HANSON AND CO.
EDINBURGH AND LONDON.

TELEGRAPHIC ADDRESS—
SUNLOCKS, LONDON.

MARCH 1891.

MR. WILLIAM HEINEMANN'S

ANNOUNCEMENTS

AND

NEW PUBLICATIONS.

Early in 1891.

In   Volumes, Crown 8vo.

THE

POSTHUMOUS WORKS OF THOMAS DE QUINCEY.

VOLUME I.

SUSPIRIA DE PROFUNDIS.

WITH OTHER ESSAYS,
CRITICAL, HISTORICAL, BIOGRAPHICAL, PHILOSOPHICAL,
IMAGINATIVE, AND HUMOROUS.

VOLUME II.

CONVERSATION AND COLERIDGE.

|WITH OTHER ESSAYS.

Edited, with Introduction and Notes, from the Author's Original
MSS., by

ALEXANDER H. JAPP, LL.D., F.R.S.E., &c.

THE above posthumous works of Thomas De Quincey will
form an essential addition to every library containing the
already printed works of the Opium-eater. The additional
Suspiria alone would justify this claim, some of them being
absolutely necessary to complete the significance of those
already published. There are also other essays of importance,
essays on history, speculation, criticism, and theology, and
some very remarkable *Brevia,* which will give readers a closer
access to De Quincey's private life and innermost thoughts
than anything that has ever been published.

In the Press.

THE

COMPLETE WORKS OF HEINRICH HEINE.

TRANSLATED BY

CHARLES GODFREY LELAND, M.A., F.R.L.S.,
President of the Gypsy Lore Society, &c. &c.

A WANT has long been felt and often expressed by different writers for a complete English edition of Heine's works. That this has never been done is the more remarkable, because HEINE is, next to GOETHE, the most universally popular author in Germany, and one who, although he termed himself an unlicked Teutonic savage, wrote in a style and manner which have made him a leading favourite in all countries.

Early volumes will contain the REISEBILDER, or PICTURES OF TRAVEL, probably the most brilliant and entertaining, while at the same time the most instructive or thought-inspiring, work of its kind ever written; FLORENTINE NIGHTS, SCHNABELEWOPSKI, THE RABBI OF BACHARACH, SHAKESPEARE'S MAIDENS AND WOMEN, and THE BOOK OF SONGS. Others will be announced later.

Dr. Garnett is preparing a "Life of Heine," which will be uniform with this edition of Heine's works.

**** A Large Paper Edition will be printed, limited to one hundred and fifty copies, numbered, and signed by the translator.*

Now Ready.

In One Volume, 8vo.

THE COMING TERROR.

AND OTHER ESSAYS AND LETTERS.

By ROBERT BUCHANAN.

CONTENTS.

The Coming Terror: A Dialogue between Alienatus, a Provincial, and Urbanus, a Cockney—Are Men Born Free and Equal? a Controversy—On Descending into Hell: a Protest against Over-Legislation in Matters Literary — The Modern Young Man as Critic—Is Chivalry still Possible?—Imperial Cockneydom—Is the Marriage Contract Eternal?—Flotsam and Jetsam: I. What is Sentiment? II. Emma Wade's Martyrdom. III. The Apotheosis of the Gallows. IV. The Defeat of the Total Abstainer. V. The Carnival of Robert Burns. VI. Beneficent "Murder" (1). VII. Beneficent "Murder" (2). VIII. Booksellers' Romance. IX. Professor Huxley's Miraculous Conversion (1). X. Professor Huxley's Miraculous Conversion (2). XI. "The Journalist in Absolution." XII. The Courtesan on the Stage. XIII. Goethe and Criticism. XIV. "Dramatic Criticism as she is Wrote"—Final Words: I. The Paradox. II. The Social Sanction. III. The Outcome in Minor Literary Criticism. IV. Types of Egoismus. V. "Morality" as Literature. VI. The Outcome in Idealism. VII. "Poor Humanity."

In Two Volumes 8vo, £3, 13s. 6d.

THE

GENESIS OF THE UNITED STATES.

A Narrative of the Movement in England, 1605-1616, which resulted in the Plantation of North America by Englishmen, disclosing the Contest between England and Spain for the Possession of the Soil now occupied by the United States of America; set forth through a series of Historical Manuscripts now first printed, together with a Re-issue of Rare Contemporaneous Tracts, accompanied by Bibliographical Memoranda, Notes, and Brief Biographies.

Collected, Arranged, and Edited

By ALEXANDER BROWN,

Member of the Virginia Historical Society and of the American Historical Association, Fellow of the Royal Historical Society.

With 100 Portraits, Maps, and Plans.

---

21 BEDFORD STREET, LONDON, W.C.   5

Now Ready.

In One Volume, Small 4to, 5s.

HEDDA GABLER:

A DRAMA IN FOUR ACTS.

By HENRIK IBSEN.

TRANSLATED FROM THE NORWEGIAN BY EDMUND GOSSE.

With Portrait in Photogravure.

*** *Also a limited Large Paper Edition. Price on application.*

Liverpool Mercury.—"Displays all his wonted brilliancy in dramatic development, his firmness of touch, and his unique faculty . . . free from any sign of declining power . . . and minutely drawn as only Ibsen of living men could draw it. . . . It is masterly."

Saturday Review.—"A stronger thing than any the author has done since the 'Wild Duck.' . . . The Norwegian dramatist's dialogue throws great difficulties in the way of his translators; but Mr. Gosse has, on the whole, surmounted them better than any one."

Star.—"A masterpiece of tragic art."

Globe.—"Realistic to the last degree."

Daily News.—"The translation seems literal and fluent."

In One Volume, Demy 8vo, 12s. 6d.

DENMARK:

ITS HISTORY, TOPOGRAPHY, LANGUAGE, LITERA-
TURE, FINE ARTS, SOCIAL LIFE, AND FINANCE.

EDITED BY H. WEITEMEYER.

With a Coloured Map.

*** *Dedicated, by Permission, to H.R.H. The Princess of Wales.*

Times.—"Much valuable information."

Morning Post.—"An excellent account of everything relating to this Northern country."

Nearly Ready.

In Three Volumes, Crown 8vo.

MEA CULPA:

A WOMAN'S LAST WORD.

By HENRY HARLAND.

Heinemann's International Library.

Edited by EDMUND GOSSE.

. Each Volume has an Introduction specially written by the Editor.

IN GOD'S WAY. By Björnstjerne Björnson. Translated from the Norwegian by Elizabeth Carmichael. In One Volume, crown 8vo, 3s. 6d. ; or Paper Covers, 2s. 6d.

Athenæum.—"Without doubt the most important, and the most interesting work published during the twelve months. . . . There are descriptions which certainly belong to the best and cleverest things our literature has ever produced. Amongst the many characters, the doctor's wife is unquestionably the first. It would be difficult to find anything more tender, soft, and refined than this charming personage."

Saturday Review.—"The English reader could desire no better introduction to contemporary foreign fiction than this notable novel."

Speaker.—"'In God's Way' is really a notable book."

PIERRE AND JEAN. By Guy de Maupassant. Translated from the French by Clara Bell. In One Volume, crown 8vo, 3s. 6d. ; or Paper Covers, 2s. 6d.

Pall Mall Gazette.—"So fine and faultless, so perfectly balanced, so steadily progressive, so clear and simple and satisfying. It is admirable from beginning to end."

Athenæum.—"Ranks amongst the best gems of modern French fiction."

THE CHIEF JUSTICE. By Karl Emil Franzos. Author of "For the Right," &c. Translated from the German by Miles Corbet. One Volume, crown 8vo, 3s. 6d. ; or Paper Covers, 2s. 6d.

The New Review.—"Few novels of recent times have a more sustained and vivid human interest."

Christian World.—A story of wonderful power . . . as free from anything objectionable as 'The Heart of Midlothian.'"

Manchester Guardian.—"Simple, forcible, and intensely tragic. It is a very powerful study, singularly grand in its simplicity."

Sunday Times.—"A series of dramatic scenes welded together with a never-failing interest and skill."

HEINEMANN'S INTERNATIONAL LIBRARY—*(continued)*.

WORK WHILE YE HAVE THE LIGHT. By
Count Lyof Tolstoi. Translated from the Russian by
E. J. Dillon, Ph.D. In One Volume, crown 8vo, 3s. 6d.;
or Paper Covers, 2s. 6d.

Glasgow Herald.—"Mr. Gosse gives a brief biographical sketch of
Tolstoi, and an interesting estimate of his literary productions."

Scotsman.—"It is impossible to convey any adequate idea of the
simplicity and force with which the work is unfolded; no one who
reads the book will dispute its author's greatness."

Liverpool Mercury.—"Marked by all the old power of the great
Russian novelist."

Manchester Guardian.—"Readable and well translated; full of
high and noble feeling."

FANTASY. By Matilde Serao. Translated from
the Italian by Henry Harland and Paul Sylvester.
In One Volume, crown 8vo, 3s. 6d.; or Paper Covers,
2s. 6d.

Daily Telegraph.—"A work of genius."

Scottish Leader.—"The book is full of a glowing and living
realism. . . . There is nothing like 'Fantasy' in modern literature.
. . . It is a work of elfish art, a mosaic of life and love, of right and
wrong, of human weakness and strength, and purity and wantonness,
pieced together in deft and witching precision."

Daily Graphic.—"Clever beyond all need of praise."

FROTH. By Don Armando Palacio Valdés.
Translated from the Spanish by Clara Bell. In One
Volume, crown 8vo, 3s. 6d.; or Paper Covers, 2s. 6d.

In the Press.

THE COMMODORE'S DAUGHTERS. By Jonas
Lie. Translated from the Norwegian by H. L. Bræk-
stad and Gertrude Hughes.

FOSTERING A VIPER. By Louis Couperus.
Translated from the Dutch by Clara Bell.

New Works of Fiction.

THE BONDMAN. A New Saga. By Hall

Caine. Fourth Edition (Fifteenth Thousand). In One Volume. Crown 8vo, 3s. 6d.

Mr. Gladstone.—"The 'Bondman' is a work of which I recognise the freshness, vigour, and sustained interest no less than its integrity of aim."

Count Tolstoi.—"A book I have read with deep interest."

Standard.—"Its argument is grand, and it is sustained with a power that is almost marvellous."

IN THE VALLEY. A Novel. By Harold

Frederic, Author of "The Lawton Girl," "Seth's Brother's Wife," &c. &c. In Three Volumes. Crown 8vo, with Illustrations.

Athenæum.—"A romantic story, both graphic and exciting, not merely in the central picture itself, but also in its weird surroundings. This is a novel deserving to be read."

Manchester Examiner.—"Certain to win the reader's admiration. 'In the Valley' is a novel that deserves to live."

Scotsman.—"A work of real ability; it stands apart from the common crowd of three-volume novels."

A MARKED MAN: Some Episodes in his

Life. By Ada Cambridge, Author of "Two Years' Time," "A Mere Chance," &c. &c. In Three Volumes, crown 8vo.

Morning Post.—"A depth of feeling, a knowledge of the human heart, and an amount of tact that one rarely finds. Should take a prominent place among the novels of the season."

Illustrated London News.—"The moral tone of this story, rightly considered, is pure and noble, though it deals with the problem of an unhappy marriage."

Pall Mall Gazette.—"Contains one of the best written stories of a *mésalliance* that is to be found in modern fiction."

New Works of Fiction.

THE MOMENT AFTER: A Tale of the Unseen.
By Robert Buchanan. In One Volume, crown 8vo, 10s. 6d.

Athenæum.—"Should be read—in daylight."
Observer.—"A clever *tour de force.*"
Guardian.—"Particularly impressive, graphic, and powerful."
Bristol Mercury.—"Written with the same poetic feeling and power which have given a rare charm to Mr. Buchanan's previous prose writings."

COME FORTH!
By Elizabeth Stuart Phelps and Herbert D. Ward. In One Volume, imperial 16mo, 7s. 6d.

Scotsman.—"'Come Forth!' is the story of the raising of Lazarus, amplified into a dramatic love-story. . . . It has a simple, forthright dramatic interest such as is seldom attained except in purely imaginative fiction."

THE MASTER OF THE MAGICIANS.
By Elizabeth Stuart Phelps and Herbert D. Ward. In One Volume, imperial 16mo, 7s. 6d.

The Athenæum.—"A success in Biblical fiction."

THE DOMINANT SEVENTH: A Musical Story.
By Kate Elizabeth Clark. In One Volume, crown 8vo, 5s.

Speaker.—"A very romantic story."

A VERY STRANGE FAMILY: A Novel.
By F. W. Robinson, Author of "Grandmother's Money," "Lazarus in London," &c. &c. In One Volume, crown 8vo, 3s. 6d.

Glasgow Herald.—"An ingeniously-devised plot, of which the interest is kept up to the very last page. A judicious blending of humour and pathos further helps to make the book delightful reading from start to finish."

New Works of Fiction.

HAUNTINGS : Fantastic Stories. By VERNON
LEE, Author of "Baldwin," "Miss Brown," &c. &c. In
One Volume, crown 8vo, 6s.

Pall Mall Gazette.—"Well imagined, cleverly constructed, power-
fully executed. 'Dionea' is a fine and impressive idea, and 'Oke of
Okehurst' a masterly story."

PASSION THE PLAYTHING. A Novel. By
R. MURRAY GILCHRIST. In One Volume, crown 8vo, 6s.

Athenæum.—"This well-written story must be read to be appre-
ciated."

Yorkshire Post.—"A book to lay hold of the reader."

Recent Publications.

THE LABOUR MOVEMENT IN AMERICA.
By RICHARD T. ELY, Ph.D., Associate in Political
Economy, Johns Hopkins University. In One Volume,
crown 8vo, 5s.

Weekly Despatch.—"There is much to interest and instruct."

Saturday Review.—"Both interesting and valuable."

England.—"Full of information and thought."

National Reformer.—"Chapter iii. deals with the growth and
present condition of labour organisations in America . . . this forms
a most valuable page of history."

ARABIC AUTHORS: A Manual of Arabian
History and Literature. By F. F. ARBUTHNOT, M.R.A.S.,
Author of "Early Ideas," "Persian Portraits," &c. In
One Volume, 8vo, 10s.

Manchester Examiner.—"The whole work has been carefully
indexed, and will prove a handbook of the highest value to the
student who wishes to gain a better acquaintance with Arabian
letters."

Recent Publications.

THE GENTLE ART OF MAKING ENEMIES

As pleasingly exemplified in many instances, wherein the serious ones of this earth, carefully exasperated, have been prettily spurred on to indiscretions and unseemliness, while overcome by an undue sense of right. By J. M'Neil Whistler. In One Volume, pott 4to, 10s. 6d.

Punch, *June* 21.—"The book in itself, in its binding, print, and arrangement, is a work of art."

Punch, *June* 28.—"A work of rare humour, a thing of beauty and a joy for now and ever."

THE PASSION PLAY AT OBERAMMERGAU,

1890. By F. W. Farrar, D.D., F.R.S., Archdeacon and Canon of Westminster, &c. &c. In One Volume, small 4to, 2s. 6d.

Spectator.—"Among the many accounts that have been written this year of 'The Passion Play,' one of the most picturesque, the most interesting, and the most reasonable, is this sketch of Archdeacon Farrar's. . . . This little book will be read with delight by those who have, and by those who have not, visited Oberammergau."

THE GARDEN'S STORY ; or, Pleasures and Trials of an Amateur Gardener. By G. H. Ell-

wanger. With an Introduction by the Rev. C. Wolley Dod. In One Volume, 12mo, with Illustrations, 5s.

Scotsman.—"Deserves every recommendation that a pleasant-looking page can give it; for it deals with a charming subject in a charming manner. Mr. Ellwanger talks delightfully, with instruction but without pedantry, of the flowers, the insects, and the birds. . . . It will give pleasure to every reader who takes the smallest interest in flowers, and ought to find many readers."